CRUSHED

Crushed

A PRETTY LITTLE LIARS NOVEL

SARA SHEPARD

HARPER TEEN

An Imprint of HarperCollinsPublishers

Know thy self, know thy enemy.

—SUN TZU

BAD MOJO

Have you ever gotten a bad vibe that something *terrible* was about to happen . . . only to have it come true? Like when you were on vacation and suddenly had a flash of your best friend screaming in agony—and she told you afterward she'd broken her arm at that exact moment? Or when you had that sinking sensation that you shouldn't stay at that B&B in Maine—and the roof caved in that night? Or that time you swore you heard sirens at an intersection—and the town's worst accident happened there the following week? Maybe it sounds hippie-trippy, but sometimes sixth senses are real. If a little voice in your head is telling you something is up, maybe you should listen.

In Rosewood, too many awful things had happened—especially to four pretty girls. So on a hot summer night, when one of them was randomly struck with a bad feeling that something horrible had just gone down, she tried to ignore it. Lightning couldn't have struck again.

But guess what? It did.

Although it was almost three AM in Reykjavik, Iceland, the sky was still an eerie daybreak white. The only real clue that it was the middle of the night was the lack of people—no one was on the shores of the Tjörnin pond. The Kaffibarinn bar, where Björk allegedly partied, was empty. There were no shoppers trooping up and down the main drag. Everyone was safe in bed, blackout shades pulled tight, eye masks secured.

Well, not *quite* everyone. Aria Montgomery tumbled out an open window of a dark chateau called Brennan Manor just outside town. Her hip hit the cold ground, and she squealed loudly, then popped back up and shut the window fast. Inside, the alarms were screeching, but she didn't see any police cars climbing the hill yet.

She peered through the glass for Olaf, a boy she'd just met. What the hell was she *doing* here? She was supposed to be snuggled in her bed at the guesthouse next to her boyfriend, Noel—not breaking and entering with a stranger. Not about to be arrested and locked up for the rest of her life.

Olaf appeared at the window, hefting a painting up to the glass for Aria to see. Bright, starry swirls swept across the canvas. The little town was upside down, the spires looking like stalactites in a cave. In the corner was the signature: VAN GOGH.

As in Vincent.

The dreamlike nausea washed over Aria once more. *She* had made them come here. *She* had found that painting and pulled it off the wall. But now she realized how big of a mistake that had been.

She looked at Olaf. "Put that down!" she yelled through the glass. "Get out before the cops come!"

Olaf hefted the window open a crack. "What do you mean?" he said in his Icelandic accent. "This was your idea. Or are you having second thoughts? Maybe you're more like your philistine boyfriend than I thought. More *American* than I thought."

Aria turned away. She *was* having second thoughts. She *was* American. They were on vacation, after all—all she'd wanted was a night of fun. Vacations weren't supposed to end like this.

Last spring, when Noel had announced he was putting together a trip to Reykjavik for himself, Aria, Aria's brother, Mike, and Mike's girlfriend, Hanna Marin, Aria had been psyched. She'd lived in Iceland for three years with her family after the girls' best friend, Alison DiLaurentis, went missing at the end of seventh grade, and she couldn't wait to get back.

She and Hanna also needed a trip—*anywhere.* Along with their two other best friends, Spencer Hastings and Emily Fields, they had just endured months of being stalked and tormented by an evil text-messager called A, who was the *real* Alison DiLaurentis—the Ali *they* had known was actually Ali's twin, Courtney. Courtney had been in a mental hospital most of her life, but she'd switched places with her sister at the beginning of sixth grade, doing so by pretending to be friends with Aria, Spencer, Emily, and Hanna. Real Ali got her revenge on Courtney by killing her the last night of seventh grade . . . and she got back at the girls by becoming A and nearly killing them.

So Aria and Hanna had been excited to come here when Noel planned the vacation. Real Ali was dead, and A was gone, and they had nothing to be afraid of anymore. Then their spring-break trip to Jamaica happened. A few other awful things had gone down, too. Now, in July, Aria and Hanna were keeping secrets once more. They'd barely spoken since they'd arrived. It didn't help that Noel wasn't impressed with Iceland at all, or that Mike hated the place as much as he did when they'd lived here.

Tonight, the situation had sunk to a new level. At first, Aria had simply flirted with Olaf, a scruffy Icelandic intellectual they'd met at a bar down the street, to piss Noel off. Five shots of Black Death, the local schnapps, later, and Aria found herself in the alley, Olaf's lips locked to hers. Fast-forward a few hours, and now . . . *this*.

The blaring house alarm increased in volume. Olaf tried to lift the window further up, but it caught, stuck.

Aria froze. If she helped him, she'd *really* be abetting a theft. "I can't."

Olaf rolled his eyes and tried once more. It wouldn't

To Marlene

budge. He let the painting fall loudly to the floor. "I'll use the door!" he yelled to her. "Wait for me, okay?"

He vanished. Aria peered through the glass, but all she saw was darkness. Then she heard a screeching noise behind her. She tiptoed out from behind the bushes and peeked around the side of the house. Three police cars were screaming up the drive, the lights atop their cars flashing blue against the house's elegant stonework. The cars skidded to a stop, and six cops burst out of them, guns drawn.

Aria sprinted for the thick woods. She didn't even realize Icelandic policemen *carried* guns.

The cops approached the front door and yelled something in Icelandic that Aria could only guess meant "Come out with your hands up!" She glanced at the heavy, warped back door, which she assumed Olaf was going to try to use. It wasn't open. Maybe it had an intricate lock system from the inside that he couldn't figure out. Was he trapped? Would the cops find him? Should she wait? Or should she run?

She pulled out the international cell phone she'd bought for the trip and stared at the screen. She needed advice . . . but she couldn't call Noel. With trembling fingers, she dialed another number instead.

Hanna Marin swam up out of her dreams and blinked in the darkness. She was in a long, narrow room. A picture of a stubby-legged horse hung above her head. Her boyfriend, Mike, snored next to her, his feet hanging outside the heavy duvet. The bed across the room, where her best friend Aria Montgomery and Aria's boyfriend, Noel Kahn, were supposed to be sleeping, was empty. Hanna looked at the street sign outside the window. It was *sort* of in English, but also sort of in nonsense letters.

Right. She was in Iceland. On vacation.

Some vacation *this* was. What did Aria see in this country? It was light *all the time.* The bathrooms smelled like rotten eggs. The food was crappy, and the Icelandic girls were way too exotic and pretty. And now, as Hanna lay here, she was overcome with the most ominous feeling. Like someone had just died, maybe.

Her phone rang, and she jumped. She glanced at the screen. She didn't recognize the number, but something made her pick up anyway.

"Hello?" Hanna whispered, clutching the phone with both hands.

"Hanna?" Aria's voice sang out. There were sirens in the background.

Next to her, Mike stirred. Hanna slid off the bed and padded into the hall. "Where *are* you?"

"I'm in trouble." The sirens grew louder. "I need your help."

"Are you hurt?" Hanna asked.

Aria's chin wobbled. At the front of the house, the police were trying to knock down the front door. "I'm not hurt. But I sort of broke into a house and stole a painting."

"You *what?*" Hanna shrieked, her voice echoing through the quiet hall.

"I came here with that guy from earlier. He mentioned how a priceless practice painting of Van Gogh's *Starry Night* was in a mansion on the edge of town. It had been stolen from a Jewish ghetto in Paris or something during World War II, and the thief had never given it back."

"Wait, you're with Olaf?" Hanna shut her eyes tight, recalling the uncomfortable run-in she'd had with Aria and that random bearded dude making out in the alley earlier. He'd seemed perfectly harmless, but Aria already *had* a boyfriend.

"That's right." The cops broke down the door. All six of them stomped in like storm troopers. Aria gripped the phone hard. "We both went inside to find the painting. I didn't think we would . . . but then there it was. Then all these alarms went off. . . . I got out. Now the cops are here. They have *guns*, Hanna. Olaf is still trapped inside. I need you to come and get us on one of the back roads—we'll cut through the woods and find you. There's no way we'll be able to take Olaf's Jeep with all these cops here."

"Do the cops see you *now*?"

"No, I'm around the back, in the woods."

"Jesus, Aria, why are you still even there at all?" Hanna shouted. "*Run!*"

Aria glanced at the back door. "But Olaf's still inside."

"Aria, why do you care?" Hanna screeched. "You hardly know the guy! Run, *now*. I'll get on the moped. Give me the name of the street you're on once you make it through the woods, okay?"

There was a long pause. Aria's gaze fixed on the whirling police lights. She sized up the woods behind the chateau. Then, finally, she looked at the house once more. Still no Olaf. And Hanna was right. She *didn't* know him.

"Okay," she said shakily. "I'm going."

She hung up and sprinted through the woods, her heart pounding a mile a minute. She tripped over a huge log, breaking the heel of her shoe and badly skinning her knee. She slogged through a shallow creek, getting half her dress wet. By the time she was on the city road, she was cold and bleeding. She called Hanna, told her which street she was on, and collapsed on the curb to wait. She could still hear the sirens blaring in the distance. Had they found Olaf by now? Had he told them that she had been with him? What if they were looking for *her*?

When she saw Hanna on the moped at the end of the street, she almost burst into tears of joy. They rode back silently, the noise of the engine and the wind too loud for Hanna to ask any questions.

At the guesthouse, they opened the door as quietly as they could. Hanna turned on a light in the little kitchen and looked at Aria with wide eyes. "Oh my God," she whispered. "We need to clean you up."

Hanna pushed Aria into the communal bathroom, washed off her knee, and dug the twigs out of her hair. Tears streamed down Aria's face the whole time. "I'm sorry," Aria kept saying. "I don't know what got into me."

"You're sure the police didn't see you?" Hanna asked sternly, handing her a bath towel.

Aria rubbed her head. "I don't think so. I don't know what happened to Olaf, though."

Hanna shut her eyes. "You'd better hope he doesn't tell them you were with him. Because I don't know how much I can help you, Aria."

"He didn't know my last name," Aria said, placing the towel over the radiator and walking into the hall again. "Maybe I'll be okay. But whatever you do, please don't tell . . ."

She trailed off, glancing behind her. Noel stood at the bottom of the stairs by the back door, dressed in a hoodie and jeans, though they weren't the same hoodie and jeans he'd worn earlier that night. His forehead was slick with sweat like it always was after drinking, but there was a knowing look on his face that made Aria's insides seize. What had he just heard?

"There you are." Noel climbed up the stairs and patted Aria's wet head. "You take a shower?"

"Uh, yeah." Aria crossed her legs to hide the gash on her knee. "Where were you?"

Noel gestured down the stairs. "Smoking a joint."

Aria considered making a snarky comment, but she refrained—who was she to judge? She grabbed Noel's hand instead. "Come on. Let's go to bed."

Her eyes were wide open as they climbed under the covers. Noel shifted next to her, his bare legs prickly against hers. "So where were *you*?" There was bitterness in his voice. "At the bar with *Gay*loff?"

Aria turned away, the guilt oozing out of her pores as pungently as the schnapps oozed from Noel's. She bristled, anticipating a fight. But then Noel put his arms around her and pulled her close.

"Let's call a truce. This trip has been weird. *I've* been weird. And I'm sorry."

Aria's eyes welled with tears. That was exactly what she needed to hear . . . about five hours too late. She wrapped her arms around Noel and squeezed tight. "I'm sorry, too." She'd never meant something so much.

"Nothing to be sorry about," Noel said sleepily. "I love you, A . . ."

He mumbled into his pillow as he drifted off to sleep. For a split second, Aria thought she'd heard him say something else. Something strange. But then again, Noel was drunk. Even if he *had* said what she thought he had, he certainly didn't *mean* it. It wasn't like Aria would bring it up to him tomorrow, either.

She never wanted to mention this night again.

The next morning, Hanna, Aria, Noel, and Mike checked out of the guesthouse and departed for the airport. They went through the security line and stocked up on snacks and trashy magazines for the long plane ride home. If Aria seemed jittery, Noel didn't question it. When Noel complained about the puny airport not having a

McDonald's, Aria didn't snap at him. When Hanna and Aria spoke even *less* than usual, neither Mike nor Noel remarked. *I'm just tired*, they planned to say if anyone questioned them. *It's been a long trip. I miss my bed.*

The plane had satellite TV, and Aria flipped to CNN International after boarding. Suddenly, there it was: a shot of the chateau. It was even more ramshackle and haunted-looking than she remembered. *Break-in at Brennan Manor*, read the headline.

A video showed the shadowy, closed-up, spiderwebbed rooms. Then there was a blurry insurance photo of *Starry Night* . . . and a police sketch of Olaf. "This is the thief who got away with the painting, as described to the police by a witness who lived down the road," said the reporter. "Authorities are on the hunt for him now."

Aria's mouth hung open. *Olaf made it out?*

Hanna stared at the TV screen in horror. The situation had changed. Valuable art had been stolen, and Aria had helped facilitate that. Hanna thought of the art-theft cases her father had worked on when he practiced law: Even people who knew about the crime were guilty. Now she was one of those people.

Aria touched Hanna's forearm, sensing what she was thinking. "Olaf was smart, Han. He won't get caught . . . meaning he'll never say I was with him. The police will never be able to connect me to the crime. No one will ever know that you know, either. Just don't tell anyone else, okay? Not even Emily and Spencer."

Hanna turned away and stared at the runway, trying to lose herself. Maybe Aria was right. Maybe this Olaf guy, whoever he was, could evade the police. That was the only way Aria's secret would remain safe. That was the only way Hanna would remain safe, too.

And, mercifully, they *were* safe, for almost a year. The story surfaced in the news from time to time, but there weren't many details, and the reporters never mentioned an accomplice. One time, Hanna watched a report with Spencer and Emily in the room, the secret like hot lava inside her. But she didn't say anything. She couldn't betray Aria's trust. Aria didn't dare tell them, either—the less those girls knew, the better.

After a while, what happened didn't haunt Aria as much anymore. Olaf had disappeared into oblivion, and he'd taken the painting with him. Things had improved between her and Noel, too, that Iceland trip a distant memory. She was safe. No one knew.

Wishful thinking. Someone *did* know—and that person was keeping this secret very, very quiet until the time was right. And now, at the end of the girls' senior year, that very same someone decided to make it public.

The third—and scariest—A.

1

WATCH YOUR BACK

On a sunny Monday morning, Spencer Hastings walked into her kitchen and was greeted by the smell of coffee and steamed milk. Her mother; her mother's fiancé, Nicholas Pennythistle; his daughter, Amelia; and Spencer's sister, Melissa, were sitting around the farmhouse table watching the news. A coifed man was giving a follow-up report on an explosion that had occurred on a cruise ship off the coast of Bermuda one week before.

"Authorities are still looking into the cause of the explosion that forced all passengers on the cruise ship to evacuate," he said. "New evidence suggests that the blast originated in the boiler room. A video surveillance tape that was recovered shows two grainy figures. It's unclear whether the individuals in the video caused the explosion or if it was a freak accident."

Mrs. Hastings set down the coffee carafe. "I can't believe they still don't know what happened."

Melissa, who was in Rosewood visiting friends, glanced at Spencer. "Of all the cruises, it *would* be yours to have a crazy Unabomber on board."

"I'm glad *I* wasn't on that boat." Amelia, who was two years younger than Spencer and had wild curly hair, a pug nose, and a penchant for sweater sets and Mary Janes—even *after* the makeover Spencer had given her in New York City—snorted haughtily. "Were you guys on a suicide mission? Is that why you went rogue and sailed to that cove instead of to shore?"

Spencer padded toward the toaster, ignoring her. But Amelia kept talking. "That's what everyone's saying, you know—you and your three friends have cracked. Maybe you need to live in Dad's panic room twenty-four-seven, huh?"

Mr. Pennythistle gave Amelia a stern look. "That's enough."

Mrs. Hastings set a cup of coffee down in front of her fiancé. "You have a panic room, Nicholas?" she asked, seemingly eager to change the subject. She hadn't exactly learned how to discipline Amelia yet.

Mr. Pennythistle laced his fingers together. "At the model home in Crestview Estates. I built it after those mob guys moved into some of the surrounding neighborhoods—you never know. And besides, a certain kind of buyer might like that sort of thing. Of course, I doubt Spencer could attend Princeton from there. There's no Internet access."

Spencer started to chuckle, but then stopped. Mr. Pennythistle probably wasn't making a joke—he was a brilliant land developer, a real estate mogul, and a pretty good cook, but he definitely wasn't a comedian. Still, she didn't mind him—he made a wicked gumbo every Saturday, played her favorite sports radio station in the kitchen when he was cooking, and even let Spencer drive his pimped-out Range Rover now and then. If only his *daughter* were bearable.

Spencer slipped two slices of rye bread into the slots of the toaster. Amelia had a point, of course—trouble *was* following her everywhere. Maybe she *should* go to a panic room for a while. Not only had Spencer been on the *Splendor of the Seas*, but one of her best friends, Aria Montgomery, had also been in the boiler room when the explosion occurred. Equally disconcerting, Aria had come into possession of a locket on that cruise that belonged to Tabitha Clark, a girl they'd accidentally hurt in Jamaica last year. At the time, they'd thought Tabitha was the real Alison DiLaurentis, the evil twin who'd stalked and nearly killed Spencer and the others at the DiLaurentises' Poconos vacation home in an explosive fire. They'd thought Ali was back for revenge, so Aria had pushed the girl off a roof to get rid of her for good.

But then the news came out that Tabitha *wasn't* Real Ali—she was an innocent girl. That was when the nightmare began.

Tabitha's necklace connected them to the night Tabitha

was killed—the girls were sure that their diabolical stalker, New A, had planted it on Aria to frame her. They knew they couldn't just throw away the necklace on the ship— A would find it and get it back to them. So instead of evacuating to the shore after the explosion, Spencer, Aria, and their friends Emily Fields and Hanna Marin stole a motorized life raft and sailed to a cove Spencer had heard about in her scuba diving class. They buried the locket somewhere A would never look, but then their raft was punctured—surely A's plan, too. A rescue crew arrived in the nick of time.

After that mess, they decided to come clean about what they'd done to Tabitha—it was the only way to get A off their backs. They'd met at Aria's house to make the call to the authorities, but as they were on hold with the chief investigator on the case, a news flash came on TV. Tabitha Clark's autopsy report was in—she'd been killed by blunt-force trauma to the head, not from a fall off the roof. That didn't make sense, though; none of the girls had hit her. Meaning . . . *they didn't do it.*

Seconds later, they received a message from A. *You got me, bitches—I did it. And guess what? You're next.*

A charred smell roused Spencer from her thoughts. Smoke was pouring out of the toaster. "*Shit,*" she whispered, hitting the lever to pop the toast up. When she turned around, everyone at the table was staring. There was a wisp of a smirk on Amelia's face. Melissa looked worried.

"You okay?" Mrs. Hastings asked.

"I'm fine," Spencer said quickly, dropping the hot pieces of bread into the oversized marble sink. Yes, it was a huge relief that they hadn't killed Tabitha, but A still had a ton of dirt on them, including pictures of them on the roof deck that night. A could say the girls had gone down to the beach when they discovered that Tabitha hadn't died and finished her off. And A's confessional text wouldn't hold up in court—*I did it* could mean anything.

And what about *You're next*? Who *was* A? Who could want to kill them so badly? The same day they were going to confess, Emily had told the girls that she'd left the door open for Real Ali at the Poconos house, allowing her to possibly escape the blast. So she *could* be alive . . . and *she* could be A. It made the most sense: Real Ali was the only person that crazy.

Melissa stood up from the table and tickled Spencer's side. "*I* bet I know why you're spacey this morning. Someone's nervous about seeing a certain boy again?"

Spencer ducked her head. She'd let slip that Reefer Fredericks, her new boyfriend, was visiting today from Princeton, where he lived. They hadn't seen each other since the cruise. Today was an in-service day for both schools and the first day they were both free.

"It should be fun," she said nonchalantly, even though her stomach started to flip.

"Are you going to ask him to prom?" Amelia asked.

"Oh, Spence, you should!" Melissa cried. "You can't go stag in that gorgeous Zac Posen gown!"

Spencer bit her lip. She did plan on asking Reefer to prom, which was in two weeks. She'd been staring at the Zac Posen dress she'd bought on a trip to New York City with her mom all morning, dreaming about how she'd look in it on Reefer's arm.

Prom was never something Spencer had daydreamed about as a little girl—her fantasies centered more on getting elected class president and giving the valedictorian speech at graduation. But this year, prom sounded like a refreshingly normal activity in her totally *ab*normal life, and she didn't want to miss it. She already knew Reefer would say yes. She got romantic texts from him every day. He'd sent flowers to her house and her homeroom. They talked on the phone for hours every night, Reefer telling her about a new strain of pot he'd created and Spencer filling him in on the grueling after-school suspension hours she had to attend, the school's punishment for stealing that lifeboat.

Everyone cleared the breakfast dishes, and within ten minutes, they were all gone, leaving Spencer alone. She tapped her fingernails on the countertop and idly watched the news, but the weather report did nothing to calm her nerves.

The doorbell rang, and she shot up and checked her reflection in the toaster to make sure her blond hair was pulled into a neat ponytail and her pink lipstick wasn't smudged. Then she ran to the front door and flung it open. Reefer was standing on the porch, a sheepish grin on his face.

"Hey, stranger," Spencer said.

"Hey yourself." Reefer looked gorgeous as usual, a navy T-shirt pulling tight against his well-defined shoulders, his face clean-shaven, his dreadlocks pulled back to show off his high cheekbones and clear green eyes. Spencer tilted her chin up and kissed him, playfully squeezing his butt. Reefer flinched, surprised.

"Don't worry," Spencer murmured into his neck. "My mom's gone. We're alone."

"Oh, okay." Reefer pulled back. "Um, Spence, wait. I have to tell you something."

"I have stuff to tell you, too!" Spencer grabbed his hands. "So, I think I mentioned that our prom is in two weeks, and—"

"Actually," Reefer cut her off, "do you mind if I go first? I sort of need to get it out."

There was a strange look on his face that Spencer couldn't decipher. She led him into the kitchen and turned off the TV on the counter. When she gestured for him to sit down at the table, he smoothed the table-cloth again and again with his fingers, trying to get all the creases out. Spencer had to smile: Reefer probably hated the wrinkled tablecloth as much as she did. That was just one reason they went so well together.

"I got this internship I've really wanted," he announced.

Spencer smiled. She wasn't surprised. Reefer was a genius. He'd probably been offered hundreds of intern-ships. "Congratulations! Where?"

"Colombia."

"University? In New York?" Spencer clasped her hands together. "That is going to be so much fun! We can try out new restaurants, go to Central Park, check out a Yankees game. . . ."

"No, Spencer, not Columbia University. Colombia, the *country*."

Spencer blinked. "In South America?" Reefer nodded. "Well, that's cool, too. I mean, not as close, but it won't be that long before you come back for school." Then she noticed the stiff expression on Reefer's face. "*Are* you coming back for school?"

Reefer took a deep breath. "Maybe not. It's an amazing opportunity with this botanist, Dr. Diaz. He's, like, a rock star in his field. I've always wanted to work with him—everyone does—but once he takes you on, you kind of can't leave. I didn't even mention it to you, because it was such a long shot. But I got the letter two days ago offering me a position. It's for two years. I'm going to defer Princeton until I get back." He brushed a dreadlock over his shoulder. "Honestly, I was thinking about deferring Princeton anyway—I felt like I needed a few years to just, you know, *be*. But then I met you, and . . ."

A zillion thoughts zoomed through Spencer's brain. He'd heard about this *two days ago*? They'd talked on the phone a lot in the last two days. He hadn't said a word.

And two years . . . wow. That was kind of forever.

She sat back. "Okay. That's still amazing. So when are

you leaving? We still have some time together, right?"

Reefer picked at his thumb. "Dr. Diaz needs someone ASAP, so I'm leaving tonight."

"*Tonight?*" She blinked hard. "Can you postpone it a little while, maybe? I was kind of hoping you could come to my prom with me." She hated the wheedling tone in her voice.

By the look on Reefer's face, she could tell he was going to say no. "They really need me there now. And, Spencer, I'm not really sure we should . . . you know . . . wait for each other."

Spencer felt like he'd just dumped a bucket of ice over her head. "Wait a minute. *What?*"

"I'm into you." Reefer wouldn't meet her eye. "But, I mean, it's *two years.* I'm not very good at the long-distance thing. We could be different people after it's all over. I don't want you to be tied down, you know?"

"You mean *you* don't want to be tied down," Spencer blurted out angrily.

Reefer stared at the floor. "I understand that this is kind of a shock. But I wanted to tell you in person. That's why I drove all the way out here, even though I should be packing." He checked his watch. "In fact, I should probably go."

Spencer looked on helplessly as he headed toward the front door. There were a million things she wanted to say, but her mouth couldn't form the words. *So that's it?* And, *Are you seriously trying to guilt-trip me for making you drive all the way out here?* And, *What about all those romantic texts? You were the one who pursued me!*

She thought about how Reefer had promised to stick by her at Princeton and show her a good time. Who would do that now?

In the foyer, Reefer looked at her plaintively. "Spencer, I hope we can still be—"

"Just go," Spencer cut him off, suddenly angry. She pushed him out the door and slammed it shut, collapsing against it and sliding to the wood floor, her legs splayed out in front of her.

What. The. Hell. Just. Happened?

She pictured the Eco Cruise in her mind's eye. Reefer had taken her out to dinner, and they'd had their first kiss on the dance floor. It had been amazing—she knew he'd thought so, too. It was like Alien Reefer had just come over. The *one* good thing in her life had suddenly been ripped away.

Beep.

Her cell phone lay on the console table in the hall. Her heart sped up again as she pushed to her feet and looked at the screen. There was a new text from an unknown sender.

Poor little Spencer, doesn't have a date
Better find another before it's too late
Unless, of course, I happen to spill
My tale of all the folks you've killed.
—A

2

HANNA'S A ROYAL

Later that day, Hanna Marin sat at the bar at Rive Gauche, her favorite pseudo-French restaurant at the King James Mall. She was waiting for her boyfriend, Mike Montgomery, to arrive, and though the bartender wouldn't serve her, she felt classier sitting at the bar instead of at one of the booths. Besides, the booths were packed with other kids from Rosewood Day, many of them underclassmen, which made Hanna feel melancholy and sort of old. In a few short months, she would be at FIT—she'd received her acceptance letter last week. Rive Gauche would be nothing but a place to visit during holiday breaks.

Well, *hopefully* she'd get to visit Rive Gauche over the holidays and not spend the rest of her life in jail, as New A wanted. Hanna didn't like to think about that.

Her phone *ping*ed, and she grabbed it. GOOGLE ALERT FOR THE SPLENDOR OF THE SEAS ECO CRUISE. Hanna pressed READ. She'd set up an alert for the cruise she and her friends had just gone on for any news about who had set off the bomb in the boiler room. Both Aria and a boy she'd met, Graham Pratt, had been down there, but Hanna and the others were almost positive a third figure had been, too— the bomber. They were also pretty sure that person was A. If only the police could identify whoever that third person was. Then all this would be over.

Graham Pratt, a passenger on the bombed Splendor of the Seas *Eco Cruise is still in a coma after suffering multiple burns sustained in the explosion*, the first line read.

Hanna looked up, staring aimlessly at a table full of senior lacrosse players, including Aria's boyfriend, Noel Kahn, and James Freed. Graham wasn't just a friend Aria had made on the trip—he was also Tabitha's ex-boyfriend. For a while, the girls had thought he might be New A— especially when he'd started acting creepy and violent and chased Aria down to the boiler room, repeating over and over that he had something to tell her. Terrified that Graham was going to hurt her, Aria had shut herself in a back closet . . . and then the explosion had gone off.

Hanna kept reading. *Mr. Pratt has been transferred to the William Atlantic Plastic Surgery and Burn Rehabilitation Clinic outside Rosewood, Pennsylvania, for further treatment. The burn clinic has won the prestigious Best in the Tristate Area award for four years running, and . . .*

Hanna stared at her stricken expression in the mottled, old-timey mirror across the bar. Her ex-boyfriend Sean Ackard's father ran the William Atlantic Clinic, or the

"Bill Beach," and Hanna had volunteered there last year as penance for crashing Mr. Ackard's BMW after Sean broke up with her. Jenna Cavanaugh had been treated for burns there, and so had Hanna's old bestie, Mona Vanderwaal, the first A. Not that Hanna liked to think about *that*, either.

The rest of the article didn't say much more—only that Graham's injuries were severe. A chill snaked up Hanna's spine. It seemed like Graham had been caught in A's crossfire, just like Gayle Riggs, another A suspect who'd been gunned down in her driveway right in front of the girls. But why had A wanted to hurt Graham? At first, the girls all worried that Graham was A and that he'd wanted to confront Aria about what she and the others had done to his ex in Jamaica. But when they received more messages from A after Graham was in a coma, they wondered instead if he had been trying to warn Aria that A was after her. *Watching you*, he'd told Aria over and over through the heavy steel door in the boiler room. Maybe he'd meant *A* was watching her—maybe he'd seen A spying. So did he know who A was? If only he'd wake up . . .

Another e-mail popped into her in-box. NEW MESSAGE FROM SPECIAL AGENT JASMINE FUJI. Hanna squinted at the subject line. It read, simply, TABITHA CLARK.

The phone nearly slipped from her fingers. *Special Agent?*

She opened the e-mail, her heart thudding hard. Jasmine Fuji was an FBI agent on Tabitha's murder case, and Hanna's name had come up on a roster of guests who'd been staying at The Cliffs resort in Jamaica the same time Tabitha Clark had been. *I would like to ask you a few questions about what you might remember from that night*, the note read. *I'm sure you understand that time is of the essence, so please contact me as soon as possible.*

Bile rose in Hanna's throat. The girls knew now that they hadn't killed Tabitha, but A had incriminating photographs of them talking to her on the vacation—and even one of Aria shoving Tabitha off the roof while Hanna and the others stood there, watching. A had so much *else* on them, too: Hanna had covered up a serious car accident, Spencer had framed another girl for drug possession, Emily had accepted money for a baby . . . though she'd tried to give it back. Once A dumped all that in Agent Fuji's lap, she would never believe they were innocent.

"Hanna?" Mike's voice rang out behind her.

She swung around to see him. He looked adorable in his Rosewood Day Lacrosse T-shirt, fitted black jeans, and beat-up Vans. There was an excited-little-boy smile on his face.

"I have a surprise for you!"

"What?" Hanna asked warily, dropping her phone back into her bag. She wasn't really in the mood for a surprise right now.

Mike snapped his fingers, and suddenly a line of JV lacrosse players trooped in. At the count of three, in one synchronized motion, they whipped off their shirts and faced Hanna. Letters had been painted onto their rock-hard abs. First was an *H,* then an *A,* and then . . .

Hanna blinked hard. Their bodies spelled out *Hanna for May Queen.*

Someone in the restaurant applauded. Kate Randall, Hanna's stepsister, who was sitting in one of the booths, nodded appreciatively. A waitress's eyes popped wide at the boys' well-developed pecs and abs, and she almost dropped her tray. Then, Mike turned around, tore off his shirt, and grinned at Hanna. On his bare chest was an exclamation point.

"You're going to run, right?" he asked excitedly. "You've already got the lax team behind you—JV *and* varsity."

Speechless, Hanna fingered the Tiffany chain around her neck. *May Queen* was Rosewood Day's term for prom queen. Hanna and Mike were going to prom together—she'd bought her dress last month at a Marchesa sample sale. It cost more than her dad wanted to spend, but he knew how much prom meant to her—she used to wax poetic about her ideal prom night in the same way most little girls dream of a fairy-tale wedding.

But *queen?* Sure, Hanna had thought about it, *dreamed* about it, but after this crazy year, she hadn't really taken it seriously. "I don't know," she said uncertainly, looking at Mike and then the line of shirtless guys. "What about Naomi?"

Naomi Zeigler was Rosewood's queen bee. Naomi hadn't let Hanna join her clique after Mona's death, and though Hanna had begun to make inroads with Naomi on the cruise, that all had come crashing down when Hanna discovered that Naomi's cousin was Madison, the girl she'd left for dead on the side of the road after crashing her car last summer. Hanna had even suspected Naomi was A . . . but she had been wrong. When Hanna confessed what she'd done, Naomi had been so disgusted that she'd gone back to not speaking to her again.

A hand touched Hanna's arm. Kate swam into view. "Naomi's not running, Han. Her GPA isn't high enough." She smiled triumphantly. For reasons Hanna still wasn't sure about, Naomi and Kate were in a fight.

"And you're not running, either?" Hanna asked her. With Kate's long chestnut hair, even features, and runner's body, she was more than pretty enough.

Kate shook her head. "Nah. Not my thing. You should totally run, though. I'll get everyone to vote for you."

Hanna blinked hard. She and Kate had made up in the past month, but after years of being enemies, she still wasn't used to it. "What about Riley?" she asked.

Kate snickered. Mike gave Hanna a crazy look. "Riley? Are you serious?"

Hanna pictured Riley's startlingly red hair and vampire-pale skin—definitely not May Queen material. "Okay. I guess you're right."

Mike turned around and started riling up the rest of the team. "Han-*na!*" he chanted.

"Han-*na!*" The other boys joined in. Kate did, too.

Hanna grinned and started to consider it. She could already picture the fabulous, slightly spooky photo of herself and the king in the graveyard near the Philadelphia Four Seasons, a yearly Rosewood Day tradition that was printed in a special insert in the yearbook. If she won, her legacy at Rosewood would be that of a beautiful girl wearing the May Queen crown—not the girl who'd been tortured by A.

"What the hell?" she said slowly. "I'm in!"

"Great!" Mike slipped his T-shirt back over his head. "I'll help you campaign. We'll buy out a salon and offer girls free manicures. Give fashion advice. I'll even take one for the team and offer myself up for free kisses." He shut his eyes and puckered up. "Only from hot girls, though."

Hanna swatted him. "No kissing booths! But that other stuff sounds awesome."

Then, a pretty girl in the doorway caught Hanna's eye. She had sleek black hair and violet eyes, and wore a cute wrap dress Hanna had seen in the BCBG window. Hanna squinted at the girl's face, feeling a twinge of recognition.

"Whoa." Brant Fogelnest, one of the lacrosse players sitting nearby, tilted his head back to get a better look. "Chassey's smokin'!"

Hanna did a double take. "Did he just say *Chassey*?" she whispered to Mike. "As in *Bledsoe*?"

"I think so," Mike murmured, his forehead wrinkling. Kate nodded, too.

Hanna balked. Chassey Bledsoe was a dork who played with yo-yos, wore Cat in the Hat hats to formals, and favored large, limp bags that made her look like a postal worker. This girl wore Jimmy Choos and carried a dainty clutch under her arm. She looked like she was even wearing false eyelashes.

But then the girl spoke. "Oh, there you are!" she said to someone across the room. It was Chassey Bledsoe's honking-horn voice, the same voice that had called after Hanna, Ali, and the others on the playground in middle school, desperate to be part of their group. New-and-improved Chassey flounced over to her best friend, Phi Templeton, who was sitting in a booth in the corner. Though Phi was in ill-fitting Mudd jeans and an oversized T-shirt with a stain over a boob, it didn't seem to cramp New Chassey's style.

"Wasn't she out of school for, like, a month with shingles?" Hanna whispered. Chassey was in her calculus class; the teacher had taken pity on her because she'd had shingles once, too.

"I thought so." Mike drummed his fingers on the bar. "But if that's what shingles does to you, maybe more girls should get it."

Kirsten Cullen, who was sitting at a bistro table near Hanna, raised an eyebrow, listening in. "She looks amazing. She should totally run for May Queen."

More kids murmured that New Chassey *should* run— even some of the lax team Hanna-chanters called out a halfhearted "Chas-*sey*." Hanna looked at Mike helplessly. "Can't you do something?"

Mike raised his palms. "Do what?"

"I don't know! May Queen is *my* thing!"

Beep.

Hanna's cell phone flashed insistently inside her purse. She pulled it out. ONE NEW TEXT FROM ANONYMOUS.

Her stomach sank. She hadn't heard from A all week, but she'd known it would only be a matter of time. She glanced around the restaurant, hoping to spot the texter. A figure slipped behind a fountain in the courtyard. The door to the kitchen swung shut fast, swallowing up a shadow.

Bracing herself, she pressed READ.

Only losers campaign against losers. Make any effort to win, and not only will you lose my respect—I'll tell Agent Fuji about all your naughty little lies. —A

3

DEAR EMILY, I'M ON TO YOU

That same afternoon, Emily Fields and her mother entered a boutique called Grrl Power in Manayunk, a hipster neighborhood in Philadelphia. A song by a grungy girl band blared through the stereo speakers. A girl with a pierced eyebrow and a half-shaved head watched them from the other side of the counter. Two girls with hands in each other's pockets perused the jeans section. Mannequins wore tees that boasted things like I CAN'T EVEN THINK STRAIGHT! and I'M NOT GAY, BUT MY GIRLFRIEND IS.

Mrs. Fields sifted through items on a table, then held up a pair of canary-yellow leggings. "These are cute, don't you think? I could wear them on my morning walks."

Emily stared at them. Printed on the butt was I LOVE A GOOD MUFFIN IN THE MORNING. She wasn't sure whether to laugh or cry. Did her mom know what that *meant*?

Then she looked around. Everyone in the store seemed to be staring at her, on the verge of cracking up. She yanked the leggings from her mom's hand.

Mrs. Fields stepped away from the table, looking cowed. Instantly, Emily wondered if she'd been too harsh. Her mom was trying *so* hard. This was the same woman who'd banished Emily to Iowa for coming out last year. Emily had just dropped another bomb on her mom, too: She'd had a baby last summer and given her away to a couple in Chestnut Hill. For a while, her family had cut her off entirely, but there was nothing like a *real* bomb on a cruise ship and a near-drowning at sea to put things in perspective. When Emily returned from the cruise alive, her parents had given her a hero's welcome and promised to try to make things right.

So far, Mr. Fields had made Emily banana pancakes for breakfast every day this past week. Both her parents had sat at Emily's computer and looked at her cruise photos with her, oohing and aahing at her shots of glowing orange sunsets and far-off dolphin fins. Today, Mrs. Fields had come into Emily's bedroom at eight AM and announced they were going to have a girls' day: manicures, lunch, and then shopping in Manayunk. Even though mani-pedis and shopping weren't Emily's thing, she'd readily agreed.

Emily placed the leggings back on the table and selected a red pair that read GIRLS RULE on the butt. She handed them to her mom. "I think red looks the best on you."

The smile returned to her mom's face. *There*. That felt better.

Then Mrs. Fields's phone beeped, and she pulled it out of her pocket, looked at the screen, and smiled. "Carolyn just texted that she aced her biology final. Isn't that great?"

Emily pulled her bottom lip into her mouth. Her sister was now at Stanford on a swim scholarship, and Emily had heard secondhand how she'd struggled with the coursework all year. Carolyn hadn't told her *herself*, of course. Her sister had bitterly hidden Emily in Philly during the later stages of her pregnancy, and they weren't exactly on speaking terms.

Emily fiddled with a studded leather bracelet on a display tray. "So when do you think *I'll* hear from Carolyn?"

Mrs. Fields refolded a T-shirt she'd been looking at, carefully avoiding Emily's gaze. "I'm sure she'll call you soon."

"Does she *really* want to apologize?"

Mrs. Fields's eyelid twitched. "We should concentrate on you and me, don't you think? I'm so happy that we're out together. I hope we can do this more often."

Emily cocked her head. "So . . . that means Carolyn is still really mad?"

Mrs. Fields's cell phone blared, and she made a big production of rooting through her bag to find it. "I need to take this," she said briskly, even though Emily was pretty sure it was only her dad . . . or maybe Carolyn herself.

Emily leaned against a rack of jackets and sighed. Okay, so things weren't perfect yet. Mrs. Fields had told her that Carolyn wanted to let bygones be bygones, but Emily had seen no indication of that yet. Nor had she and her family had a conversation about Emily's pregnancy or the baby. But these things took time, right? Banana pancakes were still a huge gesture.

As her mom slipped through the front door, Emily pulled out her own phone and checked her e-mail. There was one new message from the Rosewood Day May Day Senior Prom Committee: *Don't forget to buy a ticket for the Senior Prom! May 7, 7 PM. The Four Seasons Hotel, 1 Logan Square, Philadelphia. Dinner and dancing.*

A lonely feeling swept through her. She'd already bought a ticket for prom; her friends were making her go. But the only person Emily wanted to invite—a girl named Jordan Richards she'd met on the cruise—couldn't come.

Thankfully, there were no new alerts about Tabitha. Emily's finger bumped the button to her photo gallery, and suddenly, a picture of Alison DiLaurentis stared back. It was the *real* Alison DiLaurentis, the girl who'd come back to Rosewood last year and later revealed herself as A. Emily had snapped the photo of Ali in her bedroom the day Ali had kissed her. *It's me, Em,* Emily could practically hear Ali saying. *I'm back. I've wanted to do that again for so long. I've missed you so much.*

Emily had continued to love Ali despite everything. Even after Ali had confessed that she'd killed her own sister, Emily held out hope that she'd come to her senses and atone for what she'd done. Her love for Ali had been so intense that she'd left the door open for her in the Poconos instead of barricading it shut and letting the girls' would-be killer burn.

She'd kept the secret for a while, but she finally told her friends last week. Now, they were starting to believe what Emily knew all along: Real Ali wasn't dead, and she was their New A. That meant that Real Ali had witnessed all of the girls' transgressions last summer, including Emily smuggling her baby out of the hospital and away from Gayle Riggs, a woman she'd thought was crazy—and a woman who was now dead. Ali might have been in Jamaica, too, and she might be Tabitha's real killer. It also meant Real Ali had been on the cruise ship last week. How had they not seen her? How had *no one* seen her?

Emily's thumb hovered over DELETE. After A had threatened her baby's life, she'd finally come to hate Real Ali. And yet she couldn't quite bring herself to get rid of the one photo she had of her. Sighing, Emily scrolled to the end of her photo gallery and looked at a picture of another girl she was pretty sure she loved. Jordan grinned into the camera. Her body was backlit by the blazing Puerto Rican sun, and blue water stretched behind her for miles. Emily touched the screen, wishing she could feel Jordan's soft cheek one more time.

"She's hot." The shaved-head salesgirl glanced over Emily's shoulder at Jordan's photo. "That your girlfriend?"

Emily smiled bashfully. "Kind of."

One corner of the girl's lip curled into a smile. "What's that mean?"

Emily slipped the phone into her pocket. *It means she's a fugitive. It means she jumped off a cruise ship in Bermuda to avoid the FBI, and I have no idea where she is now or when I'll see her again.*

She wandered toward the shoe section, which smelled heavily of leather and rubber. She would never forget those last few minutes she and Jordan were together. In Jordan's past life, she'd been Katherine DeLong, the Preppy Thief, the girl who stole boats, cars, and planes. When Emily met her, she'd just escaped from prison and changed her name, and was ready for a new start. The FBI agents, probably alerted by Real Ali/New A, chased both of them to the ship's railing. Jordan had given Emily one last look, then dived into the bay to escape.

When Emily returned home, she'd received a postcard from Jordan. *We'll see each other again.* Emily was dying to write back, but Jordan wasn't stupid enough to include a return address. Wherever she was—Thailand, Brazil, some teeny island off the coast of Spain—she was hopefully hiding well enough to evade the cops.

Emily ran her fingers over the smooth leather of a display pair of Doc Martens, getting an idea. She pulled out her phone again, opened the Twitter app, and logged into her account. Then she copy-pasted the prom invite into a new tweet. PROM IS IN TWO WEEKS, she typed. WISH I COULD TAKE MY TRUE LOVE.

She hit TWEET, feeling satisfied. Hopefully Jordan would see it and understand what it meant. And even though Jordan probably wouldn't reply, at least she'd know Emily was thinking about her.

When her phone buzzed a second later, her spirits soared—*Jordan already!* But the e-mail was from someone named Special Agent Jasmine Fuji. NEED TO SPEAK WITH YOU ABOUT TABITHA CLARK.

Emily's vision narrowed. The growling voices in the song pumping through the store's speakers suddenly sounded like vicious dogs. Pressing herself into a back corner, she opened the e-mail. *Dear Miss Fields*, it read. *I'm a special agent in charge of the Tabitha Clark murder investigation. Your name was on a list of guests at The Cliffs resort in Negril, Jamaica, at the same time Miss Clark was there. Procedure dictates that I interview everyone to get a better picture of what happened that night. Please contact me at your earliest convenience. Sincerely, Special Agent Jasmine Fuji.*

"Emily?"

Her mother was staring at her, her faux-croc purse tucked under her arm. "Are you okay?"

Emily licked her dry lips. There was no way she could talk to a cop. Jasmine Fuji would know instantly she was lying.

Mrs. Fields took her arm. "You're so pale. Let's get some air."

The street smelled of car exhaust and stale beer from the dive bar next door. Emily took heaving breaths, trying to tell herself this wasn't a big deal. But it *was*. She couldn't lie to a federal agent.

Beep.

Dizzily, she glanced at her phone again. As if on cue, a text message from an anonymous sender had come in. Emily gasped as she read the note.

Wait until I tell Agent Fuji that you and your GF are perfect for each other—you're both cold-blooded criminals. —A

4

NO ONE KNOWS WHAT
ARIA DID LAST SUMMER

"Go, Noel, *go!*" Aria Montgomery screamed from the sidelines of the lacrosse field the following afternoon at lunchtime. Her boyfriend, Noel Kahn, dashed across the grass and tried for his fifth goal in a row. Aria held her breath as the ball sailed into the net.

"Yes!" she screamed, slapping hands with Hanna. The lacrosse team was raising money for the local homeless shelter, and people had placed donation bets on which player could get the most balls past the goalie in under a minute. Naturally, Aria had ten bucks on Noel.

Once the minute was up—Noel was in second place after Jim Freed—Noel trotted over to her. "You were amazing!" Aria squealed, wrapping her arms around him.

"Thanks, babe." Noel kissed her long and hard, making the backs of Aria's legs tingle. Even though they'd been dating for over a year, Aria's stomach still flipped when she smelled his slightly lemony, slightly sweaty post-workout scent.

Hanna, who had just greeted her own lacrosse-playing boyfriend, Aria's brother, Mike, nudged Noel. "I can't believe you've turned Aria into a lacrosse groupie. I didn't think it was possible."

Noel took a mock bow. "It was hard work, but totally worth it."

"Aw, thanks." Aria pulled her cardigan tighter around her shoulders. It was chilly for late April, and the gray sky threatened rain. Hanna was right: If someone had told her at the beginning of her junior year that she'd be watching the lacrosse charity event during lunch instead of, say, working on a sculpture, she would have laughed her head off. And if that person had said she would be dating Noel Kahn, she would have fallen off her chair. Aria had crushed on Noel big-time when she and Ali were friends in middle school, but after Noel liked Ali instead, she'd sworn off him. Then, when she returned from her family's three-year sabbatical in Iceland, she was no longer the kind of girl who dated preppy lacrosse players. Or so she'd thought.

The coach blew the whistle. Noel scooped up his stick, gave Aria another kiss, and trotted with Mike toward the middle of the field to be with their team. Aria's heart swelled as she stared at his strong, straight back and taut calves. When the girls had been about to confess to the police about killing Tabitha, all she could think of was never seeing Noel again—never kissing him, holding his hand, even lying on the couch and listening to him loudly chew pretzels. Although they *hadn't* confessed, she still felt like she was on borrowed time with him.

After the boys were a safe distance away, Aria cleared her throat. "So I got a weird message yesterday."

She showed Hanna the screen on her phone. *Your name was on a list of guests at The Cliffs during Tabitha Clark's murder. . . . We need to speak as soon as possible. . . . I appreciate your cooperation.*

Hanna nodded. "I got this, too. So did Spencer and Emily—and Mike," she said. "Did Noel?" The boys had been on the Jamaica vacation with them.

Aria stiffened, glancing at Noel in his lacrosse pads and cleats. He'd just jumped on Mason Byers's back, and Mason was swinging around, trying to get him off. "Um, I haven't asked him," she said in a low voice. "Noel didn't see us talking to Tabitha, though. And he and Mike definitely didn't see . . . *you* know. It's not like they'll say anything weird."

As soon as the words came out of her mouth, she wasn't sure if she believed them. On the trip, Noel had paid no mind to Tabitha except to say that she seemed somehow familiar. Then, when Tabitha's body had washed ashore and it was all over the news, Noel often changed the channel, half the time not even registering that they'd been in Jamaica the same time she had. Only recently had he begun to perk up at the story. Now, every time her picture appeared on TV, he squinted at it curiously, saying, "Doesn't she *remind* you of someone?" What if he'd noticed how jumpy Aria was whenever a Tabitha story came on? What if he innocently mentioned that Tabitha reminded him of *Ali*? There were all sorts of inadvertent, unintentional ways Noel could incriminate her.

Aria shook out her hands. Noel would probably talk to the officer for two minutes, tops. And anyway, the girls *hadn't* killed Tabitha—A had bludgeoned her on the beach.

Of course, *they* were the only ones who knew that.

"Should we meet with Agent Fuji?" Hanna asked.

"It's not like we can say no." Aria bit a nail. "Maybe we could all meet with her together. At least then we'll all tell the same story."

Then Hanna pushed her phone toward Aria. "I also got this."

Aria read the message. *Only losers campaign against losers. Make any effort to win, and not only will you lose my respect—I'll tell Agent Fuji about all your naughty little lies. —A*

"Mike was trying to persuade me to run for May Queen," Hanna whispered. "And then Chassey Bledsoe walked in looking all fabulous."

"I saw her!" Aria exclaimed. "She looks sort of . . . airbrushed, doesn't she?"

Hanna shrugged. "I don't know. The weird thing is, A sent this practically the moment I saw Chassey's makeover . . . *like A was watching.* There were tons of kids at Rive Gauche that day, but I didn't see anyone texting."

"A is everywhere," Aria whispered, shivering. They'd been through so many different New A suspects, but each had resulted in a dead end—one of them literally—or a horrible injury. Like Graham, the guy Aria had befriended on the cruise who also happened to be Tabitha's ex-boyfriend. For a little while, Aria had worried that Graham might be A—he certainly had motive, and he'd begun acting so strangely, insisting that he had something to tell her. She now realized he'd wanted to tell her that someone was watching her. But A had set off a bomb before Graham had said who . . . perhaps because A didn't want Graham to identify him or her.

"Have you gotten any A notes?" Hanna slipped the phone back in her pocket.

Aria shook her head, then showed Hanna a new iPhone in a pink neoprene case. "But maybe that's because I got this. It has an untraceable number."

"Good thinking," Hanna said. She stared nervously at the field. "Do you think A could frame us for Tabitha?"

Aria licked her lips. A had all those horrible photos of them on the roof from that night. And who knew what else A hadn't shown them yet.

She was about to answer when suddenly the speakers mounted on top of the bleachers screeched with feedback. "Attention!" said an echoing voice. A loud cough and a lugee-hocking sound followed. It was Principal Appleton. For some reason, he always cleared his throat *into* the microphone, making noises that often sounded like belches.

"All seniors! I have some exciting news!" Appleton said. "We have our May Day King and Queen nominees! For king, it's Joseph Ketchum and Noel Kahn!"

Everyone in the bleachers cheered. Hanna nudged Aria, and guys on the field clapped Noel on the back in that jokey, let's-pretend-prom-doesn't-matter-even-though-it-sort-of-does way.

"And for queen," Appleton went on, "we have Hanna Marin . . ."

Hanna smiled nervously. Aria squeezed her arm.

". . . and Chassey Bledsoe!" Appleton finished.

A spattering of applause followed. A couple of people frowned, asking who Chassey was—as if they hadn't all gone to school together since kindergarten. Hanna set her mouth in a line.

"You're not actually worried about Chassey winning, are you?" Aria asked.

"I can't campaign!" Hanna picked at a loose string on her skirt. "There's no way I'm going to bring all you guys down just so I can be May Day Queen."

The speaker crackled again. "As for May Day decor," Appleton said, "we've gotten a lot of applications for decor chairperson. We'll make an announcement as soon as we choose!"

The crowd murmured. Hanna looked at Aria. "Did you apply for that?"

"I wanted to, but I forgot," Aria said, feeling a flutter of disappointment. Rosewood Day took its decor chairperson job seriously—those who were interested had to fill out a ten-page application with design ideas and sketches months in advance, and many applicants even included digital portfolios and personal videos explaining why they should be chosen—but people who had held the title in the past always gushed about how fun it was. Besides designing all the prom decor, the chairperson also did the prom blog and took pictures of goofy-but-exclusive prom rituals, like the big conga line, and of the king and queen at the graveyard near the Four Seasons hotel in Philly, where the event was held every year. Aria had been so consumed with A that she'd missed the application deadline.

"*But* I can tell you that we've decided on a theme!" Appleton went on. "Student Council has decided on . . . *The Starry Night!*"

People cheered. Hanna rested her spine against the fence behind them. "That's a pretty good theme, don't you think?"

Aria just stared at Hanna, the blood draining from her head. On second thought, thank goodness she hadn't applied. It was a *terrible* theme.

"What?" Hanna blinked. "They could do big Van Gogh paintings and . . . *oh.*"

The painting. Aria could see the thought flashing across Hanna's mind as if it were in neon. Aria and Hanna had never spoken about that night . . . but that didn't mean Aria had forgotten. She could tell Hanna hadn't, either.

Aria put her hands over her eyes. The trip to Iceland had been such a disaster from the very start. They'd sat on the runway for almost two hours before taking off. Then no one's ATM cards worked in the Keflavik Airport, which meant they had to scrape together traveler's checks for a bus to the hotel instead of a cab. The hotel lost their reservation and referred them to a guesthouse down the street, which was damp, smelled of fish, and so small and overbooked that they all had to share a room.

Then Noel started complaining about everything—how weird the milk tasted, how the backyard hot tub was probably full of bacteria, how uncomfortable the duvet felt against his skin. Aria had just chalked it up to jet lag, except he bitched the next day, too. And the next. He didn't seem impressed by their romantic walks around town. He didn't compliment the delicious local beer. He didn't even find the penis museum interesting. He thought the native horses were ridiculous, and when Aria pointed at the gorgeous Mount Esja in the distance, Noel had said, "Eh, the Rockies are better."

Mike got into the act, saying that the bars in town seemed even lamer than when they lived there. When Hanna whined about the lack of boutiques, Aria had gone into the bedroom and screamed into a pillow. *Typical Rosewoods*, she'd thought bitterly.

By the last night, the air had crackled with tension, and they'd all gone to a bar down the road to let off steam. When Aria sat down next to the shaggy-haired, emo-bearded, bespectacled boy named Olaf, who struck up a conversation about an Icelandic poet Aria loved, she'd almost hugged him out of relief. *Here* was someone who knew there was more to life than Rosewood. Someone who liked interesting music, had his own pony, and loved Iceland as much as she did.

Of course Noel and Mike thought he was ridiculous. They called him Gayloff behind his back—not quietly, either—as they also drank shot after shot of Black Death schnapps, told stupid jokes, and acted so American and idiotic Aria wished it wasn't so obvious she was with them. Then they tried to infiltrate Aria and Olaf's conversation. "You're an art student?" Noel slurred at Olaf. "Hey, I like art, too."

Olaf raised an eyebrow. "Who's your favorite artist?"

Aria wanted to hide. Football, Noel could talk about. But art? *Disaster.* "Uh, that painting with the trippy stars and swirls," Noel answered. "By that dude who cut off his ear?"

"You mean Van Gogh?" Olaf said it like *Van Gock.*

Noel smirked at his pronunciation but didn't comment. "Did you hear there's a top secret painting by him stashed in a mansion not far from here? It was stolen by this German baron from a rich Jewish guy during the Hologram."

He'd said *Hologram* instead of *Holocaust.* Aria covered her eyes. "Where did you hear something that idiotic?" she mumbled, mortified.

"Actually, I heard *him* saying it." Noel jutted a thumb at Olaf.

Olaf raised an eyebrow. "It wasn't me."

"Well, it was *someone*," Noel slurred. Then he puffed out his chest, which only made him lose his balance and topple off the stool. Mike laughed long and hard while the bartender eyed the two of them wearily, surely thinking, *God, I'm so* sick *of American kids.*

But then Olaf had touched Aria's arm. "He's right, though. There is a painting in a mansion not far from here—a practice study of *Starry Night.* No one has ever seen it."

"Really?" Aria raised an eyebrow.

"Really." Olaf peered out the window thoughtfully. "The woman who owns the house is very stingy with her money and her things. Word has it she has all kinds of priceless possessions in that house that should be in museums, but she wants them all to herself."

"Well, that's just ridiculous." Aria put her hands on her hips. "That's the most bourgeois thing I've ever heard. The masses deserve to witness great art just as much as rich people do."

"I agree," Olaf said. "Art like that should be owned by the world, not just one person."

Aria nodded emphatically. "It should be *liberated.*"

"Liberated?" Noel guffawed from the floor. "It's not a caged tiger, Aria."

But Olaf's eyes twinkled. "That is the most beautiful thing I have ever heard," he said in his delicious Icelandic accent.

The next thing she knew she was leaning against a brick wall outside the bar, Olaf's beard scratching her face, his lips searching for hers. When the door creaked, they shot apart. A figure was standing in the doorway, and Aria's heart stopped. *Noel?*

It was Hanna who'd walked out. She'd stopped short when she saw them, a disgusted look on her face. "Please," Aria had begged, stepping away from Olaf. "Don't say anything, okay?"

Now a whistle blew, yanking Aria from her memory. She glanced at Hanna and saw her biting her nails as though they were made of chocolate. Down on the field, Noel was laughing with Jim Freed. He probably didn't remember that night's conversation—he'd been so wasted. Thank goodness he had no idea what *else* had happened that night—no one did except Hanna. Sometimes, in dark moments, Aria dared to think of Olaf. There had never been a story about the police catching him—she assumed he and the painting were still out there. But how had he escaped the chateau? Where had he gone?

Bloop.

Aria looked down and frowned. There, on her new phone's screen, was an alert for a text message. Only she hadn't given anyone the number yet.

Her heart began to pound. Nervously, she opened the text. It was a picture of the *Splendor of the Seas* cruise ship on fire. A message accompanied it.

That was one smokin' cruise, Aria—I'm sure your BFF Graham thinks so too. Better hope he pulls through! —A

LET THE QUESTIONING BEGIN

On Wednesday afternoon, Spencer stood in front of the full-length mirror in her bedroom, inspecting her reflection. Agent Fuji was coming to interview all of them in a few minutes, and Spencer couldn't remember the last time she'd agonized over her outfit so much.

Was a pin-striped blazer too corporate? She frowned and pulled it off and tried on a pink blouse, but that just made her look like a big square of bubble gum. She needed casual but serious. Girl next door—no, *smart* girl next door. Someone who would never, ever break the law.

Her gaze drifted to the shimmering pearl-gray Zac Posen gown that hung in plastic in her closet. The tag was still on, but she didn't have the heart to return it. Two days later, Reefer's rejection still stung. Spencer had sent him a few plaintive texts, begging for another conversation. Maybe she'd misinterpreted what he'd meant when he said they shouldn't be tied down. Maybe he'd had a change of heart. But Reefer hadn't written back, and she'd begun to feel foolish and desperate. What she needed, she decided, was a prom date to take her mind off things. But who? All the eligible boys had been claimed months ago. Spencer considered calling her old boyfriend, Andrew Campbell, who had graduated early and was now at Cornell, but they hadn't spoken since last spring.

The doorbell rang, and she shed the blouse, changed again, and padded downstairs in a blue oxford shirt and skinny khakis. Aria, Emily, and Hanna stood on the porch, bouncing and quivering like a trio of shaken-up soda bottles. They rushed inside.

"We've got to do something," Hanna said.

"I think A's reading my e-mails," Emily wailed at the same time.

"I got a note on an *unlisted phone*," Aria blurted out.

"Hold up." Spencer stopped at the border of the hall and the living room. "Start over."

Each girl explained that they'd all gotten A notes in the past forty-eight hours. All of them had to do with telling the cops on them, like Spencer's had, and several mentioned Agent Fuji by name. Aria's was especially disconcerting—A had cracked her unlisted number in a matter of hours.

"Does A have an in with Verizon or something?" she moaned. "And I think A is trying to frame us for hurting Graham. As if *I* set off that explosion."

"A could try to do that with Gayle, too," Emily said.

"We were in her driveway when she was shot. I'm sure A has something up his or her sleeve about all of that."

"Don't forget A's threat to kill us," Hanna added.

"This is getting ridiculous. It's like A's everywhere." Spencer thought about how A had texted her almost the minute Reefer left. But how had A known? Spencer had been inside her house. It was like A had bugged the place or something.

She blinked. Was it possible? She peered into the corners of the room, the spaces under the couches, at the high windowsills. A rearing horse in the garish Civil War painting Mr. Pennythistle had hung in the hall leered at her.

Suddenly, she hit on an idea. "Come on," she commanded the others over her shoulder, heading toward the backyard.

Everyone followed her out the sliding door. It was wet and gray outside, and the air smelled like freshly cut grass and the swampy creek in the woods at the back of the property. A big blue tarp covered the family's swimming pool. An eerie haze hung over the trees where the Hastingses' refurbished barn had once stood—before Ali burned it down. To the left was the DiLaurentises' old house, though the only reminder that they'd lived there was the big boulder in the middle of the backyard that they never dug up—the new family had removed all other traces of them by now, including their old deck, and there was no longer an Ali shrine on the front curb.

Spencer marched to the shed Mr. Pennythistle had

installed a few weeks ago, unlocked the door, and looked around. An orange leaf blower leaned against the left wall. She grabbed it, dragged it to the middle of the yard, and pulled the starter chain. Her three friends stared at her like she was crazy, but there was a method to her madness. Everyone's hair flew about until Spencer pointed the nozzle at the ground. The air filled with the noxious scent of gasoline. The best and most important part was the deafening noise the thing made. No one, not even A, would be able to hear the girls over it.

Spencer gestured for the girls to move in closer. "This has got to stop," she said angrily. "If A knows where we are at all times, then A must be bugging us somehow. A's trying to pin all these crimes we didn't commit on us, and if we don't act soon, A might just succeed."

"What do we do?" Hanna yelled over the leaf blower.

"I say we go rogue," Spencer declared. "We get rid of our current phones and phone numbers. If we need cell phones for absolute emergencies, we can get a burner cell, but we can't tell one another *anything* critical on calls or voicemails. We should use a code phrase."

"What about *not it*?" Emily piped up.

"That's perfect," Spencer said. "And we can't give the number out to anyone else except for our parents."

Aria shifted her weight. "What about boyfriends?"

Spencer shook her head. "It's too risky."

Aria frowned. "Noel won't tell anyone."

"He might leave his phone out somewhere that A

might see, though. And you'll have to explain to him *why* you got a burner phone."

"How am I going to explain why I'm not using a phone at all?" Aria asked, hands on her hips.

Spencer stared at her, exasperated. "I don't know! Say you're doing it for a school project about living for a week without technology."

"What about e-mail?" Hanna asked.

"We can still use school e-mail for schoolwork—maybe we could carry our old phones around but only use WiFi. I'm pretty sure WiFi usage on phones can't be tracked in the same way as usage on a data plan. And we shouldn't use the Internet on our home computers—for all we know A has hacked into our systems. We need to use computers that won't be linked to us and definitely don't have any spyware installed."

Emily glanced at the spot where the barn had stood. "All that sounds well and good for A not knowing where we are *now*. But A could *still* frame us."

"That's the second part of my plan," Spencer shouted over the leaf blower. "As soon as possible, we need to go somewhere really secret and safe and sit down and figure out who A could be. There are probably all kinds of clues that we aren't even thinking about. And now that we know what happened the night of the fire, A could be Real Ali."

The leaf blower sputtered. The trees at the back of the property swayed, and for a moment, Spencer swore she saw a figure in the woods.

"That sounds like a good idea to me," Hanna said. "Where should we go?"

Everyone paused to think. Then Spencer's gaze drifted to a light on inside Mr. Pennythistle's office in the house. "The other day, Mr. Pennythistle told me that his model home at Crestview Estates has a panic room. Aren't those places, like, soundproof?"

"I think so," Hanna said. "And sometimes they have video surveillance, so you can see if someone is on your property."

"Perfect," Emily said. "A will never hear us in somewhere like that."

Aria squinted. "Crestview Estates isn't far from here, right? In Hopewell?"

"Yeah," Spencer said. Hopewell was a town about fifteen minutes from Rosewood. "And I bet I could steal the key to the house." Mr. Pennythistle kept copies of all of his properties' keys in his home office. It would just be a matter of finding the right one.

Emily's eyes gleamed. "Should we drive together?"

Spencer shook her head vehemently. "We need to all go separately to confuse A. It would be even better if we could go by different modes of transport—like bus or SEPTA or car."

Aria ground her toe into the grass. "Well, the public transport goes to Hopewell."

"And if some of us drive, we can take different routes," Emily said. "A won't know which one of us to follow. And if it seems like someone is following us, we could speed up or pull off or do a quick turnaround, maybe catching A in the act. Then we might see who A is."

"Great," Spencer said. She looked hard at the others. "How about tomorrow night?"

Everyone nodded. Then Spencer caught sight of a black sedan rolling up the long driveway. Her stomach turned over. *Showtime.*

The car cruised to a stop at the front of the house. A tall, thin woman with long, wavy, black hair and sharp features started toward the front door. When she noticed Spencer and the others in the backyard, she stopped and waved.

"Miss Hastings?" She looked questioningly at the leaf blower. "Doing some yard work?"

Spencer turned off the leaf blower and dropped it to the ground. She tramped through the wet grass toward the house. "Something like that."

The woman extended her hand. "I'm Jasmine Fuji." She looked at the others with wide gray eyes. "Let me guess. Hanna, Aria, and Emily," she said, pointing at each girl in turn. Then again, it wasn't hard—the four of them had been plastered all over *People* magazine last year after Real Ali allegedly died. Even a made-for-TV movie called *Pretty Little Killer* had been filmed, documenting Real Ali's torment and near killing of the girls.

When no one said anything, she cleared her throat. "How about we go inside and talk?"

Spencer led the way through the kitchen, nervously trying not to trip over anything. Then they lined up on

the living room couch, squeezed together tightly. Aria
flicked a tassel on a pillow. Emily crossed and uncrossed
her legs. Everyone's hair was a windswept rat's nest from
the leaf blower.

Fuji sat across from them on a striped ottoman, pulled
out a yellow notepad, and flipped to a clean page. Her
nails were impeccably groomed and painted pink. "Well.
Okay. Thanks for meeting me, for one thing. This is just a
formality, but I appreciate your cooperation."

"Of course," Spencer said in her most mature, profes-
sional tone. She wished she had something to do with
her hands.

"Your names were on a list of guests who were staying at The Cliffs resort in Jamaica the same time Tabitha
Clark was murdered," Fuji said, looking at a separate sheet
of paper. "March twenty-third to March thirtieth. Can
you confirm that?"

"Yes." Spencer's voice cracked, and she started again.
"Yes. We were there. We were on vacation for spring break
with a lot of our classmates."

Fuji gave them a tight smile. "Must be nice."

Spencer twitched. That sounded kind of bitter. *Must
be nice for you spoiled rich girls*, maybe. *You think you can
get away with anything, huh?* But then Fuji pointed to a
watercolor of a pastoral farm scene above the piano. "My
grandmother has one a lot like that, except a little bigger."

"Oh, neat. I've always loved that painting," Spencer
said quickly. *Calm down*, she scolded herself.

"So." Fuji took out a pair of glasses from her purse and perched them on her nose, then studied her notes again. "Did you meet Miss Clark while you were staying there?"

Spencer exchanged a look with the others. They'd briefly talked through what they'd say on the phone last night, but her mind suddenly was blank. "Sort of," she said after a moment. "I had a passing conversation with her, nothing big."

Fuji removed her glasses and put one of the stems in her mouth. "Can you tell me what it was about?"

Spencer's insides fizzed. "She thought we looked familiar. Like long-lost sisters."

Fuji cocked her head. Her teardrop earrings fluttered. "*That's* a strange thing to say."

Spencer shrugged. "She'd had a lot to drink."

Fuji wrote something down and turned to the other girls. "Do you remember Tabitha as well?"

Emily nodded. "We danced near each other." She swallowed hard.

Fuji turned to Hanna and Aria, and both of them said they'd met Tabitha in passing but didn't have a long conversation. Fuji didn't ask them to elaborate, so Emily didn't mention Tabitha's eerily similar Jenna Thing bracelet, Aria didn't talk about how Tabitha had hinted that she knew her dad was a cheater, and Hanna didn't tell her that Tabitha had known Hanna used to be a loser.

Everyone answered articulately. If Spencer were a bystander to the conversation, the girls would have seemed truthful enough. Distraught and quiet, maybe, but that was okay: A girl they'd met had been murdered a few feet from where they'd been sleeping.

Fuji capped her pen. "It seems like a lot of people are telling me the same thing—Tabitha must have gotten around that night, chatted everyone up. Everyone remembers her, but no one can connect her to anyone in particular." She put down her notebook and met their gazes. "I heard you girls were on the cruise ship that exploded, too."

"That's right," Spencer croaked.

"*And* I heard you were on Gayle Riggs's property when she was murdered." She stared unblinkingly at the four girls.

Hanna nodded faintly. Emily coughed. "We've been in the wrong place at the wrong time," Spencer said.

"Sounds like you guys have had a rough couple of years." A sad smile spread across Fuji's face. "Conspiracy-theory crackpots would probably have a field day with you girls, huh? They might say you're cursed."

Each girl laughed, though their chuckles were mirthless and forced. When Fuji gave them a strange, knowing glance, the moment felt spiky and electric. What if A had already told Fuji everything? What if she was just toying with them, waiting for them to slip up?

But then Fuji pressed her palms flat on the top of her notebook and stood. "Thanks for your time, girls. If you think of anything else, please let me know."

Spencer jumped up, too. "I'll walk you out."

Fuji bid her another good-bye at the door, walked down

the path, and climbed into her car. When she backed out of the drive and turned off the cul-de-sac, Spencer whirled around to face her friends, who were sitting stock-still on the couch.

Hanna broke the silence. "I thought she was going to nail us."

"I know." Aria collapsed into the back cushions. "I was convinced she knew more than she was saying."

Beep.

It was Spencer's phone. All of the girls' spines went ramrod straight. A *bleep* soon followed from Emily's phone. Then Hanna's buzzed. Aria's phone made a slide-whistle sound. Their screens all flashed with an alert that a new text message had come in.

Taking a huge breath, Spencer looked at the screen.

I do love some freshly planted lies on a lovely spring after-noon. I wonder if Agent Fuji feels the same . . . —A

Spencer squeezed her eyes shut. Letting out a wail, she hurled the phone across the room, where it crashed against a small side table. The battery flew out and skidded across the floor. Then she eyed the others. "Tomorrow?"

"Tomorrow," Aria growled. Emily and Hanna nodded, too.

It was their only hope. They were going to solve this, once and for all.

6

THE SITUATION ROOM

On Thursday, after the last bell rang, Hanna scuttled toward the parking lot, her leather tote bumping against her back. When she heard someone call her name, she turned. Chassey Bledsoe stood at the curb, smiling eagerly, every inch of her formerly pockmarked skin eerily blemish-free.

"We're shooting campaign videos," Chassey chirped. "Aren't you coming?"

Hanna glanced toward the lot, then back at Chassey. "Um, I can't."

Chassey looked disappointed. "Do you want me to tell them to reschedule?"

Hanna chewed on her lip. All she wanted was to make a video that was a zillion times better than anything Chassey could do. But then she thought of A's note about campaigning. It was painful to see all the VOTE CHASSEY posters on the wall when she couldn't put up a single

HANNA FOR MAY DAY QUEEN one. What if Chassey won by a landslide? Hanna would be humiliated.

"That's okay. I have an appointment I can't miss," she said. "It's sort of hard to explain. Good luck, though!"

"But . . . ," Chassey started, but Hanna just waved, turned, and jogged up the hill to her car. Before she got in, she pulled a black knit cap over her head and shrugged into a black peacoat she'd stashed in the back of the Prius. Time to get into secret-mission mode.

She climbed into the car, gunned out of the lot—well, as fast as a Prius could gun—and pulled onto the highway. She threw the new burner cell she'd picked up at Radio Shack in the console, then glanced at the car's GPS. The next turn wasn't for a few miles yet, but what was with that black SUV on her tail? She squinted in the rearview mirror, trying to get a glimpse of the driver. The windows were tinted. Her heart began to bang. Black SUVs were a dime a dozen here in Rosewood—it could be *anyone* in there.

She took the very next exit. *Recalculating,* the GPS said. The SUV followed. Hanna slowed at a stop sign and took a left. The SUV did the same. "Oh my God," Hanna whispered. Was it A?

She spied a Wawa ahead and pulled into the parking lot. The SUV whizzed past. Hanna reached for a pen to scribble down the license plate, but the car was out of view before she could read the last two letters. Shifting into reverse, she peeled out and took the back way to the highway. When she merged into traffic, the black SUV was nowhere in sight. She wished she could call Mike and tell him about how much of a badass she was. But as of now, Mike didn't even have the number for her burner cell, a hideous flip-phone thing that Hanna couldn't even buy a bejeweled Tory Burch case for.

Twenty minutes, three more suspicious vehicles, and several more evasive turns later, Hanna pulled up to a secluded street of huge, cookie-cutter mansions. A man-made lake glittered in the distance—even the plump, brilliantly colored mallard ducks looked like models. A few athletic-looking people were out walking their dogs, even though a steady rain had started to fall. Hanna pulled into the long slate driveway of number 11, noticing a light on inside.

She got out of the car and tiptoed toward the door. The heavy scent of pine bombarded her nostrils. For a neighborhood in the middle of the bustling Main Line, it was eerily quiet, the only sounds the chirps, crunches, and flutters of nature.

Before she could ring the bell, a hand grabbed her arm from behind. She started to scream, but a second hand in a black glove clapped over her mouth. "*Shh*," Spencer whispered, pulling the hood off her face. "Didn't I tell you not to go in the front?"

"I forgot," Hanna said, suddenly irritated. She'd lost four tails! She couldn't be expected to remember *everything*.

Spencer led her through a side entrance and into a

mudroom that smelled like 409 cleaner and cinnamon candle. Then she guided her down a flight of stairs into a finished basement with a game room, wine cellar, and home theater. To the left was a heavy iron door with a spinning bank vault handle. Spencer wrenched it open. "Go," she whispered, pushing Hanna inside like she was a hostage.

Hanna squinted in the dim light. The room had thick, solid walls. There was a small denim couch, a few chairs, and a card table in the corner, along with a bookcase that held some magazines and board games. On two walls were video cameras of the house's massive front and back yards. Hanna watched them for a few minutes. Trees brushed back and forth. A rabbit hopped in front of one of the cameras.

One of the screens showed a cab pulling up to the driveway. Aria, wearing a black hoodie like Spencer's, slunk out of the car and crept toward the house. Spencer appeared on the screen and led Aria to the same entrance Hanna had come through.

Emily arrived a few minutes later. Then Spencer unfurled a large piece of blank paper and taped it over the closed vault door. "Okay. Let's get started."

She pulled a black marker from her purse and wrote *A* at the top of the piece of paper. "What do we know so far?" she asked.

Hanna jiggled her leg. "Well, A killed Tabitha. So it's someone who was in Jamaica."

Jamaica, Spencer wrote. "What else?"

"Do you think A was a friend of Tabitha's, or an enemy?" Emily asked. "I would say an enemy since A killed her, but maybe that's what A *wants* us to think."

Aria nodded. "A was poised on the beach, so A knew Tabitha was going up to the roof to talk to us. Do you think A told Tabitha to say all those Ali-like things to us, too? Like how you guys seemed like long-lost sisters, Spence? Or how you used to be chubby, Hanna?"

"Maybe. And A could have given that string bracelet to Tabitha, too," Hanna said. "But why would someone want us to think Tabitha was Ali?"

"To pique our curiosity, so we would *definitely* go on the roof deck with her when she asked?" Aria said. "And then . . . what? Orchestrate things so that we'd push Tabitha off? How would A know that was going to happen? A's not a mind reader."

"It might have just been an accident that Tabitha fell," Hanna decided. "What if A really asked Tabitha to push *me*? But then Aria stepped in and pushed her instead. Everything went wrong, until A realized how to make it *right*. A killed Tabitha when she fell and then blamed it on us."

Spencer capped the marker. "That could be how it went down, I suppose. But who would do something like that?"

Emily looked at the others. "It's obvious, isn't it?"

Hanna swallowed hard. "Real Ali?"

Emily shifted her weight on the couch. "It makes sense. First of all, she knew our weaknesses—it would have been easy for her to tell Tabitha what to say. She wanted revenge once and for all. *And* it makes sense how she knew Tabitha—she met her at The Preserve. But how did she get Tabitha to do all that—even potentially murder for her? What did Tabitha have to gain from it? Do you think she paid her?"

"Tabitha's family was rich." Hanna leaned toward the TV screens. "Besides, does Ali *have* money? Even if she had some sort of trust account, she couldn't draw from it—I'm sure her accounts are being monitored, if her family hasn't already taken back all the funds."

"Maybe someone else is giving her money." Spencer tossed the marker from hand to hand.

There was a silence. It was so quiet inside the panic room that Hanna could hear the ticking of Spencer's Cartier watch. "It doesn't explain why Ali would have bludgeoned her to death, though," she said. "I mean, someone *could* have seen her. She took a big risk."

Aria breathed in. "Someone could have seen Real Ali, *period.* How was it that *no one* noticed her in Jamaica? Isn't that weird?"

"That brings us back to the money thing," Spencer said, writing *money* on the sheet of paper. "Now that I think about it, the DiLaurentis family definitely didn't have cash. When I found out all that stuff about Ali and Courtney being my half sisters, part of it was about how the DiLaurentises were broke—probably from paying those outrageous hospital bills for all those years. So how could Ali have gotten the cash to travel to Jamaica? And if she's A, how did she come back to Rosewood and stalk us so expertly?"

"And go on the cruise," Aria added. "All of that takes money."

"She has to have someone bankrolling her," Hanna concluded. "It's the only thing that makes sense—not just for the money aspect, but because of other stuff, too. She can't be everywhere at once. It's just not possible."

"So she has a helper, then," Spencer said. "Just like we thought."

Hanna nodded. "Honestly, who's to say Ali has *ever* been working alone? Maybe she had someone help her drag Ian's body out of the woods that night after we found him. Remember how quickly he was gone?"

She shivered, thinking back to that cold, creepy night. They'd come upon Ian's bloated, blue body and had run back to get Officer Wilden, only to find a matted patch of grass when they'd returned. The mechanics of it had always bothered Hanna. Ali was tough, but she wasn't strong enough to drag a six-two, one-hundred-eighty-pound guy away from a crime scene in under ten minutes.

Spencer sat down on the couch. "Someone could have helped her carry Ian up the stairs and put him in the closet at the Poconos house, too. That same someone could have been the one to kidnap Melissa."

"*And* kill Jenna Cavanaugh," Hanna said, shifting to the edge of the couch excitedly.

"And set that fire in Spencer's backyard," Aria added.

Everyone stared at each other. It seemed so obvious now. Ali wasn't superhuman. Of course she had help. But who was crazy enough to help her?

"It has to be someone who loves her, obviously," Aria said faintly.

Spencer wrote *love* on the paper. "Like a friend or a boyfriend, right?"

"Sure." Emily sounded a little pained. "But that could be *anyone.*"

Hanna sat back to think. "Well, Real Ali was in The Preserve for a long time. So maybe it was someone she met while she was there."

"Like Graham?" Emily asked, looking at Aria.

Aria hunched her shoulders. "Graham seemed more into Tabitha than Ali, and he told me he never visited The Preserve. And I'm not sure he's A—he's been in a coma since before the latest notes came in."

"But maybe *Ali* wrote the most recent notes," Spencer suggested, writing down Graham's name anyway.

"And potentially bugged our houses? I don't know about that." Aria tucked her feet under her butt. "And anyway, A is threatening to frame us for hurting Graham. My money is on Graham *seeing* Ali's helper. I bet that's what he was trying to tell me in the boiler room."

Hanna perked up. "Ali *did* have some good friends at The Preserve, though. Remember Iris, Ali's roommate? When I was there, she talked about Ali—well, she called her Courtney—all the time."

"Ooh, that's good." Spencer wrote *Iris* beneath Graham's name.

Then Hanna tapped her lips. "Although I'm not sure Iris could *be* Ali's henchman. She was at The Preserve when Ian was killed. I don't know how she could have snuck out to haul Ian's body to the Poconos, either. We'll have to figure out a way to see if she was there when we were in Jamaica, too."

"Still, she could know something." Spencer turned back to their list. "Who else?"

"We can't leave off Jason," Aria volunteered.

Hanna frowned. "Ali's brother? Do you really think he'd help her?"

"Who knows?" Aria shrugged. "That family is beyond weird."

Hanna raised an eyebrow as Spencer wrote it down. That was big of Aria to suggest it—she'd had a crush on Jason forever.

"What about Cassie, Ali's field hockey friend?" Spencer asked. "Remember, before Ali died, how she bragged about Cassie nonstop? How she was going to high school parties. How Cassie was the coolest. How Cassie was going to be her new BFF."

Emily didn't look convinced. "I ran into Cassie last

Christmas, and she seemed okay. And anyway, that was *our* Ali's friend, not Real Ali."

Spencer smacked her forehead. "Right. God. It's hard to keep track."

They wrote down a few more names, including Darren Wilden and Melissa, only because the two of them had been involved in Ali's case from start to finish. But they didn't seem like very likely suspects. Spencer scratched her chin. "I still feel like we're missing something huge. Maybe Ali's helper is right in front of us and we don't see it. Is there anyone besides the four of us who has been around this whole time? During Ian's death, Jenna's death, the fires, Jamaica, that summer, all of it?"

Hanna cleared her throat. "Well, I can think of two people, but I don't think either of them would be Ali's helper."

"Who?" Spencer's eyes widened.

"Mike." Hanna looked guiltily at Aria. " . . . and Noel."

Aria burst out laughing. "Never in a million years."

Spencer's marker hovered over the paper. "We can't rule anyone out, though."

She wrote Noel's name at the bottom, then capped the marker once more. Aria glowered at her. "Why aren't you writing Mike's name?"

Spencer sank into one hip. "Do you seriously think your brother would do that to you?"

Aria pressed her lips together. "Well, maybe not. Besides, Mike's an idiot."

Hanna let out a small squeak. "Hey! He's my boy-friend!"

"Well, Noel's *my* boyfriend." Aria peered at everyone anxiously. "You guys, this is crazy. Just because Noel was everywhere with us doesn't make him guilty—it's just a terrible coincidence."

"We know," Spencer assured her. "We just have to write down everyone, okay? That's the point of this meet-ing. We'll probably be crossing him off the list in days." She turned back to the list. "This is a good start, don't you think? We should investigate some of these people. Graham, Iris—there are some good leads here."

Emily looked at Hanna. "You should take Graham. You've volunteered at the Bill Beach before—maybe you could get your job back."

Hanna shot up straight. "I don't want to go there again!"

"Em's right, Hanna," Spencer said. "You make the most sense. You want to figure this out, right?"

A foul taste welled up in Hanna's mouth. She thought of the clinic's horrible antiseptic smell. The yellow pee in the bedpans. Dealing with Sean, her ex. Then again, it was a better option than going to The Preserve. It would be just her luck that they'd readmit her or something.

"I'll do it," Hanna mumbled.

"And I'll talk to Iris," Emily volunteered. She looked at Hanna. "Do you think she's still at The Preserve?"

Hanna closed her eyes, remembering the last time

they'd all been to the mental hospital to question Kelsey Pierce, the girl Spencer had framed for drug possession who then almost hurled herself off Floating Man Quarry. "I don't remember seeing her," she murmured.

Spencer peered at the video cameras. The lawn was still empty. "I'll go after Real Ali herself. Maybe there's a way to find her. Maybe we're missing something. If we found *her*, we could end this even faster."

"Who should I investigate?" Aria asked, winding a piece of hair around her finger.

Spencer shifted awkwardly. "Well, you *could* look into Noel. Just to get him off the list."

Aria's eyes blazed. "A *isn't* Noel!"

"I know," Spencer said. "But you could peek around his room. Make sure he doesn't have a second cell phone or a secret e-mail account. Not that he *ever* would, of course."

Aria looked miserable. "If my relationship ends because of this, it's your fault."

They talked through a few more possibilities, solidifying their plans. After another fifteen minutes, they felt like they had worked through as much as they could. Spencer stood and stretched.

Hanna turned to the cameras once more. The picture was in black and white, and something at the very edge of the back lawn flickered into view. She inhaled sharply. Had someone just moved behind a tree?

She shot up, staring at the fuzzy image. It was difficult

to tell whether it was a person, an animal, or nothing at all. She looked at her new phone's screen. No alerts had come in.

Aria, Spencer, and Emily were peeking at their phones, too. It was as if they were waiting for A to write, saying *Gotcha!* Or, *Did you really think you could outsmart me?* One minute passed. Then another. Finally, Spencer breathed out. "I think we're good."

Hanna shut her eyes. All her life, she'd fought to not be invisible, to not be a nobody. But right now, it was the best feeling in the world.

7

EMILY'S NEW HOUSEGUEST

Even though Emily had been to The Preserve at Addison-Stevens only once before, she felt an uneasy sense of familiarity as she drove up the long road. The building's gray brickwork had definitely shown up in her dreams. She'd doodled the Gothic windows in the margins of her notebook without knowing why.

She parked in the visitors' lot and tried to slow her breaths. It was the following afternoon; she'd skipped her last period of the day, a free study, to make the drive to The Preserve. But just knowing that Real Ali had spent years here, masterminding ways to kill them, made her stomach seize. What if Ali's helper had also been imprisoned behind these walls? What if the two of them had huddled in the dreary dayroom together, plotting how they were going to ruin Emily, Hanna, Spencer, and Aria? Emily peered at the figures passing through a glass-walled hallway. *If the next person who walks by is a woman, this will go okay*, she wagered silently.

A tall man in a tweed jacket with patches on the elbows walked by next. *That* wasn't encouraging.

But she had to go through with this. Rolling her shoulders, she stepped out of the car and started toward the double doors. Earlier today, she'd called the hospital asking if she could visit Iris Taylor. The nurse had said that Iris could have visitors in the afternoon, so Emily knew that Iris was still a patient. But when Emily pressed to see how long Iris had been at The Preserve—she wanted to rule her out as Ali's helper—the nurse wouldn't give her any information.

A gust of wind slithered down Emily's back and lifted her coattails. Before she went inside, she picked up her new phone and, after a pause, logged onto Twitter. Yeah, it was breaking the no-Internet rule, but she *had* to check. There was her prom invitation and note, but no one had responded or retweeted. What made Emily think Jordan had even *seen* it?

She shut her eyes and tried to imagine what Jordan was doing right now. Sitting at an Italian café in big sunglasses? Lounging on a deserted beach in the tropics? She longed to be stirring her coffee next to her or splashing her with sea foam. The desire was so strong, it physically *hurt*.

Sighing heavily, she trudged inside the marble lobby. A woman in a white lab coat greeted her with a big smile. "I'm here to see Iris Taylor," Emily said. "I'm Heather Murphy." It was her default name; she'd used it when she was a waitress at the seafood restaurant on Penn's Landing the summer she was pregnant. Gayle Riggs, the woman she'd almost given her baby to, *only* knew her as Heather . . . until A got involved, that was.

The woman smiled. "I'll let her know."

With a gesture of her arm, she directed Emily toward the patient area. Emily walked slowly, bracing herself, and shuddered at the heavy *click* of the bolt on the door that separated the lobby from the ward. The hallway was quiet, had stained beige carpet, and smelled of hot dogs. A chilling laugh pealed from one of the rooms. A wild-haired girl passed, going the other direction. When she caught Emily watching, she stared back at her blankly. "*Boo!*" she shouted. Emily jumped, and the girl laughed.

Emily pulled open the double doors to the dayroom. The same faux-cheerful construction-paper balloons and stars were on the walls from when the girls had visited Kelsey. Worn jigsaw puzzles were stacked on a shelf, and there were a few books on an industrial-looking metal bookcase. A sign on top of the TV read NO CABLE.

When Emily pulled the door shut, a few girls, all dressed in white pajamas, turned excitedly, perhaps hoping that Emily was here for them. An overweight girl who had a visible bald spot attempted a smile, but it looked more like a grimace. A frail-looking ashen girl lowered her head and muttered. Emily looked around for Kelsey, but she didn't see her anywhere. She'd been too nervous to ask the nurse if Kelsey was still here.

Then Emily spied a girl with ice-blond hair in the corner. She matched the description Hanna had given her of Iris. Clearing her throat, Emily called out Iris's name. The girl, who couldn't have weighed more than ninety pounds, whipped around and gave Emily a long, knowing look.

"Your name isn't Heather Murphy," she said in a dry, craggy, tough voice. Her white pajama bottoms inched down her hips when she stood. "You were one of *her* friends, weren't you?" She moved closer. Her breath smelled like sour candy. "That bitch who stole Alison's life."

Emily flinched. She could feel everyone in the day-room staring at her, but she didn't want to give them the satisfaction of seeming uncomfortable. "That's right, I'm Emily," she said. "I was Courtney's friend." It was still weird to call Their Ali *Courtney*. "And I heard you were Ali's friend—and roommate. I have a couple of questions about her. Is there somewhere we could talk in private?"

Iris crossed her arms over her chest. For a moment, Emily was sure she would refuse, but then she shrugged. "I don't know what I can tell you about her, but sure. Let's talk."

Then she turned on her heel and headed for the door. Emily followed her, trying to ignore the prying eyes on her back. She wondered if they were even *allowed* to leave the dayroom, but there were no nurses around, no one to stop them.

Iris padded down a hall and opened a door near the fire exit. Inside were two unmade twin beds. One side had posters of teen bands on the wall–Justin Bieber and a few Disney Channel stars–and an assortment of pink stuffed animals on the bed. The other side was bare and impersonal, like a hotel room. Iris flopped down on the generic side and glanced disdainfully at the Bieber posters. "My new roommate is *such* a loser." Then her bright green eyes turned back to Emily. "So? Why do you want to know about Ali?"

Emily perched on a scratchy corduroy chair. "I think she's still alive."

Iris snorted. "Bullshit. She was trapped inside an exploding house."

"Maybe not."

Iris crossed her legs. Her bony knees poked through the fabric of the pajamas. "Do the cops know this?"

Emily shook her head. "We wanted to try to find her ourselves."

"Why?"

Emily stared fixedly at the digital clock across the room. How could she make this sound innocuous? Iris didn't seem like an idiot; if she'd heard about Real Ali dying inside that house, then she'd probably also heard that Real Ali had tormented them as A. Why else would they want to find her except to stop her forever? This was Iris's friend Emily was talking about. She wouldn't want to sell her out.

"Forget it, I don't really care," Iris said, as if sensing the reason for Emily's hesitation. And then a light came on in her eyes. She inched closer to Emily's side. Her sudden proximity made Emily flinch. Though Iris was small, she radiated with angry energy.

"So what do you want to know?" Iris asked. "I could tell you all sorts of things about her."

"Really?" Emily sat up straighter.

"Uh-huh. But there's only one way I'm going to do that. You're getting me out of here."

Emily laughed nervously. "*Out* of here?"

Iris nodded. "I've already told the nurses that I have an ailing grandmother in the hospital. That's the only way they let you out for a few days, you know—to see sick relatives or go to funerals. Really happy, huh?" She rolled her eyes. "I was just waiting for the right opportunity—and guess what? You're it. Now, go back to the front desk and explain to them that you're my cousin and you've come to sign me out so we can see Nana together."

"*Nana?*"

"We have to make it convincing!" Iris sounded exasperated.

"And then what?" It was slowly dawning on Emily that Iris was serious. "Do you want to go home?"

"Actually, I was thinking I could stay with you."

"*Me?*"

Iris crossed her arms over her chest. "No questions, okay? I've been cooped up in this hellhole for four years with no break. You can't even imagine what that feels like.

I have *really* good stuff on Ali, but you're not going to hear a word of it if you don't help me. Are you in or out?"

Emily bit her thumbnail. "Wait. You've been here for four years *straight*?"

Iris pointed at a folder hanging from a plastic slot on the door. "Check my records if you want."

Her gaze remained on Emily. After a pause, Emily marched over to the door, ripped out the file, and leafed through it. Sure enough, there were patient records for Iris dating back four years ago. Nowhere were there signs that she'd ever been released, not even for a weekend. Iris was telling the truth.

Emily dropped the file back into the slot. If Iris had been here for four years without a break, that meant she couldn't be Ali's helper, killing all those people last winter and murdering Tabitha in Jamaica last spring. Feeling better, she cleared her throat. "You don't have a vendetta against anyone on the outside, do you? You're not going to go on some sort of rampage if I check you out?"

Iris scoffed. "They don't allow people like that out *ever*. Why do you think Alison never went home?"

Emily had never thought of that. "Okay," she said quietly. So Iris would stay with Emily for a few days. If it meant finding out more about Ali—about A—it would be worth it.

But her legs were still shaking as she walked back down the hall toward the lobby. The same woman who'd checked her in smiled from behind the desk. "Um, I forgot to mention," Emily began, her voice trembling, "I'm Iris's cousin. I'm taking her to see our grandma."

She figured the receptionist wouldn't buy it, but after a few quick checks with some nurses and Iris's case manager, Iris was cleared to leave. When she appeared in the lobby, she'd changed into a pair of jeans that were slightly too short, as if she'd bought them a few years back. Coupled with a pink parka and a lumpy leather purse, she looked sort of . . . dorky, like a girl who sat alone in the cafeteria.

They exited the hospital together. The grass squished beneath their feet as they walked toward the parking lot. It was so quiet outside Emily could hear her own ragged, nervous breathing. She looked around, certain A was watching, but there wasn't a single car on the road or pedestrian on the little trails that circled the property. The only sound was the bubbling fountain close by, the one dedicated to the memory of Tabitha Clark.

"Let's do this, bee-yotch!" Iris whooped as Emily unlocked the Volvo. She climbed into the passenger seat, slammed the door shut, and pulled a crumpled piece of paper from her pocket. "Okay. First stop, the Metropolitan Bar in Philly."

"Ex*cuse* me?" Emily stared at her. "Why are we going there?"

Iris held up the paper. It looked like a list, written in craggy, frenzied script. *Have cocktails at the Metropolitan Bar. Pretend-hump the dinosaurs at the Franklin Institute. Run up the Art Museum steps like Rocky. Find Tripp.* "These are the things I've wanted to do for four years. And you're going to take me to do them."

"*All* of them?" Emily bleated, scanning the list. It was at least fifty items long.

Iris raised an eyebrow. "If you want intel on Ali, every single one."

"Okay," Emily said quietly. There was nothing like the promise of Ali secrets to shut her down. And she had a feeling Iris knew that, too.

She started the engine, gritting her teeth. *This is all for a good cause, this is all for a good cause.* Still, her throat was dry. She glanced at her new cell phone, certain A had sent a text about how she wasn't going to get away with this.

But there was nothing.

8

A MONSTER IN THE CLOSET

Aria's last class of the day was newspaper editing, which was held in the journalism barn. Even though the school paper had gone digital ages ago, the building still smelled like ink and newsprint. Old headlines of important Rosewood Day events decorated the walls, everything from the 1982 Rosewood Day Boys' Soccer Team winning the state championship to a hundred trees being planted on the school's perimeter to honor the victims of 9/11.

Ten minutes into class, Noel slunk through the back door. "Where were you?" Aria asked as he slid into the seat next to her.

Noel shrugged. "I tried to text you, but this message came on saying your phone was out of service."

Aria stared at the grooves in her desk. "I told you. I'm not using technology this week as part of a science project." The lie felt awkward on her tongue. Noel wasn't going to buy *that* story for very long.

The PA crackled, and a familiar throat-clearing sound signaled that Principal Appleton was about to speak. "Students?" he boomed. "Would everyone mind turning to our school station? We have some important May Day Prom news."

Mr. Tremont, the teacher, rolled his eyes but dutifully switched on the television that hung on the wall next to the whiteboard. Penny Dietz, who did the morning news, appeared. "Good afternoon, Rosewood Day students!" she chirped, her cheeks looking extra shiny. "The May Day Prom is approaching, and today we're going to hear from some of the candidates for prom king and queen. First up, prom queen. We haven't received Hanna Marin's video as of yet, so let's hear from Chassey Bledsoe."

Noel frowned. "I can't believe Hanna didn't make a video yesterday."

Aria looked away. *She was busy meeting in a secret room, figuring out who A might be.*

Chassey Bledsoe appeared on the screen, talking over-enthusiastically about how she was thrilled to be running and that she was hosting a Vote Chassey Pasta Dinner tomorrow at the local Olive Garden franchise, which her uncle owned.

Then it was time for the candidates for king. When Noel's image popped up, Aria's heart did a proud flip. His hair was pushed back from his forehead, showing off his bright green eyes. The black button-down he was wearing popped against his olive skin.

Aria poked him playfully. "No *wonder* all the girls want you."

Noel smiled lazily. "But I got the best one."

Aria squeezed his arm, but then her smile dimmed, and she turned away. Spencer had written Noel's name on the suspects board yesterday . . . and Aria had *let her.* Just that alone made her feel dirty and ashamed.

All day, Spencer had been texting Aria, asking if she'd asked Noel anything yet. But what the hell was Aria supposed to ask? *Hey, did you kill a girl who was impersonating Alison in Jamaica and are you now trying to pin it on us?* Didn't Spencer realize her relationship, the only good thing Aria had going right now, would be over?

How could her friends possibly think Noel could be helping Ali out? Okay, so Noel had been in Jamaica—it was possible he could have seen the girls on the roof with Tabitha. But he never, ever would have fed Tabitha those Ali-lines. And, what, did they seriously think he'd *killed* Tabitha on the beach? Noel let spiders out of the house instead of stepping on them. He couldn't go into the SPCA, because he said he'd take every dog home with him.

Yes, he had known Ali—*both* Alis. He and Their Ali had even dated for a little while at the end of seventh grade, but Ali had broken up with him after two dates, probably because she liked Ian Thomas.

When Aria looked up, Penny was back on the TV screen. "I also have an exciting announcement about the head of the prom decor committee. In a secret meeting with Rosewood staff, students, and our generous donors, it has been decided that this year's decor chairwoman for the *Starry Night*–themed event is . . . Aria Montgomery!"

Everyone turned and stared at Aria. She blinked at the television. Images of Van Gogh's *The Starry Night* swirled, accompanied by a techno song. Then her senior picture appeared. ARIA MONTGOMERY, it read at the bottom. MAY DAY PROM DECOR CHAIRWOMAN!

"Congrats!" Devon Arlyss patted Aria on the back. "I'm *so* jealous."

"Can I help out?" Colleen Bebris asked excitedly, even though she was only a sophomore.

"This is awesome!" Noel's face popped up in front of Aria. "You've always wanted decor chairwoman, right?"

"B-but I didn't apply for it," Aria blurted out.

Noel frowned. "Do you not want it?"

Aria swallowed hard. "I . . ." Not long ago, she *would have*. But the very last thing she wanted to do was a big mural of *The Starry Night*.

Her thoughts returned to that night in Iceland. After Hanna caught her and Olaf kissing, all three of them had stumbled back into the bar. Aria had been sure that as soon as she walked in, Noel would *know* . . . but he was chatting up a couple of blond girls from Poland. The girls were making Noel and Mike say certain words with American accents; every time Noel said something new, the girls laughed and shook their boobs. Would he even *care* that Aria had hooked up with someone else? Did she even matter?

She wanted to prove something to herself that night. That she was still worldly. That she was still Icelandic Aria. She grabbed Olaf's arm and whispered, "Let's steal that painting that's locked in the chateau."

Olaf blinked. "Are you serious?"

"Yeah!" Aria jumped up and down. "We'll be art vigilantes! We'll call up the press and tell them we've saved it and we're going to put it in a museum. Maybe we could start our *own* museum!"

There were crinkles by Olaf's eyes when he smiled. "You're so cute when you get excited."

"This isn't about being cute!" Aria cried. "Will you do it?"

Olaf glanced over at Noel, as if to say, *You aren't going to involve your boyfriend in this, too, are you?* Then he shrugged. "What the hell?"

They waited another hour—by that time, Noel was barely intelligible, and he, Mike, and Hanna were getting ready to go back to the guesthouse. Aria went with him, but then said she'd forgotten something at the bar and needed to go back. Noel stumbled to bed, not even questioning her. Aria ran to the next alleyway, where Olaf was waiting in his Jeep. He gathered her in his arms, his breath smelling sweet, not boozy at all—Aria then realized she'd only seen him nurse a single beer all night. "This is *so* incredible," he whispered.

"I know," Aria said, but she pulled away. She was *quite* drunk—too drunk to kiss, even. Her head was whirling all over the place.

They skidded out of the parking space down the bumpy Reykjavik streets. Olaf gripped Aria's knee with one hand as he steered. When a stone house perched atop a hill came into view, Aria actually gasped. Some of the windows in the house were made of stained glass. A weathervane spun at the top. The house had gargoyles and turrets and a lot of ornate arches, nothing like the sporty, simple, nautical homes in town.

They parked away from the house and got out. Even though it was two AM, they could easily see the doors and windows under the midnight sun. "Look," Olaf whispered, pointing at a wide-open window on the first floor. It was like whoever lived here was *asking* to be robbed.

Aria watched his feet disappear through the window. A second later, his head popped over the sash. "You coming?"

Aria dove into the house as well. It smelled like mildew inside, and there was a fine film of dust on the floor. Sheet-covered furniture stood in every room. A grandfather clock ticked loudly in the corner. Gilded-framed paintings hung on the walls, but most were more abstract than *The Starry Night*, cubes and lines and even one that was, as far as Aria could tell, nothing but blue squiggles.

Olaf disappeared down a hall, and Aria followed. When she looked into a small, dim office, she saw a medium-sized canvas with familiar swirls and stars. She gasped and backed up, her head spinning with booze. She blinked hard, wondering if she was imagining things. She hadn't actually believed they'd find it.

"Olaf!" she cried out, leaping over an ottoman in the middle of the room and touching the frame with both hands. The painting dislodged from its hook easily. Aria steadied it in her arms. It smelled like canvas and dust. Up close, she could just make out the *Van Gogh* signature at the bottom.

It sobered her immediately. She held the painting outstretched as if it had just hissed at her. *Holy shit*, a voice screamed loudly in her mind. She was holding a *Van Gogh*. Was she insane?

"Nice!" Olaf said from the doorway. He beckoned Aria to him, but her legs felt useless. Letting out a wail, she shoved the painting at him and stumbled away.

"Aria?" Olaf had called after her. "Where are you going?" It was then that all the alarms went off.

The bell signaling the end of the period rang, and Aria jumped. Noel was staring at her curiously, but everyone else in class had gone back to their own business. Mr. Tremont opened the door, and the class filed out. Aria followed, still in a daze. People surrounded her as soon as she walked onto the grass.

"Congratulations, Aria!" said Reeve Donahue, one of the girls on the prom committee.

"Nice one!" Mai Anderson chirped, patting Aria's arm.

Riley Wolfe sniffed. "You *know* it's just because she's going out with Noel," she whispered loudly to Naomi Zeigler.

Aria blinked blearily at Noel, Riley's words ringing true. "*Did* you have something to do with this?"

Noel twisted his mouth, looking guilty. "I thought you'd be happy about it. I knew you hadn't applied . . . so I put in an application for you, using some of your art projects."

Aria swallowed hard. She knew she should be touched, but all she felt was panic. "I've just got a lot on my plate right now, that's all," she mumbled after too long a beat.

"Like what?" Noel asked.

"Like . . ." She looked around and lowered her voice. "I was questioned about that girl's death in Jamaica."

Noel shrugged. "Yeah, I was questioned, too. What's the big deal?"

Aria peeked at him, her pulse picking up speed. "You talked to Agent Fuji? What did you say?"

They reached the main building. Kids thundered past them in the halls. Someone banged a locker door shut. Noel worked his locker combination, avoiding her gaze. "I don't know. I told her that I saw Tabitha around but didn't talk to her. And I certainly didn't see someone beating her skull in on the beach."

"That's *all* you said?"

Noel pulled a book off the shelf. A muscle next to his eye twitched. "Yes. Why? What's going on?"

She licked her lips. If she continued with this line of questioning, she was going to seem really, really guilty. "I'm just freaked out," she managed to say. "After all the Ali stuff . . . it's just hard to talk to more cops."

Noel slammed his locker shut and touched her arm. "But it's over. The FBI lady won't bother you again—she said she was done with me, too. It sucks that we were there when someone died, but it's not like we killed her."

Nerves slashed through Aria's chest. "Uh-huh," she said weakly.

All of a sudden, she had to get out of here. She kissed him hurriedly. "I'm excited about the decor chairperson thing, really. Thank you so much. But now I have to go."

It took her only ten minutes to get to her mother's house, and she tried to keep her mind blank the whole drive home. She barreled up the driveway and jammed her key into the lock. But before she even turned it, the door opened. Usually they locked the dead bolt, too.

"Hello?" Aria called into the hall. No answer. She peeked into the kitchen, the backyard, and then the bedrooms. Her mother, Ella, wasn't here.

She looked in her bedroom last, and her blood went cold. There, on the bed, lay a piece of paper that hadn't been there this morning. She snatched it and looked at the words marching across the top of the page. They were in Icelandic. The bottom half of the page had been translated into English: *Wanted Reykjavik Man Missing. Murder Suspected.*

When Aria saw the face in the photo, she gasped. *Olaf.*

She swallowed hard and looked at the article. *Olaf Gundersson, 21, went missing from his house on the outskirts of Reykjavik on the night of January 4.*

That seemed like ages ago. Aria thought back. She had no idea what she was doing January fourth. Lounging around—they'd still been on winter break. Bored without Noel—his family had gone to Switzerland to ski.

She read on. *Foul play is suspected, as Mr. Gundersson's apartment was ransacked and there was blood on the floor. After extensive police questioning, locals said that Mr. Gundersson, who was "a bit of a hermit," had been in a loud and violent fight the evening before, though they couldn't identify the other person in the argument.*

Mr. Gundersson had been accused of breaking into the Brennan Manor last summer and stealing the Starry Night *study painting by Vincent van Gogh, though Mr. Gundersson had claimed in earlier questioning that he did no such thing. A police search of Mr. Gundersson's home did not turn up the painting, and one theory is that Mr. Gundersson took it with him after the attack. There is a citywide search for both his body and the priceless artwork, though nothing has been recovered yet.*

Aria's head swirled.

Then she noticed the red scrawl at the very bottom of the page. *Look in your closet.* Someone had drawn a big, bold arrow, as if Aria might not know where her closet was.

Shaking, she turned and stared at her closed closet door. Someone had been in here. They could still be here.

Should she call the police? And say . . . *what*?

She inched over to the closet door and pulled at the knob. Her shirts and dresses swung on hangers. Her shoes rested in shoe trees. But there, on the dusty wood floor, was a rolled-up canvas. Aria's fingers fumbled with it as she lifted it up and pulled off the rubber band. A familiar painting, now out of its heavy frame, unfurled. There were those iconic swirls and cometlike stars. And there, at the bottom, was a signature that took her breath away: VAN GOGH.

She dropped the painting to the floor. As it bounced on the hardwood, a small slip of paper dislodged from somewhere inside. It landed faceup, so Aria could read exactly what it said without laying a finger on it.

Dear Aria,

Isn't seeing good art truly liberating?

—A

SPENCER WAS NEVER
ONE FOR RULES. . . .

Spencer peeked through the bay window of the model home at Crestview Estates. A stone McMansion loomed over the trees across the street. A mallard waddled in the direction of the water. A car swished past on the road, but it didn't slow at the house.

She hadn't wanted to come here again—it was unnerving enough stealing Mr. Pennythistle's spare key once. Besides, she had a history paper to write, calculus homework to decipher, and potential prom dates to call and feel out—there was Jeff Grove from yearbook, though she didn't feel too excited about him, and, of course, Andrew, but she could just picture his I-knew-you'd-want-me-back tone of voice when she asked, even though he'd been the one to end things with her. But Aria had called the girls' burner phones this morning and said *Not it*. So it was back to the panic room they went.

The others hadn't arrived yet, so she settled into the

so-new-it-still-smelled-like-a-leather-factory couch in the generically decorated living room and stared at her old cell phone, which she'd removed from the data plan and was using via the house's WiFi. Taking a deep breath, she typed ALISON DILAURENTIS CONSPIRACY THEORIES into the browser.

She paused before pressing the search button. She hated resorting to the Internet for information on Ali, but she was out of options. She'd driven by the abandoned house in Yarmouth where the DiLaurentises lived when "Courtney" returned. She'd walked the whole way around the property. The deck was swept clean. There was a single Rubbermaid garbage can in the garage, but Spencer couldn't get inside to see what was in it.

She pressed the magnifying glass. Up came Google results. UNSOLVED PHILADELPHIA CONSPIRACIES was the title of the first site, along with the description A REGULAR SOURCE FOR THE PHILADELPHIA SENTINEL, THE ROSEWOOD GAZETTE, AND THE YARMOUTH YARDARM. Spencer clicked on the link, and a blog slowly loaded. The main page had a picture of the Rocky statue in front of the Philadelphia Art Museum. IS ROCKY TRULY CURSED?, the type read. READ ON FOR THIS AND OTHER PHILADELPHIA-RELATED CONSPIRACY THEORIES.

She clicked on the link. There were posts on the Philadelphia Experiment, a story about how, in 1943, a war vessel docked in Philadelphia mysteriously vanished—people were sure it was a government plot to render warships invisible. Below those were posts about Ben

Franklin being a polygamist and his homosexual dalliances, Betsy Ross working part-time as a madam when she wasn't sewing American flags, and the Liberty Bell bearing secret inscriptions from aliens. Below all of *that* were more recent conspiracy theories, including a kidnapping of a wealthy man's daughter in the 1970s, which included a lot of links to police reports and even a shout-out from a biographer who'd written a book about the crime. Finally, at the bottom, was the twisted tale of Alison DiLaurentis and her identical twin, Courtney.

With shaking fingers, Spencer clicked the bottom link. WHY ALISON DILAURENTIS MIGHT NOT BE DEAD, read a blog post. It was dated from April of last year, not long after the fire in the Poconos. The post included a police report about the fire, including a coroner's assessment that no bones had been found in the rubble. There was also some information about the Radley, where Their Ali had been, and The Preserve, including medical documents and police files most people wouldn't have access to. There were even a few tidbits about the DiLaurentises' lives *before* they moved to Rosewood; they weren't called the DiLaurentises back then but the *Day*-DiLaurentises. Maybe they'd cut off the first part of their last name in an attempt to escape their past.

When Spencer finished clicking on all the images and links, her head was spinning. Whoever this blogger was, he was legit. Working on some of those other cases must have opened some doors for the blogger, got him some connections. She wondered what *else* he knew.

The blog didn't have any conclusive evidence of why Ali wasn't dead or where she'd gone, but the post *was* from a while ago. Spencer scrolled down to see if there were any newer posts, but there weren't. The blog was still up and running, though; the latest entry was about a rumor that all of the Wawa markets in the tristate area were run by the Knights Templar. She clicked on the ABOUT ME tab at the bottom. It said the blog was run by an avid investigator named Chase M., but instead of a picture, there was a video loop of a cat slapping another cat. There was a loud, fake *kapow!* sound when one cat's paw hit the other cat's cheek. *Okay.*

Crack. Spencer looked up. What if A was here? She stared at the empty street until her vision blurred.

Then she clicked on the CONTACT US link and composed an e-mail on a generic template. *I am connected to the Alison DiLaurentis case. I can't tell you my name right now, but I will if we talk. I'm eager to know if you have more information about her.*

She signed it *Concerned in Rosewood.* In the space where the template asked for her e-mail, she used an address she'd created that morning, its password so nonsensical and impossible-to-crack that she almost forgot it as soon as she made it up.

"Spencer?"

Aria's face loomed on the other side of the window. Spencer shot out the door and pulled her inside. A cab pulled up seconds later, and Hanna tumbled out. Emily drove up at almost the same time. Spencer led them down the hall and opened the heavy door to the panic room. The video monitors flickered. The room still smelled faintly of the microwave popcorn they'd made the last time they were here. Spencer fished out the list of potential Ali's helpers and taped it back on the door. The remaining suspects glared at her. *Iris. Darren Wilden. Melissa. Jason. Graham. Noel.*

"This had better be good," Emily grumbled as she peeled off her jacket. "I had to leave Iris at my house for this. Who knows what sort of insane things she's going to tell my folks?"

"Iris is at your *house*?" Hanna repeated, staring at her.

Emily nodded, then explained how Iris would only give her Ali intel if Emily signed her out for a while. "I told my parents she's a low-income student from inner-city Philadelphia who's going through some tough times at home right now, and I'm doing this as an outreach program through Rosewood Day. Amazingly, they bought it."

Spencer looked at Aria. "So what's going on?"

Aria whipped out two things from her yak-fur bag. One looked like a newspaper article. The second was a handwritten note. Spencer recognized the scrawl immediately.

Aria showed the article to Hanna. "Recognize this guy?"

Hanna shook her head, but then her face paled. "Wait.

Is that . . . O-Olaf?" she stammered. Her eyes scanned the article. "He's missing?"

Aria nodded. "This happened in January."

"Who's Olaf?" Emily asked, hugging her knees.

"A guy I met in Iceland." Aria swallowed hard.

Hanna lowered her chin. "You didn't just meet him."

"Okay, I kind of hooked up with him," Aria mumbled. "I was really drunk."

Spencer's eyebrows shot up. Aria seemed so happy with Noel—Spencer never would have guessed that she'd cheated on him.

A crow landed near one of the video cameras, its body huge on the monitor. Spencer looked at the scrawl on the little piece of paper Aria had found. *Isn't seeing good art truly liberating?* "What does that mean?"

Aria looked back and forth nervously. "Well, Olaf and I did more than just hook up. We sort of . . . stole a painting together."

Spencer blinked. "You *what*?"

"What kind of painting?" Emily breathed, her hands at her mouth.

Spencer tried to listen as Aria laid out what had happened, but her brain stalled out once she heard the name *Van Gogh.* "How did I not know this?" she gasped. Then she glanced at Hanna, who had a guilty expression. "*You* knew?"

"It's not like I *wanted* to know," Hanna said, crossing her arms over her chest. "She called me in a panic when the police came—I picked her up. But we decided to keep it quiet."

"I figured the less people who knew, the better," Aria said softly, picking at the hem of her sweater. "And for a while, it was fine—the cops never caught Olaf, the painting was never found, and nobody ever connected it to me. But when I came home from school yesterday, that article was on my bed and the painting was in my closet. I'm sure A put it there."

Spencer's heart stopped. "A priceless Van Gogh is in your *closet*?"

Aria's eyes filled with tears. "The article says the authorities couldn't find the painting when they searched Olaf's house. Ali must have gone there, chopped up Olaf—the article says blood was all over the floor—moved his body somewhere, ransacked his place, and taken it. And then she brought it back here."

Hanna frowned. "I'm not sure if Ali could have done all that. How could she have gotten a passport? And Olaf was over six feet. It's like the Ian thing—Ali couldn't have been strong enough to strangle him all by herself."

Aria shrugged. "Maybe her helper did it, then. It doesn't change the fact that Team A killed Olaf so that they could get the painting. And now, one well-placed call from A, and I'll have a SWAT team on my lawn."

"Whoa," Emily whispered.

"Maybe you should turn the painting in anonymously," Hanna suggested, wrapping a piece of hair around and around her finger nervously.

Spencer's eyes widened. "Art theft is, like, a major crime. You could be on a surveillance camera. You could get in serious trouble."

"And now you guys could get in trouble, too," Aria cried. "All of you know what I did now. You know where a stolen painting is." Tears welled in her eyes. "You can turn me in if you want. I understand."

Emily touched her arm. "We aren't going to do that."

"We'll figure this out without any of us getting in trouble, okay?" Spencer added. "I just don't understand how A *knew* what you did."

"I guess A followed us to Iceland," Hanna concluded.

"And followed me to the chateau?" Aria held her palms to the ceiling. "There weren't any other cars even on the *road* until the police came. I suppose A could have come on foot, but—"

"What if A listened in on our call on *my* end?" Hanna interrupted.

Aria pushed a strand of hair out of her face. "You think A was staying in our guesthouse?"

Spencer leaned back in the chair and shut her eyes. Her head was throbbing, and she felt that same old rising panic that had plagued her many times before. How could A be in so many places at once? How could A know *everything*?

Then she opened her eyes. "Aria, maybe A was staying in your *room*."

She must have had a telling tone, because Aria set her mouth in a line. "A is *not* Noel."

"Are you *sure*?" Spencer threw up her hands. "Aria, Noel has been *everywhere* bad stuff has happened to us. Jamaica. The cruise. Now Iceland. Do you really think that's just a coincidence?"

"Noel was dead-drunk that night," Aria protested, her voice going high.

Spencer paced back and forth around the little room. "Maybe it was just an act. Hanna, do you remember where Noel was when you talked to Aria?"

Hanna shoved her hands in her pockets, the light from the digital clock on the wall glowing red on her face. "Well, he wasn't in bed when I woke up. And I didn't see him in the hall, which is where I was for most of the conversation. He came inside from the back when we got home, though. He said he was smoking a joint, but he didn't smell like weed at all."

Aria's eyes blazed. "Now you're against me, too?"

"Of course I'm not against you!" Hanna said. "But, Aria, it *is* weird."

Spencer shifted forward in the chair. "Remember how strange Noel was when 'Courtney' came to Rosewood?" she asked. "He was in a support group with her. He urged you guys to be friends. And you caught them making out at the Valentine's Day dance. . . ."

Aria slapped her arms to her sides. "Ali *ambushed* him! Noel didn't want to kiss her. She just made it look like he did."

"Are you sure?" Spencer asked. "It was that kiss that

made you get in the car to go with us to the Poconos. What if Noel was in on it?"

Aria's mouth hung open. "I can't believe you."

One of the surveillance monitors went dark. Everyone's gaze shot to it. There was fuzz, but then the image reappeared. The yard was empty. A few leaves drifted past the camera, and that was all.

Spencer shook her head. "I'm sorry, Aria. I don't want it to be Noel, either. I just wish we could rule Noel out for good. The article says Olaf was killed at the beginning of January. Do you know where Noel was around then?"

Aria ran her tongue over her teeth. "Switzerland. His family was skiing. He asked me to go, but I wanted to stay home and spend time with Lola."

"Are you *sure* they were skiing? Switzerland isn't *that* far from Iceland."

Aria pounded a fist on the arm of the sofa. "He posted a ton of pictures on Facebook! Do you honestly think Noel flew to Iceland, killed a guy, and came home the next day like nothing ever happened? You think he's *that* good of a liar?"

"Just see if you can find a lift ticket or something from January fourth, okay? And ask him where he was yesterday when someone snuck that painting into your house. It must have been while we were at school, right? So, basically, Noel will tell you he was in eighth period or whatever, and tons of people will vouch for him."

A worried look crossed Aria's face, but then she shook

her head. "I'm not interrogating my boyfriend. If he finds out why I'm asking him these questions, he'll dump me."

"No one wants you guys to break up," Emily said quickly.

"Look, the rest of us will see what we can discover," Spencer said, slumping against the wall. "Until then, don't do anything with the painting, okay, Aria?"

Aria's mouth made an O. "I'm supposed to keep it in my closet?"

"Just hide it." Spencer glanced at Hanna. "What's going on with the burn clinic?"

Hanna sighed. "I *really* don't want to volunteer there. But I'm talking to Sean's dad about it tomorrow."

"And how about Iris?" Spencer asked Emily.

Emily chewed her bottom lip. "I haven't found out anything about Ali yet. But Iris has been at The Preserve for four years without a break, so there's no way she can be Ali's helper."

"Good." Spencer stood up, uncapped the marker she'd brought, and crossed Iris's name off their list. "Hopefully she'll tell you who *is*."

Aria placed her hands on her hips. "And how is *your* investigation going, Spence?" she asked, a bitter tone in her voice. "Why haven't you tracked down Ali yet?"

Spencer bristled. "Um, I'm working on it." She could feel Aria's gaze on her, but she didn't know what else to say.

They shut off the lights in the panic room. Since Spencer had driven, she offered to take the girls who had come in cabs back home. As they walked out the door of the panic room, Spencer stared at Aria's straight back and wondered what was going through her mind. She felt kind of . . . betrayed. After all that had happened, after A had tormented them about so many things, how had Aria kept quiet about the painting? And now Olaf, whoever he was, was missing and maybe even dead. Aria was right: They all *could* go to jail for knowing where a stolen painting was hidden and not coming forward with the information.

Ping.

It was Spencer's old phone, still connected via WiFi. She cautiously looked at the screen. It was an e-mail on her newly created account. The return sender was PHILA-DELPHIA CONSPIRACY THEORIES.

She glanced at her friends. Hanna was peeking out the window. Aria was staring into space, lost in her own world. Emily was looking at her own phone with a glazed-over expression. Head lowered, Spencer clicked OPEN and read the two sentences. *We should definitely talk. There's a lot you need to know.*

She hit REPLY. *I'm available whenever*, she wrote back. *The sooner, the better.*

10

JUST LIKE OLD TIMES

The sky turned gloomy as Hanna steered the Prius into the parking lot of the William Atlantic Plastic Surgery and Burn Rehabilitation Clinic. She shut off the engine and looked at the squat, übermodern building. Was she seriously doing this? Part of her wanted to call up Spencer and beg for a different mission.

Her old phone bleated a new message from her school e-mail account. It was from Chassey Bledsoe: VOTE CHASSEY FOR QUEEN!

Hanna squeezed the phone between her hands, wishing she could send an alert, too. How else would people know what an awesome queen she'd make? *And* she'd heard that, as part of the *Starry Night* theme, the queen's crown would be even more bejeweled than ever.

The Starry Night. Her insides twisted. It was such an eerie coincidence that the very painting Aria had stolen was this year's prom theme—if it was a coincidence at all.

All A would have to do was tip the cops off that the paint-ing was in Aria's closet and she'd be done for. And though the police might not ever know that Spencer and Emily knew about the theft, there were Hanna's phone records from that night in Iceland. She'd be ruined, too. Who knew, maybe A would even figure out a way to blame them for Olaf's death.

What had Aria seen in Olaf, anyway? His beard was nasty. The cap he wore looked like it was from a Dumpster. But Aria was always into those grungy dudes—Hanna had been surprised, actually, when she started dating Noel. Neither of them were each other's types—a few boys on the lacrosse team even joked for a while that Noel was dating Aria because her dad, Byron, had access to good pot. Hanna was pretty sure that wasn't true, but what if Noel *did* have an ulterior motive to go for Aria? What if someone had put him up to it? Someone like . . . *Ali*? Could Noel be Ali's helper?

Hanna hated to think it, but Ali having a helper made a lot of sense. It also fit that Noel was that person—for a lot of different reasons. At the beginning of sixth grade, when Real Ali was still around and Hanna was still a loser-ish nothing, her BFF was Scott Chin. Scott was out of the closet even then, and he had a raging crush on Noel and was always jealous of his girlfriends. "What does he see in Alison DiLaurentis?" he whined at lunch one day when he spied Ali and Noel giggling at the cool table. "She's such a butter face. Everything about her is pretty . . . *but her face.*"

Hanna rolled her eyes. "She's not a butter face." Alison was the most beautiful girl ever. She'd modeled at the King James Mall spring and fall runway shows, and rumor had it she'd even been tapped by a big agency in New York City.

"Oh please, yes, she is." Scott's eyebrows, which Hanna suspected he plucked, knitted together. "I wonder if Noel has to close his eyes when he makes out with her."

Hanna lowered her PB&J. "Do you think they actually make out?" Kissing was still exotic to her. She couldn't believe kids her age were doing it.

"Oh, yeah." Scott had nodded. "I saw them doing it in the woods behind the playground."

Sighing, Hanna returned to the present and pushed through the double doors. Instantly, the familiar odor of gauze, antiseptic, and something that could only be described as burnt skin hit her like a tidal wave. She looked around, taking in the fake flowers on the tables and the patient art on the walls. Everything was the same as the last time she'd been here, down to the peppermints in the dish on the front desk. She remembered, suddenly, running into Mona in this lobby. Mona had acted all weird and cagey about why she was there, not admitting she was getting treatment for the burns from the prank-gone-wrong that Ali, Hanna, and the others had played on Toby Cavanaugh. In all the time they'd been friends, Hanna had never known Mona had been at the Cavanaughs that night, watching Ali shoot that firework into the tree house, witnessing Jenna getting blinded, maybe even hearing the fight Ali and Toby had afterward. Of course, Mona's silence had been intentional.

"Hanna?"

She looked up and saw Sean Ackard's rounded cheeks, burning blue eyes, and do-gooder smile. He stood in the doorway of one of the offices, wearing a crisp blue button-down that looked like it had come straight from his father's closet.

"Hey, good to see you!" Sean said. "Why don't you step in here so we can talk?"

Hanna fiddled with a tissue box on the front desk. "I'm waiting to see your dad."

Sean rapped on the doorjamb. "Nope. Your interview is with me."

Hanna bit down hard on the inside of her mouth. She hadn't really spoken to Sean since things crashed and burned last year. These days, he was going out with Kate. Total weirdness.

Shrugging, she followed Sean into the room and sat down on a couch. Sean sat at a desk that was populated with stacks of papers, a flat-screen computer, and empty coffee mugs. An Elmo stuffed animal sat on a shelf behind him. There was a picture of Sean shaking the hand of the governor of Pennsylvania. "Do you work here now?" Hanna asked in confusion.

"On the weekends, just to help my dad." Sean straightened some papers. "We're so overcrowded right now—a couple of local hospitals closed their burn clinics because of budget cuts." He exhaled heavily, then looked at Hanna. "So how's Mike?"

Hanna blinked, startled. "Uh, fine."

The mention of Mike made her feel squirmy. It wasn't like he knew she was here; he'd never, ever understand why she was back to beg for her old job. Every story she'd told him about the place was more disgusting than the last. She'd told him she had a hair appointment today to practice for her prom updo, but all he had to do was call up Fermata, the salon, and catch her in the lie.

"Good." Sean smiled. "So you actually want to come back?"

Hanna shifted. "I feel bad about cutting my volunteer time short," she lied. "After everything that has happened to me, I thought I should give back a little, you know?"

Sean arched an eyebrow. "Didn't you hate it here?"

Hanna clasped her hands together, trying to look earnest. "I've changed. Volunteering means a lot to me. I have a friend in here right now, actually, someone I met on the cruise. Graham Pratt?"

Sean sat back in his chair. "Yeah, Graham came in a few days ago." He shook his head solemnly. "That cruise sounded like a nightmare. I heard about what happened to you guys, too—about that life raft. Some people were saying it was a suicide pact."

Hanna didn't dignify that with a response. "It was scary to have to evacuate . . . and then get stranded at sea.

I sort of had an epiphany when I almost drowned—life's too short, I'd better make it count. So . . . please, can I help out?"

Sean bounced a pencil, eraser down, on the desk. "Well, my dad said you could volunteer again as long as you work hard."

"I can do that!"

"Okay," Sean said. He extended his hand to Hanna, and she shook it. Then, his expression suddenly became almost mournful. "You know, I never got to tell you how awful I felt about all that Ali stuff."

"Oh, uh, thanks."

"I can't even imagine what that must have been like," Sean went on.

Hanna's eyes filled with tears. It was one thing for a friend, a parent, a complete *stranger* to offer sympathy, but there was something both touching and weird about Sean saying it. "Thanks," she mumbled.

Sean stepped forward, wrapped his arms around her, and gave her a quick hug. He smelled familiar, like cinnamon and deodorant and the potpourri his mom used generously around the house. It was a nice smell, a comfortable smell. Suddenly, Hanna didn't hate him as much.

She left his office for the women's staff room, where she changed out of her Rachel Zoe print dress and snakeskin flats into hideous, oversized scrubs that smelled like puke. Then she went back to Sean's office.

"Ms. Marin?" A woman in pink scrubs appeared from

around the corner. "I'm Kelly, one of the head nurses. I'm here to show you the ropes."

"Kelly's one of our best," Sean said proudly.

"What would you like me to do?" Hanna asked pertly.

"How do you feel about bedpans?" Kelly asked.

Hanna winced, but it wasn't like she could complain with Sean still standing right there. "I *love* bedpans."

"Well, great!" Kelly pumped her fist in the air. "Let me show you what to do!"

Kelly helped her with the first bedpan, giving Hanna the opportunity to carry the pee-filled thing down the hall. A male nurse passed her going the opposite direction. Hanna couldn't help but stare—he was tall, built, and extremely handsome, with a shaved head and gleaming blue eyes.

"Hey," the nurse said to Hanna, widening his eyes at Hanna's boobs.

"H-hey," Hanna stammered back, then followed the nurse's gaze. He wasn't staring at her boobs. He was looking at the bedpan. Pee sloshed over the sides, splashing dangerously close to Hanna's scrubs. She squealed and almost dropped the thing on the floor.

Kelly giggled. "Jeff *always* has that effect on people."

They continued into the next room. Sean was right about the place being overcrowded: There were burn victims everywhere she looked. In the halls. Crammed three to a room. There was even a bed in one of the waiting areas.

"Is this legal?" Hanna asked, nearly tripping over someone's monitor stand.

Kelly shrugged. "Until the new wing is finished, we don't have anywhere to put everyone."

Then Kelly pantomimed inhaling and exhaling an invisible cigarette and said she'd be back. Hanna turned back for the supply room to grab a clean bedpan. Something behind her caught her eye. The nurse's station was empty. Every single chair was unoccupied.

She tiptoed around the desk and peered at the computer console. A program showed a list of patients in the clinic and their corresponding room numbers. *Score.* She dragged the pointer down the page. GRAHAM PRATT. According to the files, he was in room 142, which was just down the hall.

She stepped away from the desk just as Kelly swept around the corner, smelling like a Newport. "Okay, honey, time for mopping!"

Hanna added soap to the bucket and started down a hall. She gazed at the room numbers as she passed: 132 . . . 134 . . . 138 . . . and there it was, room 142. It wasn't a room, per se—more like a small partition in a corner separated by a curtain.

She held her breath and peeked in. There, on a bed, lay a boy with a big bandage on his head and neck. His eyes were shut tight, and tubes snaked into his hands and mouth. Several machines beeped. A frisson went through Hanna's body. This was what A was capable of. Hanna must have made a strange noise, because Kelly placed her hand on her shoulder. "That's your friend? I heard you talking about him to Sean."

Hanna stared at the blinking lights on Graham's monitors. "Y-yeah," she said, feeling a little bad for lying. "How is he?"

Kelly's mouth made an upside-down U. "He's in and out."

"Has he said anything?"

Kelly shrugged. "No. Why?"

For a split second, she was looking at Hanna kind of suspiciously. "Can you do me a favor?" she asked in an innocent voice. "If he starts to wake up and I'm not here, can you call my house? I want to tell him something important. Something I should have told him before all this."

Kelly's eyes softened. "He really meant something to you, huh?" She gave Hanna's hand a squeeze. "You got it."

Then Kelly disappeared back into the hall. Hanna remained where she was, staring at the figure on the bed. Graham's monitors beeped steadily. His chest rose up and down. Then, his eyelids fluttered and his lips parted.

Hanna leaned over his bed. "Graham?" she whispered. "Are you there?" *Did you see A?* she asked silently.

A puff of air escaped between Graham's lips. His eyelashes fluttered once more, and then he went motionless on the pillow. Hanna pulled away from the bed, her heart still pounding hard. Graham was going to wake up soon. She could *feel* it.

A high-pitched giggle came from the vents. Hanna stiffened and looked down the hall. Patients lay motionless. Mop water gleamed on the floor. Everything was so still and quiet that for a second Hanna felt like she was dead.

She shuddered. If she and the others didn't find Ali and her helper soon, she *might* be.

11

FAMILY BONDING TIME

As soon as Emily stepped into Saks Fifth Avenue at the King James Mall, a pin-thin girl appeared with a flower-shaped glass atomizer. "Want to try the new Flowerbomb?"

"Absolutely," Iris insisted, pushing Emily out of the way and holding out her impossibly skinny, blue-veined wrist. "Now you, Emily."

Emily shrugged and complied. After the perfume girl sprayed the fruity liquid on her wrist, Iris glanced at some-one behind them. "You should try it, too, Mrs. Fields!"

Emily whirled around. Her mom stood in the entrance, peeling her plastic, see-through rain hat from her head. "M-mom?" Emily stammered. "What are you doing here?"

Mrs. Fields stuffed the hat into her quilted purse. "Iris invited me. And since it was on my way home from CVS, I figured, why not?" Then she stuck out her wrist for some Flowerbomb and gave Iris a warm smile.

This whole Iris thing was freaking Emily out more

every second. For one thing, Emily kept waiting for The Preserve to call up and say, *Um, have you stolen our patient?* For another, she hated, hated, *hated* that Iris had to stay at her house—sometimes without Emily supervising. After Emily had returned from the panic room yesterday, she hadn't known what to expect. What if Iris had decided to tell her parents everything? What if Iris had flipped out and gone after them with a kitchen knife?

But instead, she'd found Iris and her parents sitting on the living room couch watching *Jeopardy!* and drinking tea. Somehow, that was even *more* terrifying. Iris was acting like she was just a member of the family. "I'm sure Iris is tired, Mom," Emily had blurted out in horror. "She's had a long day, and she probably wants to go to bed."

"What are you talking about? I'm wide awake!" Iris had said eagerly, moving a little closer to Mrs. Fields on the couch. She had been eating, Emily had noticed, one of her mom's Rice Krispies treats. *No one* ate those things— they always came out hard as rocks and way over-buttered. Mrs. Fields, of course, had looked thrilled.

Now, Emily poked Iris's side. "Why did you invite my mom?" she murmured.

Iris shrugged innocently. "She's cool."

Yeah, right, Emily thought, waiting for Iris to roll her eyes and say something nasty. But she didn't. Instead, Iris turned, checked to see that the perfume girl's back was turned and Mrs. Fields's attention was occupied by a free makeup sample offer, and scooped up a Flowerbomb perfume box from a display table and slid it up the sleeve of the baggy sweatshirt Emily had lent her. Emily reached forward to stop her, but Iris just gave her an I-know-what-I'm-doing look. This was the reason they were at the mall, after all. *Steal lots of shit from Saks* was number sixteen on her list of Things I Want to Do During My Time Off from The Preserve. Maybe there were bonus points for doing it in front of Emily's mom.

She trailed after Iris down the sweet-smelling corridor toward the Contemporary section. As Emily passed the handbags, someone yanked her arm. Spencer was crouched behind a table full of Marc by Marc Jacobs satchels. "*Psst,*" she whispered.

Emily ducked down beside her. "What are *you* doing here?"

Spencer's eyes darted back and forth. "I special-ordered shoes for prom at Saks." She peered down the corridor at Iris, who was now posing in front of a three-way mirror. "Has she told you anything yet?"

"Not since you *last* asked," Emily grumbled. "We've been too busy."

"Doing what?"

Emily gazed at a perfume ad across the aisle. The girl in the picture looked a little like Jordan, which made her heart ache. "Well, after I signed her out of The Preserve and before I met you at the panic room, Iris made me go to the city so she could make out with a Ben Franklin impersonator. And then, this morning, I had to drive her to her old school. Iris wanted to climb a rope in the play-ground and ring a brass bell at the top." She'd looked like a spider on that rope, all spindly arms and legs, the jeans Emily lent her held up by a child-sized belt.

"It turns out high school kids hide pot up that pole," Emily went on. "Iris came down with a huge bag. So now I've got an escaped mental patient *and* pot at my house. My parents will freak if they find out."

As soon as she said it, she realized how ridiculous it sounded. Her parents would freak even more if they found out Emily was keeping the secret that Aria had stolen a priceless painting. *And* helped shove a girl off a roof. *And* everything else.

Spencer shifted her weight. "So she's told you *nothing* about Ali?"

Emily looked around for Iris, finally spotting her blond head by a rack of miniskirts. "I'm working on it." She'd asked Iris for an Ali tidbit last night, but Iris had said that Emily hadn't done anything to really deserve information yet—she would have to prove herself. When Emily asked Iris what, specifically, she had to do to receive a blessed piece of information, Iris had tossed her hair, shrugged, and said, "I'll know it when I see it."

"And A doesn't know Iris is with you, right?" Spencer whispered.

Emily squeezed a Michael Kors clutch, angry all over again that Iris had changed the rules on her. The tissue paper inside crinkled. "No."

"What should we do about that painting?"

The cloying mix of perfumes was giving Emily a headache. "I don't know. What do *you* think we should do?"

Spencer slowly shook her head. "I don't have a clue."

Emily stared into Spencer's clear blue eyes. She still couldn't believe that Aria had kept her secret for so long, especially given that she knew about things Spencer, Emily, and Hanna had done over the summer. But now that she thought about it, there might have been one time around Christmas when Aria had tried: They were at Spencer's annual party, and after a couple of drinks, Aria had pulled Emily aside. "I've done something awful," she'd whispered into Emily's ear. "I can't live with myself."

Emily had assumed she meant Tabitha. "Any of us would have done the same thing."

Aria shook her head, her eyes glittering with tears. "You don't understand. You just don't understand. What I did will ruin *everything*, and—"

"*There* you are!" a voice said from behind them, and suddenly Noel clapped a hand on Aria's shoulder. Aria's features crumpled into something resembling a smile. "Hey, will you come meet my buddy from lacrosse camp? I haven't seen him in ages!" Noel said.

"Sure!" Aria said brightly, her mouth still wobbling.

And just like that, he was steering her away from Emily. In retrospect, perhaps a bit territorially. Like Aria was his possession.

But the next time Emily had caught up with her, she'd

been buoyant and lively. What if Aria had been trying to tell her about hooking up with Olaf? Stealing the painting?

"Ooh! These are pretty!"

Emily snapped out of her reverie in time to see Iris showing Mrs. Fields a pair of teal-blue jeans. They were a size 00—and Emily guessed they would *still* be too big on Iris.

She was about to stand up to go join them, but Spencer grabbed her arm. "Do you really think Noel was on a ski trip the weekend Olaf was killed?"

There was a determined look in Spencer's eye, the same sort of face she got when she, Ali, Emily, and the others used to put together puzzles on the floor of Ali's Poconos living room. Sometimes, they made solving the puzzles a race, and Spencer, desperate to beat Ali, shoved pieces together even when they didn't fit.

"I don't think we should go on a witch hunt quite yet," Emily said slowly.

"But Noel makes so much sense, don't you think?" Spencer whispered.

Emily shut her eyes. She didn't *want* Noel to make sense. It would kill Aria. "I don't know," she said wearily.

"Emily!" Iris crowed. When Emily looked up, Iris was coming straight for them.

Emily shoved Spencer out of the way and stood. "Hey!" she called, trying to smile.

"What were you doing on the floor?" Iris stared suspiciously at the spot where Emily had just been sitting.

Blessedly, Spencer had scampered out of sight. Then Iris pressed an armful of silk blouses at Emily's chest. "Stuff these in your bag. I already pulled the electronic tags off."

She glared at Iris. "My mom's right over there!" Mrs. Fields was holding up a leopard-patterned jacket to her torso and twisting this way and that in the mirror.

Iris scoffed. "So? She won't see." She inched closer. "I'll give you a really good Ali tidbit if you do."

"Fine," Emily growled, yanking the shirts out of Iris's arms. Glancing back and forth, she took a deep breath and shoved the shirts deep into her swim bag that sometimes doubled as a purse. She marched over to her mom and grabbed her elbow. "We're going now."

"So soon?" Mrs. Fields looked disappointed. "We just got here! And isn't this cute?" She showed Emily the leopard jacket. "I wanted to get you something special."

"That's sweet, but, um, Iris has an interview at four thirty," Emily said, steering them toward the exit. "It's a really big deal—they're thinking of offering her a scholarship."

"Really?" Mrs. Fields smiled at Iris. "Where?"

"Villanova," Emily said quickly before Iris could spout out a made-up college name—or ask what the hell Emily was talking about. "I have to drive her there, in fact. So we'd better get a move on."

Her heart thudded as she walked past the displays by the doors. As her fingers curled on the handle, she braced herself for the alarms—and her mom's wrath.

But no sirens sounded as Emily pushed through the second door fast and spilled onto the sidewalk. Her whole body was sweating. Her head throbbed. She couldn't believe Jordan used to do this on a regular basis—except with boats and cars.

"Okay, see ya, Mom," Emily said, yanking Iris toward the station wagon.

"This was lovely, girls!" Mrs. Fields looked so pleased Emily almost felt sorry for her. She waved as she headed toward the family minivan. "Let's do it again!"

Emily's swim bag felt like a lead weight in her hand. She was certain that any minute someone was going to pounce on her and make her return everything. Only once they were in the car and moving did she breathe out.

Iris kicked her legs. "Whoa, what a rush!"

Emily squeezed her hands on the wheel. "I can't believe you made me do that in front of my mom."

Iris rolled her eyes. "Stop being so dramatic."

"I've definitely done my part," Emily insisted. "Now tell me something about Ali."

Iris rubbed her palms together. "What do you want to know?"

Emily's mind scattered in a thousand different directions. She hadn't been prepared to get to choose her question. "Did Ali have a boyfriend?"

Iris ran her fingers across one of her newly stolen shirts. "Everyone adored Ali. Guys *and* girls. Everyone wanted a piece of her."

"Was there someone special? Someone who would do anything for her?"

A knowing smile spread across Iris's face. "You were the one who was in love with her, weren't you?"

Emily flinched. "Who told you that?"

Iris's eyes locked on Emily's. "Ali talked about you all the time when she was at The Preserve. She was like, *My sister has this one friend named Emily who's got it bad for her. That's how I'm going to win her over. She'll be a piece of cake.*"

Emily focused on the lines on the highway until they blurred. That was exactly how Ali had won Emily over; she'd kissed Emily as passionately as Emily had kissed Their Ali in the tree house at the end of seventh grade. And then Ali had said how much she'd always loved Emily, even when she was trapped in The Preserve. Of course Emily had bought it. It had been what she'd always wanted to hear.

"Aw, did I hit a nerve?" Iris asked, stroking Emily's forearm.

Emily ripped her arm away. "It doesn't matter."

"Do you still love her?"

"I'm not talking about this with you," Emily snapped. "But no, I don't love her anymore." Again, Jordan's face flashed in her mind. She felt a pang of sadness.

"But you did after the fire in the Poconos, didn't you? Someone snuck an iPad into The Preserve around the time all that Ali stuff went down, and I remember watching a lot of the footage. I saw your face on the news. You looked crushed that she might be dead. Your true love . . . *gone*. That had to hurt."

Emily turned her head so sharply toward Iris that Iris cowered. "What do you know about true love?" Emily snarled.

Iris's bottom lip trembled. "I was in love once, too."

The moment suddenly defused. There were tears in Iris's eyes. She pressed her lips together so tightly they were translucent. Emily did the same thing when she was trying to hold it together.

Emily faced front again, feeling bad for lashing out. "Sorry," she muttered. "I thought you were teasing me. Do you want to talk about it?"

Iris sniffed. "I'm not talking about this with you," she said in the exact same tone Emily had used.

"Touché," Emily said softly.

They passed a Wawa and a flower shop, and then the road that led to Aria's house. Emily tried to imagine the person Iris had been in love with, but when she tried to picture a face, she only came up with a question mark.

"Okay, fine." Iris broke the silence. "Ali *did* have someone special. A guy."

Emily's heart started beating faster. "Okay . . ."

"She talked about him all the time. They were really tight."

Emily was so excited that she pulled over onto the shoulder. Cars whipped past. She shifted the car into park and stared at Iris. "Was he a patient at the hospital? Or just a visitor? Do you know his name?"

"Ah, ah, ah!" Iris wagged her finger. "You just wanted to know if she had a boyfriend, not what his name was." She patted Emily's thigh. "All in good time, honey. Now, I believe we have more things on my bucket list to get to, don't we?"

Then she yanked the list out of her bag and consulted it. Emily bit down hard on the inside of her lip, trying to swallow her frustration. After all, she had no choice but to play Iris's game.

Especially if it led to some answers. And Ali.

12

KISSING AND TELLING

On Monday, Aria stood in the Rosewood Day gym. The bleachers had been folded up to make more room on the basketball court, the air smelled like rubber sneakers, and a flickering fluorescent light in the rafters was doing its best to break her concentration. The six girls on the decorations committee, all with smooth, long hair, perfectly toned bodies, and matching Tory Burch flats, stood in a circle around her, awaiting instructions. Aria knew she should be thrilled to be bossing around Typical Rosewoods, but instead she just felt on edge.

"Um, okay, so the theme is *The Starry Night*," Aria said shakily, holding up a big picture of the Van Gogh painting in a library book. Just holding it, pointing at it, made her feel like a marked woman. She was sure all the girls could tell exactly what was hiding in her closet—and exactly what she'd done.

She coughed and continued. "So, I'm going to hire a

company that specializes in papier-mâché sculptures to do some big moons and stars for us—since we have to do this by the end of the week, we need some outside help." That was the nice thing about Rosewood Day: They had a big budget for decorations. "I've also called up a company that custom-dyes table linens and can even make interesting slipcovers for the chairs. But the seven of us should definitely paint at least one of the murals. But, um, I was thinking *The Night Café* instead. It's much more romantic, don't you think?"

A pert-nosed blond girl named Tara raised her hand. "Um, the theme is *The Starry Night* for a reason," she said in a haughty, nasal voice, glancing derisively at Aria's thigh-high pleather boots.

The other girls murmured their agreement.

"Um, I guess you have a point," Aria mumbled, even though the idea of painting a *Starry Night* mural made her twitchy. It was like she'd have a big bull's-eye on her forehead, saying, *Hey, cops! Want to know why I know this painting so well? I've got the practice version in my closet!*

Off Spencer's suggestion, she'd moved the painting to the very back of her closet, behind a box of old sweat-shirts. Her mom had knocked on the door as Aria was finishing up.

"Whatcha doing?" Ella had asked, bursting into her room just like she always did.

"Don't come in here!" Aria shrieked before she could restrain herself. "I'm cleaning!"

Ella stopped in the doorway. "Aria Montgomery,

cleaning? I thought I'd never see the day." She tossed something into the room. "This came for you today."

It was a letter with Aria's address on the front, nothing else. For a seizing second, Aria feared A had written to her again, but when she opened it up, it was an invitation to an art apprenticeship in Holland next year. Which would be amazing . . . except Aria would never go so far away from Noel. She threw it into her drawer, then stared at her mom's disappearing figure down the hall. *What a disaster.* Not only were her friends guilty by association, but was her mom, too? If the cops came for the painting, what if they didn't believe Ella didn't know it was here?

And how the hell had someone gotten into the house? There had been no sign of forced entry, which meant whoever got in had a key. Byron and Meredith had a spare key. Spencer had a key from the time she'd fed Polo while the family was away. The cleaning lady had a key, too.

And so did Noel.

Of course, that didn't mean *Noel* was A. Though she could hear the other girls' voices in her head: *Ask Noel where he was the day you found the painting in your closet.* It was weird that Noel had been late to the newspaper editing class. Aria had asked where he'd been, too, but he hadn't given her a straight answer. *And what about Tabitha's necklace, the one that Noel supposedly "found" on the beach in St. Martin?* her friends might say next. *With a little digging, Noel could have figured out who Graham was—he'd been all over the Tabitha memorial site. Or if he was in touch with Ali, she could have just told him everything, since Ali and Tabitha had been friends!*

Aria shut her eyes. Even the idea that Noel had been friends with "Courtney"—aka Real Ali—made her shiver. There were a lot of things about "Courtney's" return to Rosewood that she'd tried her hardest to forget, and Noel's involvement with her was one of them. It *did* seem like a strange coincidence that they'd been in a support group together, and Noel had really encouraged Aria to give "Courtney" a chance. What if he'd known she was Real Ali all along and was helping her out with her plan?

"Earth to Aria!" called a snooty voice in the corner. Aria snapped out of her thoughts and blinked. The committee girls snickered.

She forced a smile, mumbling something about re-creating Van Gogh paintings on big canvases using an overhead projector. The girls shrugged and got to work gathering up supplies and finding copies of the paintings online. Suddenly feeling exhausted, Aria flopped onto a folding chair in the corner and let out a breath. Her palms were shaking. Her head felt faint. She was losing it. Noel absolutely could *not* be A—he was her boyfriend. He didn't know Courtney was Real Ali. He wouldn't do that to her. End of story.

As if on cue, two strong arms wrapped around her waist. "You're such a liar," Noel growled into the spot between her neck and her shoulder.

Aria stiffened. "W-what?"

Noel pulled her up and spun her around. "You told me you needed a ride home, but then I saw your car in the student lot . . . and I find you here!" He cuffed her arm and gave the stink-eye to the Van Gogh portrait on Aria's laptop. "Are you cheating on me with Vincent van Gogh?"

"What? No!" Aria almost shrieked, her cheeks reddening at the word *cheating*.

"I know." Noel gave Aria a crazy look. "I'm just teasing you."

Aria felt her heart slow down. "S-sorry," she stammered. "I forgot about the decor meeting."

"It's cool." Noel nuzzled her neck. "I wouldn't want you to miss this." Then he touched her hands. "So you *are* happy about the job, right?"

Aria's gaze drifted back to the committee girls, who were now priming the canvases for paint. "Uh-huh," she murmured, trying to sound sincere.

Noel cocked his head. "That didn't sound very convincing."

Aria's head felt muddied. She looked up at Noel, then marched toward the hall. "I need to ask you something." After a moment, Noel followed her.

The freshly mopped floors sparkled and smelled like lemon. Outside the floor-to-ceiling windows, Aria swore she saw someone duck behind the journalism barn. She stared out fixedly, her heart in her throat. No one appeared.

Then she faced Noel, who smelled like cologne and looked adorable in his Rosewood Day Lacrosse hoodie. "You were late to class the day they announced I would be the decor chairwoman."

Noel's expression hardened. "So?"

Was he acting defensive? *Guilty?* Aria rubbed out an imaginary spot on the floor with her toe, contemplating how to ask the question. *Where were you?* was so distrustful; it might make things worse. Instead, she found herself blurting out, "Do you ever think about Ali? *Both* the Alis?"

Noel blinked. "What do you mean?"

"Well, it affected you, too. You were friends with her—with *them*. Did you ever . . . I don't know, *suspect* anything after Courtney and Ali switched places? How about when the real Ali returned to Rosewood after Ian Thomas died?"

A muscle above Noel's eye twitched. "I . . ." He trailed off, looking totally flustered. "Why are you asking me these things?"

Aria swallowed hard and looked across the hall into a chemistry classroom. Someone had stuck a daisy into an empty Bunsen burner. "I've just been thinking about Ali and Courtney lately, that's all. Actually, *you* and Ali—the real Ali. You know, that time when you kissed at the Valentine's Day dance."

Noel stepped back, his shoes squeaking on the polished floor. "That's a funny way of saying it. Ali kissed *me*, remember?"

Aria pressed her lips together and said nothing.

Noel made a noise at the back of his throat. "Haven't we been through this? She, like, *pounced* on me."

Aria picked at her nails. "I know, but you were so nice to her. You kept urging me to give her a chance. You were in her support group. You . . ."

Noel's mouth hung open. "Are you asking me if I *liked* her? If I, I don't know, *knew*?"

Aria stared at him. "Maybe. Yeah."

In the background, a bunch of band kids rushed past, giggling and shoving. Noel blinked. He scratched his ear. But he didn't answer her question. Aria's whole body felt snappy. It seemed like Noel was trying to figure out how to word something. But if he had a simple, honest answer, wouldn't he just come out and say it?

Noel jingled his keys in his pocket. "I don't know where this is coming from all of a sudden. *Or* how it relates to being the decor chairperson," he said finally.

"Just answer the question," Aria said. "I need you to tell me you didn't like her at that time."

"I didn't." The annoyed look melted from Noel's face, and he gently took her hands. "I liked *you*, and I would never cheat on you, not even with Courtney or Ali or whoever that was. I was horrified when she kissed me. And when I found out it was all to manipulate you to go with her to the Poconos . . ." He shut his eyes and grimaced. "It's too awful to think about."

"Okay, okay," Aria said. But the prickly feeling didn't go away. It felt like Noel was almost being too melodramatic, like he was acting or something. But was she just thinking that because Spencer and the others had planted suspicions in her mind?

She broke Noel's grip and turned toward the door. "I need some air." Maybe it was rehashing Real Ali's return, maybe it was the panic she'd felt when she thought Noel was lying, but she felt like she couldn't breathe.

Noel had the good sense not to follow her outside. A misty rain was falling, and the strong scent of grass tickled her nostrils. As she climbed the slope, she saw her family's brown Subaru looming in the distance. Even from down the hill, she could tell there was something caught under the windshield wiper. It looked like a note.

Aria started to run. She yanked the printout, which had grown soggy from the mist, from under the wiper and stared at it, her fingers trembling. It was another news article. *Investigation of Prized Van Gogh Study Painting Reopened.*

Aria drew in a breath. There was the *Starry Night* practice painting. She scanned the text. *Baron Brennan's priceless Van Gogh study is still missing, and authorities are reopening the case after one of the suspects disappeared. New evidence suggests two people were involved in the theft, not one. Criminologists are following up on details, including an anonymous tip. . . .*

The paper fluttered from Aria's fingers. On the back of the article was a handwritten letter. The writing was the same scrawl as on the note from the other day. Aria read the words and then rested her head on the hood, suddenly weak.

Star light, star bright,

The first star I see tonight,

I wish I may, I wish I might,

Have the cops nail Aria without a fight.

Love, A

13

A CHAT TO REMEMBER

"You want anything?" asked a pierced, green-haired, gum-snapping girl standing over Spencer's desk. She proffered a menu that read BREWHAUS INTERNET CAFÉ. Spencer took it and opened it up, but the only offerings were a small, medium, or large cup of coffee. She peeked at the mugs on the shelf behind the counter. They looked dusty and stained.

"You don't have coconut water, do you?" Spencer asked hopefully.

The girl rolled her eyes. "What do *you* think?" Then she stomped away, the laces on her Doc Martens slapping against the checkerboard floor.

Spencer looked around, questioning once again why she was here. The Brewhaus Internet Café was nothing more than a dated coffeehouse across from the Yarmouth train station. Every train that passed rattled the old walls, the scent of stale coffee filled the air, the chairs weren't level, and there was grating electronica playing over the speakers. But word had it that this place had the most password-protected Internet service anywhere in the tristate area, meaning that the connection was spy-proof.

As Spencer slipped her burner phone back into her purse, her fingers grazed a dinner selection menu for the prom. She'd gotten it at a Student Council meeting that afternoon. *The Starry Night*, read the dripping Van Gogh signature-like lettering, and a tiny image of the famous painting was at the bottom. Spencer pushed the card deeper into her bag. Just seeing those swirly clouds made her ill. She'd assured Aria that they'd figure this out, but would they? Even with A's threatening notes, even if they could find evidence that someone had broken into Aria's house to plant the painting there, would the police believe that a Van Gogh had just shown up in her closet without any involvement on her part?

Then again, Spencer wasn't sure what *else* they should do. Placing the artwork on a museum doorstep would only invite controversy—and besides, Aria's fingerprints were probably all over the canvas. What they needed to do was nail Ali and her helper and force them to confess every-thing. Ironically, A was their only get-out-of-jail-free card.

An IM popped up on her computer screen. *I'm here*, said someone with the handle FlyOnTheWall. It was Chase, the investigative blogger Spencer had contacted the other day. They'd planned to chat this afternoon, but Spencer hadn't been sure whether he would actually sign on.

She checked over her shoulder. Everyone else was intently staring at their own screens, oblivious to her. The IM blinked at her, waiting. *I'm here, too*, she typed back. *I like your site. You've done a lot of research.*

Thanks, Chase answered, adding a smiley emoticon. *So what's your name?*

Spencer hesitated. *I don't want to say yet. I'm trying to think of a nickname.*

Are you a guy or a girl?

Girl, Spencer wrote, feeling a little like she was filling out a dating profile.

How about Britney Spears? The reply came right away.

Spencer moved back from the screen and smirked. *She's not your favorite singer, is she?*

Hell no, Chase wrote back. *It was just the first thing that popped into my head.*

Okay, Britney Spears it is, Spencer typed.

So you're interested in the Alison case? he asked.

Spencer swallowed hard. *Sort of. Isn't everyone?*

It's definitely a weird story, a new message read. *There's something not right about the whole thing. I just don't know what it is yet.*

Are you actively investigating what happened? Spencer asked.

Just as a hobby, Chase wrote. *Since the investigation is still open, the cops asked me to keep the details secret so they can catch the real killer. But when I find out everything, I'm putting it up there anyway.*

I thought the investigation was closed, Spencer wrote. *Ali killed her sister. Didn't she?*

Yes, but there are some loose ends, Chase replied. *Like if Ali survived the fire. And the police are still gathering evidence that Ali and Ali alone killed Jenna Cavanaugh and Ian Thomas.*

Did you know Alison? Spencer asked.

Nope, but a similar thing happened to me, which is why I'm interested.

What do you mean?

There was a pause, then the screen flashed again. *I was stalked. I went to an all-boys' boarding school, and I had a psycho roommate. He became obsessed with me. He tried to kill me. His parents had a lot of money, though, and they kept the story out of the news.*

Spencer sat back. *Whoa. I'm so sorry. Were you hurt?*

A long beat went by. *I don't like talking about it.*

So did that mean his stalker *did* hurt him . . . or didn't? Suddenly, Spencer was curious as hell. She clicked on the ABOUT US link of the website again, but it was just that stupid cat video.

Still, Spencer instantly sympathized with him. She certainly knew what it was like to be tormented. *Are you still having a hard time with it?* she asked. *Do people always look at you like you're . . . contagious, or something?*

Totally, Chase wrote back. *I've definitely lost some friends because of it. But I do a lot of stuff to take my mind off things. Besides being an amateur PI, I'm into snowboarding and guitar.*

And it might sound nerdy, but I do sandcastle-building competitions in the summer.

I was in one of those! Spencer wrote. She and Melissa entered a competition when they were summering at their nana's place in Longboat Key, Florida. It was practically the only thing Spencer had beaten her sister at. *I got fourth!*

Nice—I've won a couple, Chase wrote. *Everyone thinks it's dorky—they say I should be playing beach volleyball or something.* An eye-rolling emoticon popped up on the screen. *But it's a hobby I've been into since I was a kid. I still really like it.*

Are you out of high school? Spencer asked.

Yep, graduated last June, Chase wrote. *I'm working at a bio lab in Center City for a year before I start college. We research cancer meds.*

So you're smart, Spencer wrote, adding a smiley.

You seem pretty smart, too, Chase wrote. *You in college?*

Princeton, Spencer replied. She left out the part about not actually *going* there yet.

Whoa, smart squared, was Chase's reply. *If we got together, the combined IQ in the room would be out of control.*

Spencer giggled. Was he cyber-flirting?

The screen flashed again. *But enough about me, Miss Spears—how are you connected to Alison?*

Spencer hesitated. She wasn't sure how much she should tell him. She'd never seen him, after all. And even though he said the cops didn't want him to post anything about the case, what if he exposed her anyway? *I'm just a concerned individual who knows a lot,* she finally answered. *That's all I can say right now. And I have reason to believe she's alive, too.*

Chase replied quickly. *Her bones would have been in the rubble, right? They would have found jewelry or teeth. But there was nothing. I think she got out of the house before it exploded.*

Definitely, Spencer wrote, wishing she could tell him that Emily had left the door open for Ali to escape. *But the police said that sometimes bones get ground up so finely that it's hard to distinguish them from ash.*

Maybe, Chase wrote back. *But it seems convenient—I still think she made it out.*

And did what? Spencer typed. *The house was on fire. Even if she managed to slip outside, wouldn't she have been hurt? Did she go to a hospital?*

Chase's answer was instantaneous, like he'd antici-pated the question. *I doubt it. I think she got a private nurse to take care of her. I also think she has at least one friend helping her out. Someone who was waiting for her in the woods that night the house exploded. Someone who took her away to get her the care she needed.*

A man behind Spencer grunted, but when she turned, he was staring at his screen. She turned back to her own computer, shivering at Chase's response. Someone *else* in the woods that night. It made perfect sense, especially given their theory that Ali had a helper.

Do you think she had help killing Ian Thomas and Jenna Cavanaugh, too? she typed.

Absolutely, Chase wrote. *I've found out some intel about a private nurse, too. I doubt Alison's nurse went through an employer or medical supplier, so even the supplies she got for Alison would have had to have been bought through regular drugstores. I have a friend who works for CVS who was able to get into the database of a bunch of stores in the area. There's one in Center City that has regular orders of massive amounts of gauze and bandages and wound-cleaning supplies. He also got me video surveillance of the person picking up the supplies.*

Spencer leapt on the keys. *Who is she?*

A friend from a hospital IDed her as Barbara Rogers. She's in her mid-fifties, but I haven't been able to figure out much more about her, Chase answered. *One more thing: There's also the issue of drugs. Ali wouldn't be using a prescription, so someone would have to be getting it illegally. There was a pharma theft not long ago at the William Atlantic Burn Clinic in Rosewood.*

Spencer gasped so loudly that a pale, skinny woman with dishwater-blond hair two consoles down gave her a strange look. This was all connecting in terrible ways.

She checked her watch and realized that it was getting late—she should probably get home. She signed off with Chase, making him promise that they would talk again.

As she stood, a tinkling laugh drifted through the air. Spencer shot up, but the other patrons were still staring at their screens. The pierced barista puttered behind the counter. A girl in a FedEx uniform worked a crossword puzzle at a table.

Spencer pulled out her cell phone, but she hadn't

received any texts. She gazed out the window at the train tracks again. For a split second, a ghostly image stared back at her from inside the station house. Her heart stopped. *Ali?*

The train rushed past. Spencer didn't blink the whole time, waiting for a glimpse of that station window again. But when she finally got another look, the face was gone.

14

HANNA'S THE COOLEST

That afternoon, Hanna and Mike lounged on the couch at her father's house, watching an episode of *Parks and Recreation* on DVR. She had her hands in the pockets of Mike's hooded sweatshirt, and Mike wound his socked feet around Hanna's bare ones. Mr. Marin sat behind the glass doors of his office, talking to someone about his senatorial campaign.

The doorbell rang, and she and Mike looked at each other and frowned. Hanna padded to it and peered through the glass. Standing on the other side was Chassey Bledsoe, looking perfectly put-together in a silk dress and brown boots and holding a bakery box in her hands. Hanna frowned down at her stained University of Pennsylvania yoga pants.

"Uh . . . hi?" she asked as she opened the door.

"Hey, Hanna!" Chassey smiled. "I was in the neighborhood, and I just wanted to say I'm really honored to run against you for queen."

Hanna stared at the box she was holding. Through the clear plastic top, she could see twenty iced cupcakes all lined up. Each of them bore the words VOTE CHASSEY FOR QUEEN!

"Oh!" Chassey noticed her looking and opened the lid. "Would you like one? I've been passing them around to potential voters."

Hanna snorted. "They probably have shingles germs all over them."

Chassey looked confused. "I don't have shingles."

Hanna cocked her head. "Then why were you out of school for a month?"

Chassey blinked. "My mom was doing some work in LA, so I went with her and got a tutor. I went to a lot of amazing spas, too—I bet you would have loved them, Hanna."

Now Hanna *really* didn't feel sorry for Chassey. She took a cupcake, trilled that it was nice to see Chassey, and then shut the door in Chassey's face. She turned around and handed Mike the cupcake—*she* certainly wasn't going to eat it. "*That* was lame."

Mike peeled off the wrapper and took a big bite. "She's really working hard to get votes. I thought you'd be more into it, too."

Hanna pushed a lock of hair over her shoulder. "I guess I've been busy."

Mike shoved another piece of cupcake in his mouth. "With what?"

"Honestly?" Hanna flung herself back on the couch. "I refuse to campaign against Chassey. If I don't win on my own good looks and popularity, I don't deserve to win at all."

Mike stared at her, chewing. She knew how stupid it sounded. But what could she say? *Hey, Mike, some psycho stranger who might actually be your best friend, Noel, told me that if I campaigned, he'd tell the FBI we killed a girl.*

Mike sat down and picked up the remote. "So how was the salon yesterday?"

Hanna blinked at him, struggling to shift gears. "What?"

"You know, your practice hair appointment for prom?"

Right. Hanna had forgotten about that lie. "Uh, it was good."

Mike leaned in and sniffed her head. "You don't smell all fruity, like you usually do when you come home from the salon."

"That's because I washed my hair this morning. *Duh.*" Hanna moved her head away. Then she checked her watch and jumped up. "*Shit.* I need to go." Her burn clinic shift started in a half hour.

"Where *now*?" Mike complained.

Hanna's mind scrambled for an answer, but it was irritatingly blank. She grabbed her purse and walked out the front door. "I've got to do something for my mom. I'll see you."

Mike followed her to her car. He could tell she was

lying—she just knew it. She licked her lips, about to tell him the truth—or some approximation of it. But as she turned the ignition in the Prius, a news report blared.

The search for the thieves of a priceless practice painting of Van Gogh's The Starry Night *has been reopened,* a reporter intoned, a keyboard click-clacking in the background. *At first, authorities thought there was only one thief, but now there is new evidence that the criminal might not have acted alone.* The story, the newscaster went on to say, was particularly pertinent in this area because Baron Brennan, from whom the painting had been stolen, had been a prominent con-tributor to the Philadelphia Art Museum.

Hanna's stomach flipped over. What if the *new evidence* had been a phone call from A? How long until A gave names?

She gazed at Mike, then shut her mouth tight. Yes, she was lying to him. But it was for his own good.

The burn clinic lobby was quiet when Hanna walked in fifteen minutes later. Sean jumped up from his office chair and strode across the floor to meet her. Hanna couldn't help but notice how middle-aged he looked in khakis and a checked shirt. Even her father didn't dress like such a dork.

"Kelly's not here today," he said, worry lines present on his brow. "She said you did a great job on the bedpans, though—do you think you could handle the chores on your own?"

"Sure." Hanna shrugged.

"Great." Sean looked relieved. "Thanks so much."

He patted her arm and returned to his office. Hanna heard a *ping* behind her and turned, but the lobby was still empty. She trudged into the women's staff room, unlocked her locker, and changed into the pink scrubs she'd claimed. She liked them because they had an extra-big pocket in the front—perfect to fit a cell phone.

Then she grabbed the mop bucket and some bed-pans out of the supply closet. Before she got started, she headed down the corridor to Graham's bed. She might as well check on him before making her rounds.

The partition had been partly pushed back. Graham's eyes were fluttering, and guttural, animal-like sounds escaped from between his lips. A nurse stood over him, replacing one of his IVs. She looked up sternly when she sensed Hanna's presence, but her face softened when she saw her volunteer scrubs.

"Has he woken up?" Hanna asked.

"Not yet," the nurse murmured. "But I'm hopeful that he will soon."

Hanna's hand accidentally brushed against Graham's foot under the sheet, and she pulled it away fast—it was cold and rubbery, like a corpse's. "Do patients ever speak when they're in comas? Like, say names or anything?"

"Not usually." The nurse clipped the new IV bag to the pole. Then she squinted at Hanna. "What did you say your name was again?"

"It doesn't matter," Hanna said quickly, ducking out from behind the curtain.

She stared down the hall, which was packed with cots of burn victims sporting various bandages and slings. There was barely a space for a wheelchair to fit through. The place smelled like pee and Clorox, and every few seconds, someone let out a moan.

"It's tough, huh?" a female voice said.

Hanna whirled around. Burn patients lay to the right and left. Then, someone whose whole face was covered in bandages weakly raised an arm. "Hey," the patient croaked.

"H-hey," Hanna said uneasily, not wanting to get too close.

"He a friend of yours?"

The patient, who had holes cut in the gauze so she could see out, pointed toward Graham. Hanna coughed awkwardly. "Sort of."

"He was really bad when he came in," the girl whispered. "Nothing like perfect me, of course." She waved her hands over her body, magician's assistant–style, then laughed.

Hanna wasn't sure whether she could join in on the joke. She glanced at a drainage bag leading out of the girl's groin, then looked away.

"It's okay. I hate looking at it, too." The girl pushed the bag under the covers. "The doctors told me some bullshit about it being a magical fairy pouch or something. Like

I'm freaking seven years old. Believe me, the only fairies I ever see are when they give me Percocet."

This time Hanna did laugh. "I've never seen fairies when *I've* taken Percocet," she said wistfully, "but it sounds awesome."

"Maybe that's because *you* don't have a Percocet button that feeds it straight into your vein whenever you want it." The girl held up a little button attached to a cord that lay next to her on the bed. "Didn't you know they're the number one accessory for this spring?"

"I read about it in *Vogue*!" Hanna chuckled. "Is that button a Chanel?"

"Of course," the girl said in a haughty voice. "I had to get on a waiting list for it, but only the best for me."

"Obviously," Hanna said, giggling.

"And did you see? Miu Miu socks!" The girl stuck her feet out from under the blanket. Sure enough, the cashmere socks had the Miu Miu logo embroidered on the toes.

"Where'd you get those?" Hanna asked, impressed. They looked cozy and decadent.

"The hot male nurse gave them to me. You know, the one with the shaved head?"

Hanna's eyes boggled. She was sure the girl was talking about the guy she'd nearly spilled the bedpan over yesterday. "*Really?*"

The girl snorted out a laugh. "I wish. He's gorgeous, isn't he? The days he gives me the sponge bath are the *best*."

"You are *so* lucky!" Hanna squealed, then clapped her mouth shut. Had she just said a burn victim was *lucky*?

A bell rang out in the corridor, and then a voice came over the PA paging one of the doctors. "What's your name?" the girl asked. "I've never seen you before—and I would remember you. You're the coolest volunteer we've ever had."

"Thanks," Hanna said softly. "I'm Hanna."

"I'm Kyla Kennedy. Maybe when I bust out of here, we can hang for real."

Hanna raised an eyebrow. "Bust out of here?"

"Oh yeah." Kyla's tone was playful. "I have a whole black-ops mission in mind. I'm going to break out when no one's watching and take the world by storm."

She reached out her bandaged hand. Hanna tentatively shook it, then peeked at Kyla's face again. She could see long lashes beneath the gauze, but she couldn't even tell what color her eyes were. Yet she loved that Kyla said she was cool. After a moment, she realized that she thought Kyla was cool, too.

"Hanna?" Sean appeared at the end of the corridor. "There's a spill in the next hall over. Can you take care of it?"

Hanna sighed heavily. "I'd better go," she said to Kyla.

"No worries," Kyla said. Her bandaged hand clunked against Hanna's wrist. "See you again, hopefully?"

"Definitely," Hanna said.

She was a few paces away when Kyla called out her

name again. Hanna turned around. Kyla was sitting up halfway in bed, pointing wildly at the shaved-head, hot-body male nurse. She pretended to smack his butt as he passed. Hanna laughed so loud that an old lady lying on a cot down the hall squealed and jumped. Hanna and Kyla exchanged a meaningful glance—well, as meaningful as Hanna could give Kyla under all that gauze. And then they started laughing even harder.

15

UP THE CREEK WITHOUT A PADDLE

The next afternoon, Emily pulled into the main drive of the King James Mall, her heart thundering. When she first scanned the impressive entrance doors, she didn't see Iris waiting inside, like they'd planned.

She dug her fingernails into the steering wheel. Of *course* Iris wasn't there. What idiot would leave a mental patient at the mall all day? But because Emily didn't want to miss any more school, she'd struck a deal with Iris that morning: She'd drop her off at the King James before first period, Iris would spend the day doing whatever she pleased, and Emily would pick her up after the last bell. Then they'd knock a few more items off Iris's bucket list, and Iris would give Emily an Ali tidbit at the end of the day. Hopefully.

It took Iris no time to agree. After Emily dropped her off, she realized why: The Greyhound bus station was right down the street. Iris had probably planned to take off the second Emily pulled away. Emily had been her way out of The Preserve, but Iris didn't need her anymore.

She idled at the curb, her stomach in knots. No one was sitting on the benches outside the entrance. No one lurked near the metallic ashtrays. But then the double doors opened, and someone stepped onto the pavement. After the sun glare subsided, Iris shimmered into view. Emily rolled down the window. "You're here!"

Iris gave her a strange look. "Where *else* would I be?"

Emily unlocked the car doors, and Iris climbed inside. Once they were on their way, Emily glanced at the Bloomingdale's carrier bag in Iris's arms. "You went shopping?"

"Sort of," Iris sang. She tossed something in Emily's face. "For you."

Emily stared at the plaid scarf in her lap. It had a Burberry label. "Is this *real*?"

"I hope so," Iris said. "I got your mom one, too."

"Iris . . ." Emily trailed off. She'd always wanted a Burberry scarf . . . but not a stolen one. Still, she was oddly touched that Iris had thought of her. *And* her mom.

"The light's green," Iris said loudly. "Turn left here."

Emily turned on her signal. They were driving in the direction of Delaware. She glanced sidelong at Iris. "Where are we going, anyway?"

"To Keppler Creek," Iris answered. "I want to take out a paddleboat."

Emily rolled to a stop at another light. "I don't think the boats are open for the season yet."

Iris scoffed. "So we steal one."

Emily looked at her hard. "I'm not stealing a paddle-boat."

Iris gave her a warning stare. "Come on. And besides, we're not stealing it—just borrowing it for a little bit."

Emily felt a pang of longing. She and Jordan had borrowed a beautiful glass-bottomed boat in Puerto Rico—and it *had* been easy, for Jordan at least. They'd had their first kiss out on the water. It was the most public kiss Emily had ever had with a girl—there were tons of other sailboats, Jet Skis, and party ships nearby, with many people on board—and yet she hadn't felt uncomfortable in the slightest. She missed Jordan so much she'd taken to sleeping in one of the T-shirts that she'd let her borrow for the cruise. If Emily breathed in hard enough, she could still smell Jordan's jasmine perfume.

She must have sighed dreamily, because Iris giggled. "Who are you thinking about? A girl?"

"No," Emily said quickly.

Iris crossed her arms over her chest. "You can tell me. I'm not gonna judge you."

Emily felt her cheeks flush. "Fine. I was thinking about this girl I met a few weeks ago."

"What's her name?"

"Jordan."

Iris crossed and uncrossed her legs. "What's she like?"

Emily smiled, trying to think of a simple way to sum up Jordan. "She's funny. And brave. And beautiful."

"Is she the first girl you've liked since Ali?"

Emily slowed down to take a turn. "I had a girlfriend for a little while last year. Her name was Maya. She was cool, but she was also a little pushy."

Iris twisted a silver ring around her finger. "Sounds like you fell for Ali all over again."

Emily laughed uneasily, then glanced at Iris. "Was Ali pushy with you?"

Iris wrapped a tendril of hair around her finger. "I guess. She was always manipulating me into doing things I didn't want to do."

"That sounds like her," Emily said. Until she remembered: They were talking about two different Alis.

They came to a T in the road, and Iris told her to turn right. "So will you tell me about *your* crush?" Emily asked, remembering what Iris had said the other day.

Iris twisted her mouth. "It's boring."

"Come on. I told *you*."

Several houses flew past the window before Iris spoke again. "His name is Tripp," she said softly.

Emily nodded, suddenly remembering Iris's list. *Find Tripp*, it had said.

"He was a patient at The Preserve, too," Iris went on. "We were really great friends, and things were definitely going in a romantic direction. Until they let him out. He promised to visit me every Saturday, but he never did. And we can't make calls or send e-mails at The Preserve, so I had no idea where he was. I never heard from him again." She sniffed loudly. "Then again, who wants a girl-friend in the loony bin?"

"So you have no idea what happened to him?"

"Nope." Iris tied the Burberry scarf she'd stolen for Emily's mom into a messy knot. "Which is why I want to find him. He owes me an explanation."

Emily paused at a stop sign, waiting for two girls walking a standard poodle to pass. "Why were you at The Preserve in the first place?" she asked, choosing her words delicately.

Iris snickered. "Isn't it obvious?" She waved her hands up and down her frail, skinny body. "*Anorexia nervosa.* Sometimes, I choose not to eat. For *days.*"

Emily blinked hard. "Has being there . . . helped?"

Iris's shoulders rose and fell. "Some days yes, some days no. My therapist insists that I do the eating thing for attention. My dad left when I was really little. My mom had to work a bunch of jobs to support us, and then she started dating all these guys, each one worse than the last. She had no time for me anymore. Getting skinnier and skinnier got her to sit up and notice. But then I got dehydrated and ended up in the hospital for malnourishment. The doctor had this whole medical plan for me, and my mom tried to be there for a while, but she just couldn't do it. So off to The Preserve I went." She sucked in her teeth. "My home away from home."

"Is she paying for you to be at The Preserve?" Emily asked.

Iris smiled crookedly. "Her new boyfriend is. He's rolling in cash—lucky me!"

Emily knew Iris wanted her to laugh, but it really wasn't funny. Thinking of Iris's mom, she felt a renewed sense of gratitude for her own family. Imagine if, instead of caring for Emily with ice cream and storybooks when she'd had her appendix out in sixth grade, her mother had declared Emily a burden and sent her off to a facility. Even Emily's banishment to Iowa after she'd been outed by A had been short-lived: Her parents came to their senses quickly and begged for Emily's forgiveness.

Up ahead on the road was a wooden sign that read KEPPLER CREEK STATE PARK. Emily pulled into a space in the parking lot and shut off the engine. A lake shimmered in the distance, but there was no one in the water; it was still too cold. The rental booth was shuttered, and there wasn't a single paddleboat anywhere. Only a few fishermen in Woolrich plaid jackets sat on the other side of the pond, staring at their fishing poles.

Iris got out of the car and surveyed the scene. "Well, this sucks," she grumbled. "*Now* what are we going to do?"

Emily wandered over to a shed where the boats probably were kept, but when she tried the lock, it was bolted tight. "Is there something else you want to do instead?"

Iris didn't answer. When Emily turned around, Iris was standing next to a tall oak tree, its branches still bare. There was a strange, faraway look on her face.

"What is it?" Emily asked, walking over to her.

Iris turned. "I used to come here when I was a lot younger with school friends. When Ali and I were at The Preserve together, we found out that she used to come here, too."

"She did?" Emily asked, cocking her head. That didn't make sense—the DiLaurentises had a bunch of kayaks, but they took them to Pecks Pond, which was much closer to Rosewood.

Iris nodded. "She said she loved it here. She said she couldn't wait to come back when she got out of the hospital."

Emily shoved the toe of her sneaker into a tuft of dried grass. "Do you think she came here after she was released?"

"Definitely." Iris leaned against the tree trunk. "She even made plans. We weren't allowed to watch TV at The Preserve, but we heard things. Even the nurses wanted to know what happened to poor Courtney DiLaurentis's murdered sister. One had a portable radio, and we gathered near her office when the report came in that Ian Thomas had been arrested. Ali got this excited look on her face, and she kept glancing at her watch. *My parents are coming*, she kept saying. *I just know it. They're coming today. And then I'm going to Keppler Creek Park.* We had no idea how she knew for sure that she was getting out."

"I know how she knew," Emily interjected. "Ali's parents hid her away at The Preserve because they feared *she* had killed her sister—which, of course, she did. But when

Ian was arrested, they thought they'd made a horrible mistake and immediately had her released."

"That makes sense," Iris said. "She seemed thrilled that Ian was arrested, too. At the time, I thought it was because she was glad someone had gotten caught, but maybe she was just glad that someone else had been pegged for something *she* did."

"Wait a minute." A brisk wind kicked up, blowing hair into Emily's face. "You didn't know Ali killed Courtney?"

Iris looked at her crazily. "No way." She turned back to the tree, chipping away a piece of bark with her nail. "Anyway, her parents *did* show up that day, just like she predicted. As they were signing paperwork to check her out, Ali was packing up her stuff in our room. And she mentioned Keppler Creek again. She was like, *This is awesome. I'm going to Keppler Creek as soon as I'm free. I'm going to see my best friend in the world. I can't wait to see him.*"

A chill whizzed up Emily's spine. *Him.* "She was coming to meet a guy. Her boyfriend?"

"I think so."

"So her boyfriend *wasn't* a patient. He was on the outside."

The corners of Iris's mouth twisted into a smile. "Aren't you clever? You're right. It was someone on the outside. He used to visit her all the time. And I bet he carved this."

She stepped away from the tree and pointed at something in the bark. There, etched into the wood, were the words *I love Ali D* in a heart. At the bottom was the date.

It was November of last year, a few days after Ian had been arrested.

Emily's breath caught, thinking of the time *she'd* carved Ali's initials into a tree. If only whoever had cut this heart into the bark had added his initials, too, like Emily had. She touched the letters, then looked around for any video cameras on the nearby snack bar and bathroom structures. Unfortunately, there were none. Nothing had recorded Ali and whoever this person was meeting . . . but it *had* happened. *I'm going to see my best friend in the world.* Who? Had this guy transformed into Ali's helper, the new A?

She grabbed Iris's hand. "Please tell me his name."

A torn look crossed Iris's face. For a moment, she looked like she was going to tell, but then she yanked her arm away and started running toward the beach. "Hey, I know what we can do instead of take a boat out!" she called over her shoulder. "Skinny-dip!"

And at that, she started peeling off her clothes, first her T-shirt, then her shoes and socks, then her jeans, which were Emily's. Her legs and arms looked so pale. The knobs of her spine stuck out prominently.

"Iris!" Emily protested, running after her toward the water, dodging the pile of clothes she'd left in her wake. "You'll freeze!"

But Iris had already plunged into the lake. She surfaced and shrieked at the cold, then laughed. "C'mon, Emily!" she called out. "It's a rush!"

Emily stared at Iris, then turned back and looked at the

carving on the tree. It *was* a rush, finding out something new about Ali. And Iris's admission suddenly made her feel charitable. Daring and invincible, too. She pulled her sweater over her head, kicked off her jeans, and waded into the frigid water after Iris, not caring that the fishermen were staring. There was a flicker in the trees, and Emily stopped, goose bumps rising on her bare stomach. *Ali?* The word froze solid as it left her lips.

But when she looked again, the forest was still. Whoever had been watching had vanished.

16

MEETING OF THE MINDS

On Tuesday night, Spencer sat at the kitchen table with Amelia, their schoolbooks spread in front of them and the classical station on at low volume. Spencer liked doing her homework at the kitchen table. As it turned out, so did Amelia, meaning the kitchen had turned into a turf war.

An IM popped up on Spencer's laptop. It was Chase. *Hey there, Britney.*

Spencer smiled. Chase's nickname had grown on her. But she hesitated before replying. It was one thing to break the Internet rule on a super-safe connection, but A probably had been bugging her laptop for months.

She jumped up from the table and ran into her mother's office, a carved-out nook behind the pantry. Mrs. Hastings's computer was on a vegan recipe website. Spencer exited out of it, logged into her mother's instant messenger screen name, RufusAndBeatrice—Mrs. Hastings liked to IM Spencer that dinner was ready and things like that. She found Chase's screen name, friended him, and told him that it was *Britney*, just using her mom's account instead of her own.

After a moment, another message from Chase appeared. *Two things: One, I've reached out to Billy Ford to see if he had any interaction with Alison before he was arrested.*

Spencer almost dropped her bottle of coconut water. Billy Ford was the guy who'd been framed for murdering Their Ali—he'd been one of the guys who'd dug the hole where Ali's body had been found. People thought he was A, too. The cops found pictures of Spencer and the others on the laptop in his truck. But Real Ali had planted them there.

Did he tell you anything interesting? Spencer asked. If she remembered correctly, Billy told the cops that the only time he'd seen Alison—or, rather, *Courtney*—was when he'd worked on her gazebo when the girls were in seventh grade. He had no idea how Real Ali had gotten those files onto his laptop.

He told me that a few days before all that stuff was found in his truck, someone from Geek Squad came to his door and offered to do a free security scan. Maybe that person helped frame him. Perhaps they were working with Alison.

Spencer's eyes lit up. *Was it a guy or girl?*

He said it was a guy. But he barely remembers him. Couldn't pick him out of a lineup.

Spencer laid her head on her mom's desk. Another dead end.

There was another *ping. Two, I just received some interesting photos of Ali and her sister when they were younger. Maybe they'll spark a connection.*

Spencer glanced over her shoulder in case Amelia was watching from the kitchen. *Where did you find them?* she typed.

The text box lit up again. *You wouldn't believe the sorts of people who come out of the woodwork when you run a conspiracy theory blog. I get all kinds of weird stuff about all sorts of topics. These I got anonymously, but I really think they're legit. Exciting, right?*

Spencer swished a gulp of coconut water in her mouth. Whenever anything was done anonymously, her first thought was that it was A. But why would A send DiLaurentis twin pictures to a conspiracy blog?

It is exciting, she wrote back—and she meant it. Not only finding new evidence, but also talking to someone who was just as jazzed about it as Spencer was. Not just someone, either, but a smart, interesting, funny, intriguing guy. Not that Spencer had a crush on him or anything.

Okay, maybe she did.

The idea of him was just so *alluring.* All the investigating he'd done on Ali, his tragic story about being stalked, even his choice of words in their chats. Last night, he'd used the phrase *if I had my druthers,* which was so adorably old-fashioned Spencer had squealed with delight. Chase was smart and funny . . . *and* they both wanted to bring Ali down. It sort of felt like they were a superhero duo, connected via Internet. Surely there was a picture of him online, right? But Spencer had spent hours last night searching all sorts of avenues. The work he'd done with the police. The stalking story. There wasn't a single image of him *anywhere*—of course, it would help if she knew his last name.

She *had* to meet him.

She looked at the screen and took a deep breath. *I really want to see them*, she wrote. *But I don't want you sending them over the Internet. Do you think we could meet in person?* It might be a risk to reveal who she really was, but she was willing to take the chance.

The cursor blinked . . . and blinked . . . and blinked. No new message appeared. Spencer's cheeks burned. This felt just like the time in seventh grade when Spencer and Ali were competing over who could kiss the greatest number of older guys. Spencer had walked up to Oliver Nolan, the champion rower at St. Francis Prep, and asked him to kiss her, and he'd flat-out refused. Ali had been watching—she'd laughed her head off.

There was a knock on the front door. Spencer jumped up from her mom's desk chair, ran through the kitchen and down the hall, and peered through the sidelight window. Emily stood on the porch. Her Volvo wagon chugged at the curb; Iris's blond head could be seen in the passenger seat.

"What's going on?" Spencer whispered as she opened the door.

Emily looked right and left. Then she pulled Spencer down the hall and into the powder room. She shut the door and turned on the overhead fan, which rattled noisily, and ran the faucet at full volume.

"What are you doing?" Spencer frowned at Emily's reflection in the mirror. "What about Iris?"

"She'll be okay," Emily assured her. "I want to make sure no one hears. I just found out that Ali *did* have a special boyfriend, someone on the outside. The two of them met as soon as she was let out of The Preserve after Ian was arrested. There's a carving at Keppler Creek State Park that says *I love Ali D* with last year's date."

"Keppler Park?" Spencer leaned against the pedestal sink. "That's almost in Delaware."

Emily chewed on her thumb. "I know. Maybe the boyfriend is from there. Ali said he was her best friend in the world. What if this friend is her helper?"

Spencer thought about what Chase had just said about Billy Ford: The Geek Squad employee who'd planted that stuff on his laptop was a guy, too. "She didn't say who he was?"

"No. But maybe whoever this is hated us as much as Real Ali did. Maybe he was pissed that we put Real Ali in The Preserve and let Courtney go free. It sounds like we're looking for a guy, right?"

"So it could be Jason," Spencer said. "Or Wilden. Or . . . hold on." She darted out of the powder room, up the stairs, and grabbed the rolled-up list they'd made in the panic room that she'd stashed in a padlocked box under her bed. She spread it out across the sink and crossed off the girls' names. Jason and Wilden were next on the list.

"If it was someone who was pissed that Real Ali was locked up, this guy would have had to have known Real Ali *before* Courtney made the switch, right?" Emily murmured as she stared at the list. "Jason makes sense, obviously, but I just can't see him killing for her."

"That's how I feel about Wilden," Spencer murmured. "He hates Ali with a passion—and anyway, Ali-as-A kind of embarrassed him with all that Amish stuff last year." A had sent Emily on a wild-goose chase to Amish country, where Emily had exposed Wilden's roots there.

Emily nodded. "That was something he definitely didn't want people to know about. If he was Ali's helper, I don't know why he would have allowed that."

Spencer put a question mark next to Jason's name and drew a faint line through Wilden's. They looked at the list again. *Graham. Noel.*

Spencer glanced at Emily's pale face in the mirror. "Have you talked to Aria lately?" she asked in a quiet voice.

"She won't answer my calls." Emily swallowed hard. "I think she's upset that we're asking her so many questions about Noel."

"I feel terrible about it," Spencer said into her chest. "But . . ." She trailed off, her thoughts still unfocused.

She'd revisited a lot of memories about Noel over the past few days, and some worrying details had surfaced. Like how on the day after they'd pushed Tabitha off the roof, the girls had gathered together in Spencer's room to discuss what they should do. As they were panicking, Spencer heard shuffling sounds in the hall. She peered through the peephole and saw Noel standing at the door, staring at something on his phone. She whipped open the door and glared at him. "Can I help you?"

"Oh!" Noel looked surprised. "I was just seeing if Aria was here. I want to take her to breakfast."

Aria had rushed to Noel's side, and the conversation had ended. Spencer hadn't thought much of it—she'd just been glad Noel hadn't overheard anything. But what if he *had* overheard? What if he already knew what they were talking about because he'd been there the night before?

"What about your search?" Emily whispered. "Have you figured anything out?"

Spencer straightened up. "Well, if Ali *did* escape the explosion, there might be a lead on a private nurse she hired to help her recover from her burns. I'm trying to track down where the nurse lives and what she knows."

"Wow." Emily sounded amazed. "How'd you figure all that out?"

"Oh, you know." Spencer nervously folded the hand towel again and again. She could just hear Emily's response if she told her she was corresponding with a conspiracy blogger: *Are you out of your mind? That's so dangerous!*

"Do you think Ali knows you're looking for her?" Emily whispered.

Spencer picked up a scented candle and put it back down. "I hope not."

Emily glanced at the Nike watch on her wrist. "I'd better get back to Iris before she decides to drive off without me. At least we're making progress, though."

"We just have to keep pushing," Spencer said.

She walked Emily to the door, her brain swimming. When she turned the lock again, the telltale *ping* of an IM rang through the hall. She ran back to her mom's office. The screen was flashing. Chase had written back.

Okay, Britney. Let's meet. Mütter Museum in an hour?

"Yes!" Spencer whooped, exiting out of IM. She strolled out of the kitchen, a huge smile on her face. Amelia smirked at her. "What are *you* so happy about?"

"Nothing," Spencer snapped, sashaying down the hall. But there was a little spring in her step and a zillion butterflies knocking against her stomach. Okay, maybe she *was* happy to be meeting Chase.

Just a little.

Forty-five minutes later, Spencer paid the parking meter on Twenty-First Street and headed for the brownstone down the block. MÜTTER MUSEUM OF MEDICAL ODDITIES, read an old-fashioned sign on a post. Spencer had been here once two years ago on a school trip and almost puked several times. Not only did the place smell overwhelmingly like formaldehyde, but one of the attractions was a large set of drawers of various objects people had swallowed. There was also a huge human digestive tract stored in a large jar. Not exactly her thing.

She plopped a blond Britney Spears wig on her head—it only seemed fitting, after all—and pulled a pair of Ray-Bans over her eyes. Even though the museum docents looked at her like she was crazy, she paid the fee with her head held high.

The museum was essentially only one large room with displays around the perimeter. A couple stared at the hanging skeletons. An old woman examined the world's largest colon. It seemed pretty clear that A wasn't here, but what about Chase? Spencer eyed a stooped, lecherous-looking old man grinning at the preserved Siamese twins and got a sinking feeling.

"Um, hello?"

She jumped and whirled around. Standing next to a security guard was a tall guy with tousled brown hair, a square jaw, broad shoulders, and long, lanky limbs. He pulled off his sunglasses, revealing piercing green eyes.

"I'm Chase," he said. "You're . . . ?"

Spencer walked toward him dazedly. Chase had thick, expressive eyebrows. His body was strong and taut under his T-shirt and cargo pants. And when he smiled, his whole face lit up.

"H-hi," she said shakily when she got close, feeling ridiculous in the wig and sunglasses. "I'm, um, Britney." She motioned to her wig and smirked.

"It's great to meet you." Chase held out his hand for her to shake.

"It's great to meet you, too," Spencer said back, her hand tingling where Chase had touched it.

They stared at each other for a few beats. Spencer was glad she'd worn a printed silk minidress, which showed off her long legs. She couldn't tear her gaze away from Chase's biceps. He looked like the type of guy who could lift her up and spin her over his head without breaking a sweat.

Then Chase smirked. Spencer giggled nervously in response. "Sorry," Chase admitted. "It's just that I normally don't meet people like this."

"I know. Me, neither," Spencer said.

Chase sat down on a bench near the gift shop, his eyes still on her as though she were the only interesting thing in the room—maybe the world. When his phone buzzed, Spencer smiled awkwardly and stepped away. Chase glanced down at the screen. He flinched and immediately started typing.

"Sorry," he muttered, tilting the screen of his phone away. "This'll just take a second."

"No problem," Spencer said. "Got a conspiracy theory blog emergency?"

"Something like that," Chase murmured.

He slipped the phone back into his pocket and gazed at her again, from her blond wig to her pointy Loeffler Randall boots. After a moment, he touched the silver bracelet around Spencer's wrist. "That's really pretty."

"Oh, thanks." Spencer spun it around. "My mom gave it to me. It's from Prendergast's."

"On Walnut?" Chase asked. "I used to get my girlfriend stuff from there all the time."

Spencer peeked at him. "Is this a . . . current girlfriend?"

"Nah." Chase wrapped his hands around his knees. "It was over a long time ago. Before the, um, stalker thing."

Spencer nodded quickly. By the look on Chase's face, it seemed like he didn't really want to talk about it. She didn't blame him; she didn't like talking about what Ali had done to her, either.

"What about you?" Chase asked. "Dating anyone?"

Spencer studied her feet. "There was someone, but . . ."

Suddenly, the Reefer story spilled out of her. As she explained it, though, she realized she didn't really miss Reefer as much as she had even a few days ago. She'd had too much else on her mind to think about him.

"That sucks," Chase admitted when she finished. "He's got to be a real idiot to drop someone like you, Miss Spears."

Spencer wound a piece of fake hair around her finger. "You know, the worst thing about being dumped was that he did it two weeks before prom. There's no one for me to ask. I'm going to have to go stag, which is just beyond depressing."

"What a jerk," Chase said, shifting his weight. When Spencer looked up, there was a hopeful little smile on his face. Suddenly, an idea flickered in her mind. Could she ask *Chase* to the prom? He would look amazing in a tux. But no, that was crazy. They barely knew each other.

Buzz. It was Chase's phone again. This time he stood and walked a few paces away before checking the screen and typing back.

When he was done, he was all business again, reaching into his pocket. "Anyway. I have the photos you wanted to see."

He handed her three glossy five-by-sevens. They were various images from parts of what she assumed was Real Ali's life. The first one was a picture of blond twin girls of about five. Both wore purple overalls, had pink ribbons in their hair, and were smiling. Spencer could see a hint of Ali in both their faces. It was impossible to tell who was who.

"I think this is from when they lived in Connecticut," Chase explained. "It doesn't really tell us much about the case, just that the twins didn't always hate each other." He sniffed. "They sounded psycho, didn't they? Then again, those parents must have been whack-jobs, too. Who doesn't notice when their daughters switch places?"

"Seriously," Spencer mumbled, wondering what Chase would say if he knew those very twins were her half sisters.

She flipped to the next photo and gasped at the familiar image. Two blond girls stood in the DiLaurentises' Rosewood backyard. Ali—or was it Courtney?—faced the camera, and the second blonde, who they'd all thought was Naomi Zeigler once upon a time, turned away. An innocent-looking Jenna Cavanaugh was next to them, a trapped expression on her face. Spencer had seen this photograph before: Real Ali-as-A had sent it to Emily along with a note that said, *One of these things doesn't belong. Figure it out quickly . . . or else.* They'd never quite figured out why Ali had sent it to Emily. To frame Jenna, perhaps—she'd died shortly after and probably knew way too much for her own good.

Spencer looked up. "Are you going to post these on your blog?"

Chase shook his head. "I'm not posting anything until I have more proof."

"I wish you knew who sent you these. There wasn't a note with them? Nothing?"

Chase shrugged. "They just showed up."

Spencer shivered. Had Real Ali sent them? Only, why? To tease them? To show them how invincible and evasive she was?

She flipped to the last photo. In this one, Ali faced the camera. She looked older, nearly as old as the girl they'd met last year, and she wore a pair of white pajamas. She stood in The Preserve's dayroom—Spencer recognized the construction-paper cutouts on the wall. Someone stood next to her, too, but Ali's raised palm blocked out his face. Was it another patient? Her boyfriend? Helper A?

Chase's phone beeped again. He typed a response, then put the phone away. "I'm so sorry, but I have to go."

"Already?" she blurted.

Chase seemed surprised by her reaction. "W-would you want to hang out more?" he asked, a note of hope in his voice.

Spencer nodded quickly, then felt like a desperate idiot. "To talk about the Ali case, I mean. You have some really good ideas."

For a split second, Chase almost seemed disappointed, but then he smiled. "Definitely," he said. "I'd like that . . . a lot." He stuck out his hand for Spencer to shake, but Spencer pulled him in and gave him a hug. He smelled like leather and citrus-scented deodorant. It took all of Spencer's willpower not to run her fingers through his hair.

Chase pulled away from Spencer, studied her once more, and let his thumb trail across her cheek. Tingles shot up Spencer's spine. "Maybe next time you'll tell me who you are, Britney," he teased. And then he turned around and strode out of the museum, his sneakers barely making a sound.

Spencer followed him from a distance and watched as he strolled up the side street and made a right on Market. When he was gone, she melted to the stoop of a building in a full-on swoon. That. Was. *Amazing.*

Crack. Something sounded across the street. Spencer shot up, suddenly alert. An empty Diet Coke bottle rolled under a car. A face appeared in the windshield of a van to her right, but when she turned to see, there was no one there.

When her phone beeped, she almost expected it. But

it was her old phone ringing—she'd received an e-mail on her school account. Although it wasn't from A, Spencer blinked hard at the words.

Spencer, I have a few more questions for you. I'm coming by tomorrow to have a chat. Your house, 4 P.M. Please reply to let me know you got this message.
Sincerely,
Jasmine Fuji

Spencer's finger hesitated over the REPLY button. But then, swallowing a lump in her throat, she pressed DELETE.

17

AND THE WINNER IS . . .

On Wednesday morning, just three days before prom, all of the Rosewood Day Upper School students gathered in the auditorium. Girls were texting and playing Plants vs. Zombies and a group of drama kids near the left exit were acting out a duel from *Macbeth*, which the school had put on the month before. A big banner over the stage read MAY DAY PROM KING AND QUEEN. Two ancient-looking, gold-plated, fake-jeweled crowns that had adorned the heads of kings and queens from years past waited on a table. Two royal scepters, which the king and queen carried to prom, sat on the stage, too. Voting had occurred that morning, and Rosewood Day had tallied the votes immediately. The assembly was to announce the winners.

Hanna sat with the other candidates up on the stage, her heart going a zillion miles an hour. She glanced around the filling auditorium. Where the hell was Mike? He wouldn't miss this assembly, would he? She'd seen him before first period this morning, so she knew he wasn't sick.

Then she peeked at Chassey Bledsoe two stools down from her. Chassey kept peering at the crowd, giving everyone hopeful, gracious smiles. Then Chassey turned to Hanna, and her eyes lit up. "Are you excited?" she asked, her voice trembling slightly.

Hanna nodded in response. She was too hyped up and freaked out to speak. All the days of noncampaigning weighed heavily on her. What if Chassey *won*? Would she ever live it down?

Noel, who sat next to Hanna, stretched his arms behind his head and yawned loudly. Hanna turned to him. "*You* don't seem very nervous."

Noel shrugged. "This isn't as important for guys." Then a serious look settled over his features. "Hey, do you know what's going on with Aria?"

Hanna blinked. "What do you mean?"

"She's acting . . . strange." He tugged on the sleeve of his Rosewood Day blazer. "I thought she'd be into the prom decor chairman thing, but it's almost like she's pissed that I got her the job."

Hanna sat back. "*You* got her that job?" Aria hadn't told them that.

Noel nodded. "Has she said anything about why she doesn't want it?"

Hanna studied her nails, avoiding his gaze. "Maybe she just feels overwhelmed."

"That's what she said, but I think there's another reason." Noel stared into the crowd. "She's acting just like she did when we got back from Iceland."

Every muscle in Hanna's body went still at Noel's words. What was he getting at? Spencer and Emily had shared their theory that Ali's helper was a guy, and she'd agreed. Well, *Noel* was a guy. A guy who already knew too much because of his association with Aria. What was he capable of?

With every passing day, more weird memories about Noel had tugged at her. In sixth grade, after Scott Chin had inferred that Noel and Ali were getting hot and heavy, Hanna had gotten weirdly obsessed with spying on them. During the second week of school, when she was supposed to be in music class, she'd looked out the window and noticed two heads running toward the playground. One of them was Ali, and one of them was Noel.

She'd grabbed the bathroom pass and snuck outside. What would they do when they kissed? Would they close their eyes, or keep them open? Where would their hands go? When—*if*—Hanna ever kissed anyone, she wanted to be ready.

But when she'd climbed the hill to the playground, they were sitting side by side on the swings. Ali's head was down, and Noel had his hand on her back. After a moment, Hanna realized she was crying. It was even more shocking than seeing them kiss—she'd assumed that Ali had never cried a day in her life.

"I can't believe it's happening," Hanna had heard Ali say.

"It will be okay," Noel had answered. "I promise."

Hanna had had no idea what they were talking about at the time. But what if it had been something to do with her twin sister? Courtney, *Their* Ali, was still at the Radley then, but the switch had happened only days later. Maybe Ali had found out that Courtney was coming back. Maybe she'd been worried. And maybe she'd confided in Noel about everything.

And maybe, just maybe, Noel had promised to help her—in any way possible.

Everyone in the auditorium began to applaud as Principal Appleton stepped onto the stage. Hanna blinked hard and snapped out of the memory. The girls of the prom committee followed him. Aria pulled up the rear, looking fidgety, awkward, and out of place next to the smooth-haired, lip-glossed, Tory Burch bag–toting clones to her left. Hanna tried to catch her eye, but Aria wasn't looking in her direction.

Appleton took the microphone. "It's time to announce the May King and Queen."

Hanna's heart started to hammer. She glanced around for Mike again but still couldn't find his head of dark hair.

Appleton pulled a shiny white envelope from the inside breast pocket of his blazer and sliced it open with his nail. He took great care in unfolding it and then had to spend a few seconds adjusting his glasses. *Get on with it!* Hanna wanted to scream.

"First, prom king." Appleton adjusted the microphone, and a screech sounded through the speakers. "The winner is . . . Noel Kahn!"

Everyone cheered. Noel rose and strode toward the podium, giving everyone his easy, I'm-cool-and-I-know-it smile. Hanna glanced at Aria. She was clapping, but there was something off about her expression. Hanna thought again about how Aria hadn't told them that Noel had gotten her the decor chairwoman job. Was that all she hadn't told them?

After the crown was placed upon Noel's head and the applause died down, Appleton faced the students once more. "And now for the name you've all been waiting for: prom queen." He squinted in the bright lights. "The winner is . . ."

The hot lights beat on Hanna's forehead. A bead of sweat trickled down her back. She peered out at the crowd. Everyone's eyes were on the stage. A zillion thoughts zinged through her head at once, and none of them had anything to do with A: Did she look flushed and nervous, or poised and amazing? What if she won? What if she *didn't*?

"Hanna Marin!"

Hanna placed a hand over her mouth to control an excited squeal. The audience applauded thunderously. As she rose to shake Appleton's hand, her legs trembled.

Suddenly, a hand grabbed her arm. "Congratulations," a voice said. "You make the perfect queen."

Chassey's eyes were watering, but there was a wide smile on her face, like she was actually glad for Hanna.

"Th-thanks," Hanna stammered, taken off guard. Most runners-up trash-talked the winner. It was practically mandatory.

She turned and headed to the podium. With a *snap*, hundreds of blue-and-white balloons fell from the net on the ceiling and bounced onto her head. She batted them away, laughing. The crowd roared. The prom committee girls beamed. Aria strode forward and gave Hanna a hug.

As Hanna turned around and accepted the crown, the scepter, and even a little faux-fur, royal-blue shrug for her shoulders, all her troubles drifted off. For one shining, brilliant second, she was prom queen and nothing else—not a secret-keeper, not a victim, not a framed killer. A couldn't touch her. Her life was simple, and charmed, and absolutely perfect.

The assembly adjourned, and Hanna walked down the aisles to hundreds of congratulations. When someone grabbed her hand at the back of the auditorium, she assumed it was another well-wisher. A woman in a dark blue suit frowned down at her, her eyes flinty and sharp. A scream froze in Hanna's throat. Agent Fuji.

"Congratulations, Hanna," Agent Fuji said smoothly. "I don't mean to sully the moment, but I have a few more questions for you, and you're a hard girl to track down.

Would you mind if I stopped by your house tomorrow afternoon, maybe about four thirty?"

Hanna's bottom lip trembled. Why did Fuji want to speak with her again? "I-I probably have prom queen stuff to do after school tomorrow."

"I'm sure they can let it slide. It will take only a few minutes, I promise." A weird smile swam across Fuji's face. "Besides, you want to get all of this out of the way before prom, don't you?" She shifted her briefcase strap higher on her shoulder and gave Hanna a nod. "See you then!"

And then she was gone. Hanna watched her go, her heart thudding. But suddenly, something occurred to her: Agent Fuji was going to meet Hanna at her house . . . but she hadn't said *which* house. All Hanna had to do was hide out at the mall for a few hours. Whichever house Fuji called from to ask where she was, Hanna would just say she was at her other parent's for the day.

It was brilliant. Hanna's mood buoyed again, and she practically skipped down the hall. Until she realized: Newly crowned prom queens did not skip, they *glided*. Which was exactly what she did.

Later that afternoon, Hanna was still gliding. This time, though, it was down the burn clinic hallway with a bottle of Mr. Clean swinging from her hand.

"I'm gonna be prom queen," she chanted melodically, pausing in the middle of the hall to do a pirouette. She thought of perks other prom queens had enjoyed. Last year's queen, Angelica Anderson, had gotten her picture in the style section of the *Philadelphia Sentinel*. The paper even interviewed Angelica about her prom dress and pre-prom day, like she was an It Girl on Oscar night. Would Hanna get that opportunity, too?

She peeked into Graham's room. Today he was sleeping so soundly he almost looked dead. But even that didn't sully her mood.

"*Someone* sure is happy to be on bedpan duty."

Hanna looked up. Kyla lay on her cot in the same spot in the hall where she'd been the other day. There were fresh bandages on her face, and she'd taken off her socks to reveal coral-painted toenails. The last summer before Mona became A, she'd been obsessed with the exact same shade.

"Hey!" Hanna said brightly, surprised and pleased by how excited she was to see her. "I just got the best news at school." She plopped down on a metal chair next to Kyla's bed. "I was voted prom queen!"

"Are you *serious*?" Kyla squeaked. She groped for Hanna's hand. This time, Hanna let her hold it. "That is so incredible!"

"I know," Hanna gushed.

"And I bet you have a super-hot date, too, huh?" Kyla asked, propping herself up a little on the bed. "You are *so* lucky."

Hanna blushed. "I'm going with my boyfriend. And, yeah. He's pretty hot."

Kyla squealed. "Spill it! What does he look like? How

long have you been going out? I want to know *every-thing*."

Hanna felt another rush of pleasure at Kyla's interest. "I'm actually pissed at him right now," she admitted. "He missed the assembly where they announced that I won. He's going to have to give me back rubs for hours to make up for it."

Kyla clucked her tongue. "You deserve better than that."

"I know." Hanna rolled her eyes. "But usually he's amazing, and . . ."

Someone tapped her on the arm, and she stopped. "Miss Marin?" It was Kelly. "There's a call for you at the front desk."

Hanna frowned. The only people who knew she was here were her parents. She glanced at Kyla. "I'll be back in a sec."

"I'll be here," Kyla trilled.

A receiver was sitting on the front desk when Hanna arrived. "Hello?" Hanna said worriedly into the phone, wondering why her parents were trying to track her down.

"So you *are* there," Mike's voice boomed over the line.

Hanna's blood went cold. "O-oh!" she chirped after a moment. "Um, hi, Mike! What's up?"

"What's up is that you've been lying to me. You haven't been doing stuff for your mom or going to hair appointments. You've been at the burn clinic." His tone was clipped and accusatory.

Hanna wound the cord around her finger. The sharp smell of the bleach they used to clean the floors stung her nose. How did Mike find out she was at the burn clinic? Had A contacted him? But that made no sense—A didn't know about this, either. Right? She hadn't received a single note.

"It's to be with Sean, isn't it?" Mike said when she didn't answer. "I don't get it. What do you see in him? He wasn't even *nice* to you."

Hanna slumped into the leather chair next to the front desk. "Wait, you think I'm with Sean?" she whispered. "Why would you think *that*?"

Mike scoffed. "Why have you guys been talking a lot? *Hugging?*"

Hanna blinked hard, remembering the tender moment she and Sean shared about Ali. "Okay, we hugged *once*," she admitted. "But it was totally platonic. Who told you that happened?"

"It doesn't matter," Mike said stiffly. "It just matters that you're lying to me."

"I have a good explanation for why I'm here!" Hanna cried.

"Great. I'd like to hear it," Mike demanded.

Hanna's gaze drifted toward the circular drive. At that very moment, the nurse who'd changed Graham's IV bag the other day swept past the lobby, her lips pursed tightly. "I can't."

"Why not? Are you having top-secret treatment for a burn?"

"No . . ."

"Are you having plastic surgery?" Mike sounded incredulous.

"Mike, *no*. It's just . . ."

"It's Sean," Mike concluded. "That's the only reason that makes sense."

Hanna's head was starting to hurt. "It's not Sean! It's just . . ."

"You know what, Hanna?" Mike sounded weary. "I don't really want to have this conversation. Until you actually give me a reason, I'm not taking you to prom."

"Jesus, Mike!" Hanna shouted into the phone, so loudly that a nurse at the station gave her a sharp, there-are-no-personal-calls-allowed-in-here look. "Wait! Don't be like that!"

Then he hung up. Hanna wheeled around, tempted to kick the side of the desk, then noticed a piece of paper stuck to her shoe. Frowning, she kneeled down and picked it up. A familiar smiling face stared back at her. *Ali*. Hanna could almost hear her giggle echoing through the air.

Hanna faced the receptionist. "Who was standing here before me?"

The woman blinked at her. "No one," she said after a beat.

Hanna's heart thudded hard as she looked at the paper. It was the picture of Real Ali that ran in the *Philadelphia Sentinel* when she'd returned to Rosewood last year.

Someone had drawn a crown on her head with a pink
Sharpie. And underneath her chin was:

> You don't deserve the crown, bitch, and you know it. Here's
> the real queen. —A

18

NO FUN FOR YOU, MS. FIELDS

The following morning, Emily pulled into the now familiar neighborhood of Crestview Estates. The glimmering pond greeted her on the left. A huge gazebo and flower garden were on the right. The mansions looked even more enormous today, the chandeliers in the foyers twinkling through the windows.

"What are we doing *here*?" Iris's nose was pressed to the window like a little kid.

"I told you. One of my friends lives here," Emily murmured. "I need to pick up something from her for school."

"One of your friends lives *here*?" Iris seemed impressed. "Is her dad, like, Bill Gates or something?"

Emily steered into the circle, feeling bad that she couldn't tell Iris the truth. Sure, she was lying to her about a *lot* of stuff, but things with them had become easier since they skinny-dipped in the lake on Tuesday. They'd even developed an inside joke about Emily's dad's old, stinky fleece slippers. But it wasn't like she could bring her inside the panic room while she and her friends had yet another talk about Real Ali and her helper.

Emily turned into the long driveway and parked next to the four-car garage. "Are you going to be okay in the car for a sec?" she asked Iris. "I won't be long, I promise."

Iris slumped down in the seat and looked at a copy of *Us Weekly* she'd stolen from Wawa. "Why can't you just get whatever it is from your friend at school?"

"Because, um, she's sick," Emily said stupidly.

Iris gave her a strange look, but Emily fled the car before she could ask anything else.

Spencer pulled her inside and once again led her down into the basement. Aria was already inside the panic room, pacing back and forth. And Hanna, who looked even more made-up and coiffed today, was sitting on the denim couch, looking at Aria plaintively. "So Mike didn't ride to school with you? Do you know where he is right now? How can I talk to him if I can't use my stupid cell phone?"

"He was at Byron's last night—I was at Ella's." Aria looked apologetic. "What were you guys fighting about, anyway?"

"Guys, we don't have much time," Spencer interrupted, and everyone looked at her. "I got another note from Agent Fuji," she continued worriedly, her eyes darting around the security screens. "She says there's something we didn't tell her. She wanted to talk to me."

"She wants to talk to me, too!" Hanna whispered. "Are you going to?"

"What do *you* think?" Spencer looked horrified. "I deleted the message. I'm going to pretend I didn't get it."

Emily sat down next to Hanna. "Do you think A said something?"

Spencer sank to the metal swivel chair next to the monitors. "I don't know. Has anyone heard from A?"

Hanna tentatively raised a hand. "A sent me a note. It was about prom, but A left it at the front desk of the burn clinic."

Spencer widened her eyes. "So A knows you've been volunteering there?"

"I guess." Hanna's face was ashen. "But that doesn't mean A knows *why*, right?"

"The only notes I got were the two about the painting investigation," Aria said, perching on the couch's arm. "Which is scary. They've opened the case back up. Maybe *that's* what Fuji wants to talk to us about."

Emily shifted worriedly. "Maybe A is pissed off because he or she doesn't know our new cell numbers. Maybe he gave Fuji some intel as punishment."

"That's what I was worried about, too," Spencer said. "What do you think A told Fuji?"

"Who knows?" Emily mumbled.

For a moment, no one said anything. On the monitors, Emily could see her Volvo parked at the curb. Iris turned a page of her magazine, looking like she was about to fall asleep.

Then Spencer pulled the suspects list out of her bag and pinned it to the wall. Quite a few names had been crossed off—all the girls. There was a wiggly line through Darren Wilden and a question mark next to Jason. Only Graham's and Noel's names were unmarked. Emily caught Aria staring at it. It wasn't a surprise to her—last night, Emily had stopped over at her house to tell her they'd narrowed down the list to only guys. Aria opened her mouth to say something, then shut it fast.

"What?" Emily asked.

Aria shook her head. "Nothing."

Emily cleared her throat. "So does anyone have any thoughts about who Ali might have met at Keppler Park?" She'd shared her discovery with Hanna and Aria last night.

Hanna shook her head. Aria cleared her throat awkwardly and turned away. "Nope." Her voice squeaked.

Emily watched Aria's face, but she gave nothing away. Spencer was watching, too. "Are you *sure*?" she pressed. "Maybe Noel has been there?"

Aria fiddled with the grommets on the couch. "I said I was sure, didn't I? Noel isn't A."

"I know you don't want to believe it, Aria," Spencer said soothingly. "But the more we find out, the more sense Noel makes."

Aria's eyes flashed. "All we've found out is that A might be a guy and that Ali had a boyfriend. That could be anyone."

"There's more than that." Spencer twirled the pen in

her hands. "It turns out that someone stole a bunch of prescription medications from the Bill Beach last spring. It might have been the person who was taking care of Ali."

Aria wrinkled her nose. "So? Noel doesn't have a connection to the Bill Beach. As far as I know, he's never even *been* there."

"He knows Sean, though," Spencer pointed out. "They run in the same circles. Maybe Noel got Sean to slip him the passcode to get into the building."

Aria burst out laughing. "Are we talking about the same Sean? He'd never do that."

"True." Hanna shoved her hands in her jacket pockets. "But, Aria, Noel *was* acting weird at the assembly yesterday. He asked if there was anything going on with you. Then he brought up Iceland out of the blue. Why would he do that?"

Aria pressed her lips together. "That *is* kind of strange," she admitted. But then she shook her head vigorously. "It still doesn't mean anything. I asked Noel about whether he sensed that the 'Courtney' who returned wasn't who she said she was, and he got really upset and defensive. After that, there was no way I was going to ask him if he'd taken a little jaunt to Iceland to murder Olaf over winter break. We've hardly talked since. Don't you guys see? A *wants* us to suspect Noel. A wants to ruin what Noel and I have. Then we'll break up, it's *not* going to be Noel, and A's going to win again."

"If that happens, you can blame us for everything,"

Spencer said. "We'll do everything in our power to get Noel back for you, okay? But can you please do a little more digging?"

"None of us want it to be Noel," Emily added. "We're not against you."

Aria stood up from the couch. Her eyes were flinty and cold. "Fine," she said gruffly. "I'll see what I can do. But I'm not going to find anything, believe me."

She whipped around, turned the handle of the panic room, and left. Emily heard her footsteps on the basement stairs and felt a twinge of regret. The last thing she wanted to do was pull their friendship apart. What if Aria was right—what if suspecting Noel, wrecking everything, was just part of A's master plan?

Then Spencer touched her arm. "Try to get something out of Iris soon, okay?"

Emily nodded. "I will."

Then she headed out of the house, across the driveway, and climbed into her car. Thankfully, Iris was still sitting in the passenger seat, flipping through *Us*. Emily slid the key in the ignition and started the engine.

"How's your sick friend?" Iris asked without looking up from the magazine.

"What?" Emily snapped her head up. Then she remembered the lie she told. "*Oh.* Uh, feeling much better!"

Iris slapped the magazine closed and gave Emily a knowing look. "God, Emily. If you're going to lie, at least do a better job."

"I'm not lying," Emily said quickly.

Iris waited a beat. When Emily didn't say anything more, she tossed Emily her cell phone, which was sitting in the center console. "This beeped while you were out," she said woodenly.

Ice ran through Emily's veins. She peeked at the screen. There was a new message for her on Twitter. Her mouth dropped open as she read the words. THOUGH I CAN'T BE THERE WITH YOU IN PERSON, I'LL BE THERE IN SPIRIT, an unfamiliar Twitter handle had written to her. I'M GOING TO SEND YOU A SECRET MESSAGE, MY LOVE. BE READY AT 10 PM!

"Is that from the girl you're into?" Iris asked, still staring straight ahead.

Emily knew she should be annoyed that Iris was snooping, but she was so thrilled she let it slide. "I think so!" she whooped. "I can't wait for prom now!"

Iris's neck twisted around so she was facing Emily. Her eyebrows furrowed. "Who says you're going to prom?" She tilted her chin. "If you want answers from me, then we're sticking to *my* schedule. *My* list. No balls for you, Cinderella."

Emily blinked hard. "But . . . I thought maybe . . . I mean, this is *important*. I thought you'd understand. As, you know, a friend." As soon as she said it, she realized she meant it. They sort of *had* become friends, in a weird way.

Iris crossed her arms over her chest, a look of hurt passing across her face. "Friends don't lie, Emily."

Emily stared at her. Iris looked genuinely shattered—over such a small lie. Then again, maybe it wasn't small to her. Emily suddenly wondered how many friends someone like Iris could have made in The Preserve. Probably not many.

She opened her mouth, wishing she could tell Iris the truth, but then reality slammed back. She swallowed the thought and stared out the windshield. "Okay," she said quietly. "Your list it is."

19

ARIA OPENS UP

After school that day, Aria climbed the stairs in her house holding a lacquered tray her father had brought back from a trip to China. On it were two plates of fried tofu spring rolls that she'd specially made for her and Noel. She'd garnished each dish with basil, green onions, soy sauce, and even two red roses she'd plucked from her mother's vase in the kitchen. Ella's boyfriend, an artist named Francis who was on a month-long trip to Berlin, had sent them to her, but he sent her roses all the time, so Aria figured Ella wouldn't miss a couple.

She kicked open the door to find Noel splayed on her bed, reading *ESPN* magazine. "Dinner is served," she chirped in a faux French accent. "I think I even got the wraps right." They'd learned to make them in a cooking class they'd taken together.

Noel smiled at the steaming food. "This smells way

better than when we made it in class. Have you been practicing?"

Aria propped up a fringed pillow against the headboard. "Maybe a little . . . for you." She touched his hand. "We haven't seen each other much lately. And the last time was so . . . weird."

It was hard to spit the word out. *Weird* didn't begin to describe her Ali-terrogation. Since she wasn't texting or calling, she and Noel had barely spoken in the past few days. Aria hadn't realized how much they relied on technology to communicate.

But maybe it was good: She needed some space to clear her mind. Though she'd never admit it to her friends, there were a few other things about Noel she couldn't get out of her head. Like how Noel's house was filled with pictures of the family at the picnic grounds at Keppler Creek—Mr. Kahn said the fishing there was the best in the state. Noel had gone hiking and fishing there with his brothers a few times last winter, spring, and summer. Some of the trips had been before Real Ali reappeared, some of them after. He'd never invited Aria, and she'd thought nothing of it. *Should* she have?

Noel popped a spring roll into his mouth and swooned. "You can even make tofu taste awesome."

"That's one reason to keep me around," Aria teased, trying to make her voice sound carefree.

"I can think of a few other reasons, too." Noel set his

plate on the end table, grabbed her around the waist, and pulled her on top of him. "The only tastier thing than this dinner is you."

Aria snuggled into his neck. Noel ran his hands through her hair and kissed her lips. She shut her eyes and tried to relax. A traitor wouldn't touch her like this. Even the best actor in the world wouldn't be able to caress her so affectionately.

Beep.

Aria shot up in bed. She stared at her new phone. It wasn't blinking . . . but Noel's, which was sitting on Aria's desk next to his wallet, was. He sat up and studied the screen. "Huh. Is this an international number?" he asked, showing her.

Aria tried to process the long string of numbers in the text box, but before she could, Noel opened the text. Normally, Aria would have looked away, but she caught sight of her name in the message. As she read the words, a sinking feeling crept over her skin.

Look in Aria's closet. She has something to show you.

Noel snorted. "Freaking international spam. They're getting so good they know our names now." He hit DELETE. "*Look in Aria's closet,*" he said in a mock-ominous voice, punctuating it with a Dracula laugh. "What's in there?"

"Nothing," Aria squeaked. She tried to take a breath but hiccupped nervously instead.

Noel pulled away and searched her face. "Are you sure about that?" he teased.

He was still laughing, which made Aria feel even worse. "Yes!" she said, but her voice was too loud and high-pitched.

A beat passed. Noel swung his legs off the bed and started toward the closet. He had the same look on his face he got when he was about to tickle her. "Is it the bogeyman?"

"Don't open it. It's a huge mess in there."

Noel shrugged. "I bet mine's messier."

Aria glanced at Noel's phone lying faceup on the bed. What the hell was she supposed to do now? She couldn't tell him about the painting. It was bad enough the case had been reopened and that the police had new evidence and an anonymous tip—which Aria was sure was from A. She couldn't involve Noel in this. The last thing she wanted was for him to go away for life, too.

"Come here," Aria said, pulling Noel back to the bed.

She kissed his neck softly, hoping it would distract him. But his muscles were stiff; he pulled away from her and inspected her carefully. "What's with you?"

"What do you mean?" Aria peppered his cheek with kisses. "I'm fine."

Noel sat up. "You're totally not fine. I don't get you lately. Like, *really* don't get you. And it's starting to scare me. I'm starting to think you're . . . I don't know. Not telling me something."

Now it was Aria's turn to tense up. "Don't think that," she squeaked.

Noel sat back. "Whatever it is, I'll still love you. But don't lie to me anymore. There's something. I can tell."

Aria's jaw started to tremble. It felt like Noel could *see* her secret, ugly and wrinkled inside her. If she insisted it was nothing, he would just keep asking . . . or maybe check the closet for real. Besides, coming clean would eliminate some of A's power: A would surely let it slip to Noel about Olaf soon enough if Aria didn't.

She took a deep breath, staring at one of the prisms hanging in the window to steady her nerves. "Okay, I have been keeping something. Something I'm not really proud of."

Noel pressed his lips together. "Okay," he said in a brave voice.

Aria cleared her throat, her heart hammering fast. "The reason I was asking you about kissing Ali the other day is because . . . I was feeling guilty about something I did. And, um, if you would have said you liked kissing Ali— even a little bit—it might have made me feel a little better." As she fumbled her way through the words, she was surprised to realize they were actually true.

Noel's brow furrowed. "Excuse me?"

Aria held her up her hand to stop him. "Just let me finish. So, uh, you know Olaf, from Iceland?"

"The bearded dude?" A hint of a smirk appeared on Noel's face. "Yeah."

Aria started to tremble. "Something sort of . . . *happened* between us when I was there. I meant to tell you a long time ago, but I was afraid. But you need to know."

A car engine grumbled out the window. The house made a settling sound. Noel turned away sharply. "I *knew* it."

"You did?" Aria bit her lip hard. Was she *that* transparent? Had Noel seen them?

When Aria and Olaf had snuck outside, the door had creaked a few times, like it was about to open, but then it hadn't. Perhaps Noel had peeked out and saw them. But why wouldn't he have stormed into the alleyway, punched Olaf in the face, and broken up with Aria on the spot? Noel could have easily taken Olaf in a fight. So maybe he didn't know that night—maybe A *had* told him later. But if that was the case, why wouldn't he have said something as soon as he found out?

Noel paced the room. He stopped at Aria's desk, laced his hands over the back of her swivel chair, and glared at her. "You accused me the other day of cheating on you with Ali, and here you cheated on me for *real*. Jesus, Aria."

Tears rolled down Aria's cheeks. "I'm sorry. I shouldn't have done it. I've felt terrible ever since. I love *you*, Noel. I was really drunk. It meant nothing."

Noel scoffed. "Are you upset now because you really feel bad, or because you got caught? I always suspected something happened, but I hoped . . ." He trailed off and bit his lip. Then he whirled around and kicked the garbage can under her desk hard. It made a metallic clang and rolled against the wall. Aria gasped and jumped back.

Then Noel swiveled around and grabbed his cell phone. "This is an Icelandic number, isn't it? Is it from Olaf? Are you still in touch with him? You gave him *my* number?"

"No!" Aria cried. "I'm not in touch with Olaf. Olaf is . . ." She couldn't say *missing* or *dead*. Noel would ask how she knew that, and then she'd have to bring up the newspaper article she'd found on her bed . . . or else she'd have to pretend she'd *Googled* him, which would make her seem like she liked him. Nor could she say who had *really* sent Noel that text just now—she couldn't put Noel in jeopardy.

"I don't know who that text is from," she admitted. "Maybe Olaf, though I never gave him your number. I guess it was someone's way of getting me to tell you the truth."

"*Look in Aria's closet. She has something to show you,*" Noel repeated nastily. "A skeleton."

Tears pricked Aria's eyes. "I'm so sorry." She hated the way he was looking at her.

"Is that *all* you have to tell me, or is there something more?" Noel demanded.

Aria's stomach swirled. "Th-that's all. I swear."

Noel raised one eyebrow, like he didn't believe her. Then he turned and stomped out of the room.

"Noel!" Aria cried, chasing after him.

"I have to go," Noel said gruffly as he thundered down the stairs. He grabbed his keys off the table near the door, whipped it open, and ran out onto the porch.

"Wait!" Aria yelled. By the time she was at the door, Noel was in his car. Its headlights snapped on, and he backed out jerkily, without bothering to look if anyone was on the road. The taillights disappeared down the street quickly.

Aria stood in the chilly night, rubbing her bare arms. It felt like there was a huge weight sitting square on her chest, preventing her from taking a full breath. Noel's words swam back to her. *Is that all you have to tell me?* What did *that* mean?

Another memory flickered into her head, faded and almost forgotten. A Reykjavik cab had picked them up to go to the airport the morning of their flight home. As they drove out of the city, they passed the huge chateau on the hill. Police cars surrounded the place. Cops stood on the driveway, and sirens whirled. Aria slumped down in her seat, but Noel stared straight at it, fascinated. "Huh," he had said in the croaky voice from a night of too much drinking. "I wonder what happened *there*." And then he'd looked pointedly at Aria.

But he *couldn't* have known. *Right?*

She swallowed a huge lump in her throat and went back inside the house. The stairs creaked noisily as she climbed back to her bedroom. She pushed open the door, nearly bursting into tears at the two unfinished plates of food on the table. She walked over to the closet, whipped the door open, pushed the sweatshirts aside, and stared at the rolled-up canvas. If only she could just burn it.

A square wallet on her desk caught her eye, and she straightened. It wasn't hers, but she knew it well. She picked it up, tracing the embossed NAK—*Noel Alexander Kahn*. Noel always took his wallet out of his back pocket when they made out—it was much more comfortable that way. But he'd never forgotten it before. And Aria had never looked through it.

Don't, she told herself. But her hands inched toward it anyway.

The wallet made a squeaky-leather sound as she opened it. Inside the pockets were two credit cards, Noel's driver's license, a couple of twenties, and some singles. His student ID was tucked into a back slot. So was a free pass to the Rosewood Go-Kart track and a receipt from Wordsmith's Books for a coffee.

Aria stared at the ceiling, suddenly feeling oily and gross. Noel wasn't hiding anything. This was just A being A and ruining everything.

But then she noticed a faded ticket stub behind the bills. THE WOODS CINEMA, it read in purple ink. Aria had never heard of it before. The stub was a pass to a *Spider-Man* movie. Aria frowned. The latest *Spider-Man* had come out the last summer she was in Iceland—before junior year. Why would Noel keep this?

She turned the stub over. There was faded handwriting

on the back, but Aria could still make out the words. *Thanks for believing in me! Next time, I'll get the popcorn.*

The note was punctuated by a little doodle. At first, it looked like just a blob, but when Aria brought it into the light, it was of a girl playing field hockey, her hands curled around a stick, the ball shooting through the air. Aria sank onto the bed. She'd seen this exact doodle before—on someone's piece of the Time Capsule flag. She'd been given it accidentally, and she'd hidden it in her room ever since.

It had been Ali's.

20

THE STING

That same afternoon, Spencer, clad once again in her Britney wig and sunglasses, paced back and forth in front of a Philly brownstone near the Schuylkill River. Boats honked. A double-decker bus full of tourists in faux Ben Franklin glasses and Liberty Bell sweatshirts swept by. Rain had just fallen, and the air smelled like slick cement and exhaust. She checked her school e-mail on her old cell phone, piggybacking off someone's unencrypted WiFi. A new message had come in. *Dear Spencer, Perhaps our wires crossed. I was hoping to see you at your house yesterday, but maybe you didn't get my message. Can we try for tomorrow? Sincerely, Jasmine Fuji.*

Bile filled her stomach. Yesterday, she'd taken special care not to be anywhere near her house around four PM, when Agent Fuji said she was going to oh-so-casually drop by. She'd treated Mr. Pennythistle, her mother, and Amelia to ice cream at the King James Mall so *they* wouldn't be home when Fuji came by, either. But Spencer couldn't dodge her forever.

"Boo," a voice said. Spencer whirled around and put up her fists.

"Just me, Britney!" Chase held up his hands in mock terror, backing away.

"Don't *do* that." Spencer gave him a playful shove. Then she examined him more closely. Today, he wore skinny-ish jeans, a button-down polo, and a down vest that made him look rugged and tough. Was it possible he looked even *better* than he had the last time she'd seen him? Spencer had been thrilled when he'd sent her an IM yesterday saying, *My connection at CVS found an address for Barbara Rogers in their system. 2560 Spruce Street, Apt. 4B, 4 PM tomorrow?*

She looked at the brownstone. "Now what do we do?"

"Knock on her door," Chase said matter-of-factly.

Spencer gave him a crazy look. "Are we sure she even lives here?"

"Let's check." He climbed the steps and looked at the names on the buzzers, then frowned. "Hmm. There's no *Rogers* listed."

"It could be an outdated directory," Spencer suggested. "Or maybe she's not on the lease."

"Let's buzz." Chase reached toward the 4B button.

Spencer caught his arm. "Wait! Maybe we shouldn't let her know we're coming."

Chase squinted at her. "Then how are we going to get into the building?"

At that very moment, the red door opened, and an old man with white hair walked out. Spencer tried to catch it, but the door banged shut and locked behind him. She turned to the man instead. "Um, I'm Barbara Rogers's niece. Can you let me in?"

The man glowered at Spencer's Britney wig. "Never heard of her." He shuffled down the stairs.

Spencer exchanged a look with Chase. Something told her the guy was lying. "Are you sure?" she called after the man.

"I said I don't know anything," he called over his shoulder, practically diving into a parked Audi. In seconds, he started the engine and pulled away from the curb. Black exhaust sputtered out of the tailpipe.

Chase climbed down the steps and stood by Spencer. "Oh-*kaaay*."

Spencer leaned against the wrought-iron railing, trying to get a look at the vanishing license plate, but it was already too far away. "It seems like he wanted to get away from us really quickly, didn't it? Almost like someone got to him, told him not to talk."

"And if people got to him, they had to have a reason," Chase went on. "Maybe Barbara Rogers *is* Alison's nurse." He glanced up at the brownstone again. "Let's wait for someone else to come out and catch the door before it shuts."

"Good idea." Spencer sat down on the first step and stared fixedly at the door, willing someone to appear. Cars honked on the main avenue. A couple of pigeons fought over a bread crust on the sidewalk. But no one emerged in the foyer. How long would they have to wait?

"So did you get your blog emergency sorted out the other day?" Spencer asked.

Chase looked at her blankly. "What?"

"You know, the reason you had to cut our first meeting so short," Spencer prompted. "Was there breaking news about Benjamin Franklin secretly running a meth lab? Independence Hall once being a whorehouse?" In some of their chats, Chase had revealed some of the ridiculous myths that his readers debated.

"*Oh*." Chase stared at his hands. "Actually, it wasn't a blog emergency at all. It was more of a family thing. My brother needed my help."

A trail of pale green leaves swirled down the street. One of them flew right into Chase's cheek. Spencer resisted the urge to brush it away. "Is your brother older or younger?" she asked.

"A year younger," Chase said. "We're pretty close. We weren't when we were little, but after the stalker thing . . ." He trailed off, his gaze suddenly distant.

Spencer rolled her jaw. "That must have been intense," she said quietly. "What happened, exactly, if you don't mind me asking?"

Chase's gaze slid to the right. "At first, the guy and I were friends. But then, something changed. He threatened me. Tried to kill me. Messed me up pretty badly."

"There's not a mark on you." Spencer allowed herself a few moments to stare.

Chase ducked his head. There was a long pause before he spoke again. "Yeah, well. Most of the scars you can't see."

Spencer knew exactly what he meant. And she *hated* that she knew. She watched the pedestrians on the street, lost for a moment in memories of Ali. "Do you know what happened to him?" she asked after a while. "Did he go to jail?"

Chase looked pained. "He was under eighteen, so no. And like I said, his parents were loaded. They kept this out of the press, paid off the cops. He left school, but that's all I know."

Spencer shook her head. "That is *so* unfair. So he's just walking the streets?"

Chase nodded. "I guess so."

He turned his head away then and made a pained noise that broke Spencer's heart. She touched his arm, all at once so sad and heartbroken, both for Chase's experience and her own. How dare someone torment him? How dare someone torment *her*?

"I know what it's like," she whispered. "I've been stalked, too."

Chase turned around, his brow furrowed. "You have?"

Quickly, before she could change her mind, Spencer removed the Britney wig and took off the sunglasses. "I'm Spencer Hastings," she said. "One of the girls Ali tried to, uh, kill."

Chase's mouth made an O. All sorts of expressions crossed his face in a single second. "I *wondered* if it was you," he said after a moment in a voice so tender it made Spencer's heart break. "But I was afraid to ask. I was afraid to scare you away."

Spencer pulled the wig back onto her head. "You can't tell anyone, though, okay? I'm trusting you. If I see this show up on your blog . . ."

"That will never happen!" Chase said, urgently shaking his head. Then he leaned back and blinked at her. "Jesus. Spencer Hastings. Now I feel like an idiot telling you all that stalker stuff. It pales in comparison."

"No, it doesn't," Spencer said firmly. "The same thing happened to both of us. Someone we trusted screwed us over in the worst way possible." All of a sudden, she felt tears filling her eyes. She'd connected with other people about Ali, confessed what Ali had done to other boys she'd been interested in, but no one had gone through it, too. She'd always laughed at the expression *kindred spirits*, but now, with Chase, she understood what it meant. If only she could see Chase on occasions other than Ali stakeouts. She had a feeling they could talk all night without ever running out of things to say.

She swallowed hard. "Will you go to prom with me?"

Chase sat back and blinked. "Wait. What?"

"We both need something fun in our lives. Something to take our minds off what happened. We could go just as friends. As whatever. And you probably couldn't tell my friends that you run an Ali blog, and you'd have to promise not to talk about any of us in it—"

"Spencer," Chase interrupted. "I already told you, I'd never do that."

Spencer nodded. "So what do you say?"

Her heart pounded as she watched Chase tilt his head back and peer down his nose at her, as if trying to see her from a different angle. The longer he didn't say anything, the more ridiculous Spencer felt. It was a horrible idea. Chase was out of high school, too cool to go to proms.

Then Chase grabbed her hand. "I would be honored. Just tell me when and where, and I'll be there with a tux on."

"Really?" Spencer's mouth wobbled into a smile.

Chase was about to say something else, but then the door behind them swung open. An old lady with a kerchief over her head and a bunch of bags in her arms struggled out the door. Chase stepped up and held it open for her. The old lady smiled at him. "That's so sweet of you, dear!"

"No problem at all," Chase said, giving her a small bow. He and Spencer scrambled through the door before it slammed closed.

The hall was dark and smelled like spicy curry. There were two apartment doors on the ground floor, then a set of stairs. Spencer could see another apartment door up the first flight. There had to be at least four or five more apartments in the building.

She looked at Chase. "So what do we do now?"

"Go to Four-B, I guess," Chase said, peering up the stairs. Then he turned to the front door again. "You go up. I'll be right behind you, keeping watch."

Spencer nodded, then bolted up the stairs, passing three doors painted red, orange, and blue. Another blue door still had a Christmas wreath, despite the fact it was May. Another orange one had a pile of mail on the mat. The railing wobbled when she grabbed it for support. She could hear Chase's footsteps on the stairs behind her.

On the top floor, light flickered behind 4B. Swallowing hard, Spencer exchanged a look with Chase, who was a few steps down, then crept up to it and pressed her ear to the door. Could Ali's nurse really be inside? What if *Ali* was inside, too?

"What should I do?" she whispered to Chase.

He shrugged. *Knock?* he mouthed.

Trembling, Spencer rapped once, then twice. Then she listened. The television's volume didn't change, but she thought she heard a sigh and couch springs squeak. There was a click in the hall, and she whipped around, on alert. "What was that?" she whispered to Chase.

"I don't know," he whispered back, eyes wide. Then he walked farther down the hall. He stopped at the second-to-last door on the right and stepped closer to it, inspecting the knob. He pressed his ear to the door, as if listening, but then he lost his balance, falling forward and softly slapping the door with his palm. Spencer covered her eyes. "Shhh!"

"Sorry!" Chase jumped away from the door as if anticipating a ghost was going to spring out.

For a moment, it was eerily silent. Then, a creak
sounded above her, and she looked up. And all at once . . .
boom. There was a crunch of metal, and a whoosh of air,
and then more banging and clanging sounds. Spencer
jumped back as an attic door in the ceiling opened and
items tumbled down. First an unwieldy coatrack, then a
mounted deer head, its antlers sharpened to knifepoints,
and then a bowling ball. The ball crashed onto the floor
next to her and careened down the steps.

"Spencer?" Chase called through the dust. "Jesus. Are
you okay?"

"I-I don't know," Spencer said, realizing she'd fallen to
the ground. When she touched her face, it was slick. She
brought her hand away—it was sweat or tears, not blood.
More dust cascaded from the ceiling. The trapdoor hung
precariously on one hinge, the screws dangerously loose.

"Come on," Chase said, catapulting over the rubble,
grabbing her hand, and dragging her down the steps.
Heads poked out of apartment doors, mouths agape.

"That was weird," Spencer said shakily as they barreled
down more stairs.

"*Weird* doesn't even begin to *describe* that," Chase said.
He glanced up the stairwell. Another loud *thunk* sounded.
"It's almost like it was planned."

Spencer shivered. She'd been thinking the same thing.
It was possible, perhaps, that Ali or her helper had planted

this address online for Chase to find. And then snuck in here and filled the attic with dangerous things. Rigging the door to fall at just the right moment . . . on just the right person's head . . .

A's evil message swirled in her mind: *I did it. And guess what? You're next.* Maybe this had all been a trap. And maybe A's warning was coming true.

21

AN UNEXPECTED GUEST

Hanna pulled into the Bill Beach parking lot, her burner phone wedged between her shoulder and her ear. Screw the no-technology rule. This was an emergency.

Mike's voicemail beeped. "It's me again," Hanna pleaded. "I can explain. I want you back. I want to go to prom with you. I have a new cell phone—this is my number. Please, please, *please* call me!"

She hung up and eyed her prom queen crown and scepter—she carried them with her everywhere. Tears pricked her eyes. She was *not* going to ruin her makeup, though. A future prom queen needed to look good even when she was cleaning up pee.

When something in her bag bleated, she plunged her hand inside again, praying it was Mike. But it was her old phone. It had auto-logged onto the Bill Beach WiFi and downloaded a new e-mail from Agent Fuji. On instinct, Hanna deleted the message without even reading it.

She stomped through the double doors, threw on her scrubs, and kicked the mop bucket down the hall toward Graham's partitioned-off area. She whipped back his curtains, not caring who saw her. Graham's eyes were closed, but his mouth was working hard. Hanna pressed her ear close to his lips, but no sound came out.

"Just tell me who you saw," Hanna growled, wanting to shake him. Couldn't they, for once, get a freaking break? They could nail A and get Fuji off their backs. They could clear up this nonsense with the painting in Aria's closet. She could make things right with Mike, too.

But Graham didn't make a sound. Hanna was so annoyed she stomped her foot hard. Her sole clacked loudly on the linoleum.

"Hanna?" a voice called out. "Everything okay?"

Hanna turned around. Kyla sat up in bed, the bandages still covering her face. There was a pot of nail polish and an emery board in her lap.

"Actually, no," Hanna admitted.

Kyla made an *mm* noise. "Guy trouble?"

Hanna walked closer. "How did you know?"

"I heard you on the phone the other day," Kyla said with a shrug. "So what did he do?"

"He won't go to prom with me," Hanna said miserably. "It's a huge misunderstanding, and he thinks I'm lying about something—but I'm not. He's being an idiot."

"So explain it to him," Kyla said.

"It's not that easy," Hanna sighed. She opened her

mouth to try to tell Kyla why, but then a wave of exhaustion washed over her.

"In that case, this will make you feel better."

Kyla groped for something on the little tray next to her bed. She handed Hanna a small picture in a frame. It was a shot of the Hot Male Nurse in the changing room without a shirt on. Hanna snickered. "Where'd you get this?"

"One of the orderlies took it with my phone." Kyla sounded proud of herself. "I uploaded it to the Kodak site and had it printed at the gift shop. But you should have it, Hanna. You need the pick-me-up more than I do."

"Thanks, but that's okay." Hanna studied Kyla's bandages and withered arms and legs. A ridiculous feeling washed over her. Here she was, making a burn victim cheer her up. Had she lost all perspective?

She leaned in closer, suddenly dying to know. "What happened to you?"

Kyla fiddled with the jar of nail polish. "My brother and I were messing around in the garage when a can of sulfuric acid fell off a shelf . . . and onto me. That stuff works just like flames—burns your skin right off."

Hanna winced. "Is your whole face . . . ?" She trailed off, not knowing how to word it.

"Gone? Messed up?" Kyla finished. She shook her head. "My cheeks are a mess. My chin, too. I need a lot of skin grafts, but you can't do them all at once. I wasn't as pretty as you, but I was okay-looking. Popular, even. But not anymore, huh? When I bust out of here, it's gonna be, *Here comes freak show!*"

She was trying to sound so brave and tough. Hanna's heart clenched. How would she treat a girl like Kyla at Rosewood Day? The Old Hanna who'd been Ali's and Mona's friend would have been ruthless. But what about the girl she was today? Was this Hanna any better?

She touched a bare spot on Kyla's arm. "Listen. When you get these bandages off, I want to give you a makeover. Hair, makeup, skin, jewelry, fashion, everything. I'm really good at that sort of stuff, I promise."

Kyla made a strange noise at the back of her throat. "Why would you do that?"

Hanna leaned closer. "Because you're the coolest girl I've met in a long time. People need to see that, you know? They need to look past some stupid scars and grafts. You're Kyla, and you're *fabulous*. Got it?"

Kyla laughed softly. "Okay," she said after a moment. "You're *amazing*, Hanna."

"I know, I'm awesome," Hanna said lightly. But she really did feel good. She couldn't wait to pick out Kyla's colors and do her hair. And who knew? Maybe Kyla's scars wouldn't be that bad. Maybe Sean's dad could work some kind of miracle.

Her phone bleated, startling Hanna so that she almost dropped it on the floor. Mike's number flashed on the screen. She stared at Kyla in amazement.

"Is it him?" Kyla whispered. Hanna nodded. "Well, answer it!" Kyla cried.

Hanna swallowed hard and turned away. "*Thank* you for calling me back," Hanna said into the phone. She scurried to the break room, even though she wasn't on break yet, and flopped down on one of the couches. "Like I said, I can explain. The truth is, I really have been volunteering at the burn clinic. I'm here right now."

Mike sighed. "Hanna, at least tell me a better lie. You hate the burn clinic. You would never voluntarily work there again."

"I'm telling the truth." Hanna picked at a loose thread on the upholstery. "The guy who got hurt in the blast is here—Graham. There's something you don't know: Just before that explosion went off, he chased Aria into the boiler room. They were both there when the bomb went off—Aria's lucky she got out safe. We wanted to ask him some questions about it when he wakes up."

She held her breath, wondering if Mike would buy her half-true story . . . and hoping her friends didn't kill her for spilling some of it. Mike breathed in. "Aria never told me she was down there."

"I know. She was afraid you'd freak."

"Do you really think it's a good idea to talk to this guy? He set off the bomb, right? What if he's dangerous?"

"Mike, he's covered in bandages and tubes—he's not going to do anything. As for the bomb—I don't really know. There was another person down there, too, at the time—it could have been him instead. That's what I want to ask Graham about—*if* he wakes up." She paused, then decided to ask: "Actually, do you remember where Noel was when the bomb went off? It would have been right when the talent show was about to start."

There was a long pause. "Are you suggesting *Noel* bombed the boiler room?" Mike sounded horrified. "What drugs are you on, Hanna? He's her boyfriend!"

"I'm not suggesting anything. I'm just asking questions."

Mike sighed. "Well, Noel and I were practicing our routine an hour before the talent show. But—okay. Right before the bomb, he said he had to go back to his room. So I *don't* know where he was, technically." There was a clunking sound on the other end. "Does Noel know you're asking these questions?"

"No, and I would appreciate it if you didn't tell him," Hanna said sharply, her heart pounding hard.

"I still don't believe that's why you're at the burn clinic, though."

Hanna stomped her foot. "Ask your sister, okay? But one thing's for sure: I'm definitely, *definitely* not with Sean. I didn't even know he'd be working here when I signed up. And he and my stepsister go to V Club together. Is that enough? Will you take me to prom?"

"Hmm," Mike said, still sounding miffed. "I'll have to check your sources."

Hanna rolled her eyes. Why was he being such a hard-ass? "Who told you about me being here, anyway?"

Mike cleared his throat. "It doesn't matter. He was just trying to be a good buddy."

The hairs on Hanna's arms stood on end. *He?* "Just tell me who. I won't be mad."

"Hanna, drop it. We'll go to the dance, okay? I have to get off. I'm getting in my car." And then, with a *click*, Mike was gone.

Hanna stared at the flashing numbers on the phone, a strange taste in her mouth.

As if on cue, a movement outside the room caught her eye. A familiar figure walked out the double doors and headed toward the exit. His head was tilted toward his phone, and he was talking too quietly for Hanna to hear. He wore fitted, dark-wash jeans; Adidas sneakers; and a black T-shirt printed messily with words in another language.

Hanna's heart started to pound. She knew exactly where that T-shirt had been purchased: the only cool boutique in Reykjavik. Mike had bought one in white.

It was Noel.

22

THE TRIP TO TRIPP'S

"*Turn left at the next intersection*," said the automated voice of the GPS Emily had suction-cupped to the windshield of the Volvo. She dutifully stopped at the light and angled the car into a development full of columned mansions. "Whoa," she murmured, looking right and left. "Swanky."

Iris, who had taken her usual spot in the passenger seat, shrugged apathetically. "I'm not surprised Tripp lives here," she said. "You have to have a lot of cash to afford The Preserve."

"Are you *sure* Tripp lives here?" Emily asked as they passed a white stone house with a miniature version of it for a mailbox. When she'd picked Iris up at the King James that afternoon, Iris had announced that she'd discovered where Tripp, her old crush, lived, and that they were going to track him down that very night. Luckily, his house was only on the other side of Philly, in a pretty New Jersey suburb that looked a lot like Rosewood. Still, there was something about this neighborhood that made Emily feel uneasy. The houses reminded her of the Crestview Manor ones, except even more soulless and spooky. In fact, this neighborhood reminded her of the big, impersonal, oddly generic neighborhood Gayle Riggs lived in when Emily had met her.

"I researched it," Iris said snootily, gazing at a notepad on her lap. "His family is listed on four-one-one." Then she pointed to a country club parking lot. "Let's park here and walk the rest of the way. I don't want Tripp to see a car at the curb and run."

Emily shrugged, then did as she was told. Things between her and Iris were back to being tense again. Iris had created an itinerary of stuff for them to do this weekend that wasn't even *on* her bucket list, the activities stretching long into the night. It was like she was purposefully keeping Emily away from prom—if Iris couldn't be happy, then Emily couldn't, either.

They headed down the quiet neighborhood sidewalk, which was swept clean of leaves and eerily unblemished by sidewalk drawings. The whole place almost felt like a movie set. "It's the next house on this block," Iris said, giving a tight smile to a passing woman walking her dog, as if *she* was the one who wasn't supposed to be here.

Finally, they stopped in front of a large brick-and-stone structure with a long strip of windows across the top level. MAXWELL, it said on the mailbox. Rolling back her shoulders, Iris marched up the front walk and rang the bell.

Emily remained at the curb. A woman Emily could only assume was Tripp's mom opened the door, and Iris's voice rose. The woman frowned and shook her head. A second later, the door shut. Iris knocked once more, but it didn't reopen.

Iris stomped back down the walk angrily. "Tripp doesn't live here anymore. That stupid bitch kicked him out."

"Did she say why?" Emily asked.

Iris angrily yanked a daffodil from the flowerbed by the mailbox and twirled it between her palms. "Tripp always used to say his mom was a hard-ass."

"Where could he have gone?"

Iris tossed the flower onto the lawn. "She said with his father. I asked where that was, and she said she didn't know." She set her jaw. "Then I said I was his old girlfriend, and that made her even angrier! She slammed the door on me!" She stared fixedly into the street. "Do you think he said bad stuff about me? Why would she have done that?"

The garage door rose, and they turned toward the house again. A silver Mercedes backed out of the drive-way. Iris pulled Emily behind a huge shrub so Tripp's mom wouldn't see them. The car backed into the street and zoomed away, the garage closing quietly in its wake.

"Well, I guess that's that," Emily said.

Iris clutched her arm. "Are you kidding? Tripp might not be there, but I bet some of his stuff still is. If I'm not going to find him, at least I want something to remember him by."

Emily placed her hands on her hips, a sinking feeling in her stomach. "And let me guess. We sneak in and steal it?"

"Aw, you know me so well!" Iris pinched Emily's cheek. Then she pirouetted toward the house. Emily followed a few steps behind, considering just leaving Iris here to do this by herself. But then she thought of Iris getting stuck inside, Tripp's mom finding her, Iris telling everyone that she'd been kidnapped . . .

Iris circled to the back of the property and climbed onto a multitiered patio. She tried one sliding glass door, then another. Then she spied a dog flap set into the French doors off the kitchen. "*Yes.*"

"Iris . . . ," Emily called weakly. Helplessly, she watched as Iris got down on her hands and knees and tumbled through the dog door. Then she unlatched the patio door, letting Emily in. "Welcome," she trilled, picking up an oven mitt that was sitting on the island and sliding it over her hand. "Would you like some fresh-baked muffins? A cup of tea? I make a good suburban housewife, don't I?"

Emily looked around the kitchen. It was massive, with a six-burner stainless-steel stove and the longest granite-topped island Emily had ever seen. An enormous fridge sat off to the left, a shiny cappuccino maker was on the counter, and a wine refrigerator filled with bottles stood near the pantry. Not even Spencer's kitchen was this luxurious. Yet it had an unlived-in quality to it, too, the appliances a little *too* clean, not a speck of dirt in the grout of the tiles, every single towel monogrammed with a swirly letter M. It was strange to think that a mental patient had grown up inside these walls—when Emily was younger, she'd assumed that nothing bad happened to people who had this much money.

"What was wrong with Tripp, anyway?" Emily whispered to Iris, who was searching through a drawer across the room, the mitt still on her hand.

Iris inspected the items hanging on the refrigerator, flipped through a desk calendar, and opened the fridge and pulled out a bottle of 5-Hour Energy. "The doctors said he was schizophrenic, but I think that's bullshit. He was the sanest person there. Super smart, too. He was always coming up with fun dates for us to go on within the hospital walls." She pulled out a picture in the drawer, squinted at it, then let it flutter to the floor. Emily scrambled after her to pick it up. An older couple were clinking wine glasses. The man wore a Santa hat on his head.

"There's *got* to be something of his," Iris grumbled. She crossed the room. "Come on. Let's go upstairs."

She headed down the hall and up the stairs as if she'd been here before. Colorful oil paintings lined the walls, including a swirly one that reminded Emily of Aria's Van Gogh. Her stomach gurgled. It was easy to forget about the painting, hidden inside Aria's closet. But what if *that* was what Agent Fuji wanted to talk to all of them about?

Iris tried each of the closed bedroom doors. When she looked through the third one, she gasped and plunged inside. Emily followed. A twin bed stood in the corner.

There were lines in the carpet from where the vacuum had swept, and the bureau was free of clutter. It reminded Emily of Iris's depersonalized room at The Preserve.

But then Iris opened the closet. A few plaid shirts hung on hangers, and a single milk crate sat at the bottom. "Bingo," Iris whispered, shedding the oven mitt and pulling the crate into the room.

Inside were paperbacks, notebooks, and an old cell phone with a cracked screen. Iris grabbed the notebooks and leafed through them. Emily ran her fingers along the pages of an old copy of *1984*. Was this all Tripp's mom kept to remind herself of him?

"Not a single frickin' thing," Iris said to the notebook, slamming it closed.

"What were you looking for?" Emily asked.

"My name in a heart. *Something*." Iris rummaged through the crate some more, tossing aside stuffed animals, an empty water bottle, a container of hand sanitizer, a hospital bracelet that said THE PRESERVE AT ADDISON-STEVENS. When she got to the bottom of the crate, her jaw wobbled. "Well, I guess that proves it. I meant nothing to Tripp."

"Maybe he brought something of yours with him when he left."

Iris snorted. "I've been kidding myself for way too long. Tripp and I never really had anything real. It was stupid to come here."

Suddenly, she tucked her head between her knees and let out a muffled sob. Emily paused for a moment, not sure what to do. Her hand hovered over the small of Iris's back, but she wasn't sure what to say to make her feel better.

Instead, she picked up the cell phone and pressed the power button. Surprisingly, a Motorola logo appeared on the screen. She clicked on the CONTACTS button. Everything had been deleted. She opened up the texts, but that folder was empty, too. A few photos had been saved, however—a penis-shaped cloud, a golden retriever, and then, the third photo, a girl Emily knew well.

"Oh my God," Emily whispered.

Ali's blond hair cascaded down her shoulders. Her blue eyes sparkled. She wore the same white pajamas that Iris had been wearing at The Preserve. Emily guessed the photo had been taken a few years ago, when Ali was maybe fifteen.

Iris wiped a tear and looked at the screen, too. She let out an annoyed sniff. "Well, I guess *you* found something."

"Why would this guy have a picture of Ali?" Emily asked shakily.

Iris leaned back on her hands. "Because we all were at The Preserve together. We were friends."

Emily stared at the picture again. Just seeing Ali's face in somewhere so unexpected made her itchy. Someone just out of the photo had an arm slung around her shoulder—the only identifying thing was a gold watch on the person's hairy wrist. She squinted at it. Had she seen it before?

She pointed to the disembodied hand. "Who's that?"

Iris brought the photo close to her face. Her mouth made an O. "You know, that might be him. The boyfriend."

Emily blinked hard. "You mean the one who came to the hospital all the time to see her? The one who she met at Keppler Creek when she got out?" Emily grabbed Iris's wrist. "You have to tell me his name. Right now."

Iris shook her head. "No can do." She stood up and headed out of the room.

Emily pocketed the cell phone with Ali's picture and followed her downstairs, out the back door, and onto the lawn. Iris was walking quickly, but Emily finally caught up with her on the sidewalk.

"Damn it, Iris!" Emily squealed. She gestured to the house. "I broke into a house with you! What's next, murder? You've been stringing me along all week—just give me something real, okay? Is it too much to ask for this guy's name?"

Iris stopped next to a tree stump. She lowered her eyes. "I can't tell you his name . . . because I don't know it."

Emily felt like the wind had been knocked out of her. "*What?*"

Iris's skin looked even paler in the sunlight. "I never knew it. I'm sorry. I wasn't lying—Ali *did* have a guy who visited all the time. But she just called him Mr. Big . . . like Carrie in *Sex and the City*. I never knew his name. It was this big secret she kept from me. I was never allowed to hang out with him, either." Her mouth tightened. "That's why I'm not loyal to that bitch, you know. She kept things from me. It's like I wasn't worth knowing the truth."

Emily wilted against a tree. "Why didn't you tell me before?"

Iris kicked at a divot in the grass. "I thought it was the only way you'd keep driving me around, taking me wherever I want, letting me stay at your family's house—the only way things could be *normal* for a little while. As soon as you found out I didn't know anything, you would ship me right back to The Preserve."

Emily blinked. She had no idea Iris was afraid of that. "So . . . wait. You *like* hanging out at my family's house?"

"Uh, *yeah*," Iris said, as if it was an obvious answer. "But whatever—it's over now. You can leave me just like my mom did. Just like Tripp did. It's cool—I'll just go back to The Preserve now and rot there for another four years. You can go to prom. Get on with your life."

She turned away. After a moment, her shoulders shook silently. Emily was so stunned that she couldn't move. She knew she should be angry, but seeing Iris there, her spindly arms wrapped around herself as she sobbed, Emily couldn't help but feel for her. She knew what it was like to be abandoned by her family, too. And to be ditched by someone she thought loved her. When Ali laughed at Emily in the tree house at the end of seventh grade, something inside Emily had died. Another piece of her had withered away when Real Ali tried to kill her in the Poconos.

She looked at Iris's quivering form. Really, she and Emily weren't that different. If Emily's circumstances had been just a bit harsher, who was to say *she* wouldn't have lied about information just to get someone to pay attention to her? In a strange way, it was almost flattering that Iris found Emily worthy of lying to, Emily's life worth living. Another surprising thought struck her: If Iris had just *asked* Emily to hang out for a few days longer, even though she didn't know Ali's boyfriend's name, Emily might have said yes.

She put a hand on Iris's shoulder. "Iris, I'm not going to send you back to The Preserve before you're ready. In fact, I think you should come to prom with me. As my date."

Iris sniffed loudly and gave her an incredulous look. "Yeah, right."

"I'm serious." Emily's voice rose. "I know prom isn't on your list, but maybe it should be. Have you ever been to one?"

Iris tucked a lock of hair behind her ear. "Well, no, but . . ."

"A lot of guys go stag. We could find someone new for you to go out with. Someone much cooler than Tripp."

Iris pinched a piece of skin on her arm. A bird chirped in the distance, and a car swished past on the road. Emily's heart pounded hard. *Please say yes*, she willed silently. Both because she wanted to see Jordan's surprise . . . and because she really thought it would do Iris some good to come.

Finally, Iris sighed. "Well, okay."

"Yes!" Emily whooped, moving in to give Iris a hug. Iris was stiff for a moment, but then she hugged back. When they pulled away, Iris's cheeks were shiny and pink.

Then Emily's burner cell rang. She picked it up and said hello.

"Miss Fields?" said a brisk voice. "This is Jasmine Fuji. We met the other day?"

Emily opened her mouth, but only a small grunt came out. She stared at the phone as if it were on fire. "H-how did you know this number?"

"Your mother gave it to me. I called your house first."

Emily's head started to spin. Her *mom*. Mrs. Fields had forced the burner cell number out of her, and Emily hadn't thought to warn her not to give the number out to anyone. Who *else* had she given it out to?

"Look, I've been trying to get in touch with you and all of your friends, but I'm beginning to feel like you're blowing me off." Agent Fuji barked out a harsh laugh. "Do you have a moment to talk right now?"

Emily glanced at Iris, who had now stopped on the sidewalk and was staring at her. "Um, I'm kind of tied up."

"It won't take long, I promise."

"I'm sorry," Emily blurted out. "But I can't right now. Maybe another time." And then, before she knew what she was doing, she hung up the phone.

23

THE COLD, HARD TRUTH

"Oh, decor chairwoman!" sang a soprano voice on Friday afternoon in the journalism barn. The room was packed with kids putting the final touches on Van Gogh murals, canvas paintings, and goody bags. Taylor Swift crooned through computer speakers, and a couple of the decor committee girls had made up an impromptu dance/cheer to "Love Story."

"Yoo-hoo!" the voice sang again. "Miss Montgomery?"

It wasn't until Aria felt a hand on her shoulder that she realized the girl was talking to her. It was Ryan Crenshaw, a Rosewood Day alumna who was helping with the prom decorations. Per Rosewood Day tradition, a recent graduate always came back and supervised, reminding the committees about the silly prom rituals like taking photos of the prom king and queen in the graveyard near the Four Seasons and organizing a massive conga line. It was an honor to come back and help with prom, but Ryan, who had mousy brown hair and freshman-fifteen, beer-drinking arms, and who whined unendingly about how college sucked, was just one of those girls who didn't want to let go of high school.

Ryan guided Aria, who had been hiding in the supply closet, freaked out by all the Van Goghs, toward a table and pointed at a huge SLR camera. "You need to start snapping photos for the yearbook, paparazzo! Let's get action shots of some mural painting! And, look! There's our queen! Let's get one of her trying on her crown!"

Across the room, Hanna was chatting quietly with Scott Chin, one of the yearbook editors. Ryan ushered Aria over. As soon as Hanna spied her, her face paled. She grabbed Aria's arm and pulled her into the hall. "*There* you are. I need to talk to you."

"What about pictures, girls?" Ryan called out.

"In a minute!" Hanna shouted over her shoulder, rolling her eyes.

They stepped onto the path that led to a small sculpture garden that a wealthy alumnus had donated to the school back in the eighties.

Hanna walked to a sculpture of a woman whose nose had fallen off years ago, faced Aria, and took a deep breath. "You know how Spencer said that Ali's helper might be connected to the Bill Beach—there was that prescription-drug theft there a while ago?"

"Yeah." Unconsciously, Aria started picking at the skin on the side of her thumb.

"Well, I saw Noel at the Bill Beach yesterday."

A bolt of cold ran through Aria. "Are you sure?"

Hanna nodded gravely. "I'm dead serious. It was definitely him."

Aria set her jaw and stared at a metal sculpture of a gyroscope a few paces away. "Maybe he had a good reason to be there."

"Like stealing prescription drugs for Ali?" Hanna crossed her arms. "If you think he's innocent, figure out why he was there."

Aria turned away. "Actually, Noel and I aren't exactly on speaking terms right now. I kind of told him about Olaf."

Hanna's eyes widened. "Why?"

Aria waited for a noisy riding mower to pass. "Noel got a text from A that said he should look in my closet. A obviously wanted him to know about the painting. Then the moment got weird, and Noel was convinced I was hiding something, and so . . . well, I spilled the beans about Olaf."

"That sucks. I'm sorry." Hanna shook her head ruefully. "Are you okay?"

Aria glanced at Hanna sharply. "Please. You're probably secretly thrilled."

"Aria!" Hanna's eyes were wide.

"Wouldn't it be easier if Noel and I broke up? Then you'd be able to continue your witch hunt guilt-free."

Hanna shook her head vehemently. "We're not anti-Noel. We're not anti-*you*. Believe me, all of us hate this. No one wants this to be happening."

Aria touched the sculpture's hand, biting back a sob. She knew Hanna was telling the truth, but it still stung every time they came to her with a new, damning Noel tidbit. She wanted to scream at them, *Aren't we friends? Don't you care about me?* It was like when her mom had warned her about dating Gunter, a boy in Iceland—he *was* trouble, and Aria had known it, and she also knew her mom had only said it to protect her. But it still didn't feel good to hear it.

Hanna leaned against the sculpture's other arm. "Has Agent Fuji called you again?"

Aria stared at the ground. "No . . ."

"She's contacted me and Spencer. Emily, too. Apparently she wants to talk to us again."

Aria raised her head. "*Why?*"

Hanna threw up her hands. "How should I know? My guess is that A said something about one of our secrets. Maybe the painting. Maybe Tabitha. Who knows?"

Aria's stomach twisted in knots. On the one hand, she was relieved she hadn't received another call, too. On the other, why *hadn't* Fuji contacted her? "What should we do?" she asked shakily.

Just then, Ryan stuck her head out the door. "Aria? We have a question about the papier-mâché stars."

Aria glanced at Hanna, then shrugged and followed Ryan back into the barn. As she instructed how the stars should look, her stomach churned. They *couldn't* talk to

Agent Fuji, not with that painting in Aria's closet. They had to figure this out *soon*.

And even though she'd lashed out at Hanna for it, the new detail about Noel scared her, too. Noel didn't know anyone at the Bill Beach. Why was he there? To see Graham?

To steal meds?

She reached into her pocket and touched the ticket stub she'd found in Noel's wallet yesterday—she'd given Mike the wallet to return to Noel this morning and prayed he wouldn't notice the stub was missing. The movie from only a few years ago, after Courtney's death, when Real Ali was definitely imprisoned in The Preserve. That weird message on the back about Noel believing in someone. Aria hadn't told her friends about it—they'd jump all over the hockey-girl doodle. Other people drew girls wielding hockey sticks, though. It didn't necessarily mean anything.

Still, she was curious. Darting to her bag across the room, she pulled out her iPad and typed THE WOODS CINEMA into Google. In a split second, the results came up. The first entry was for a cinema in Maplewood, New Jersey.

Aria's mouth went dry. Tabitha was from Maplewood. And Ali and Tabitha had clearly been at The Preserve together—and were even friends. Did this mean Noel had visited Ali when she was at The Preserve? Did he spring Ali and Tabitha out for a night so they could go to a movie? It made no sense, though—why would they go all the way to New Jersey? And why would Noel say to Agent Fuji that he'd never met Tabitha if he clearly *had*?

"Aria?"

Aria spun around. Noel stood behind her, almost like she'd conjured him. His hands were in his pockets, and there was a serious look on his face.

"H-hey," Aria said shakily, turning the iPad facedown on the table.

Noel glanced toward the door. "Can you talk?"

Aria nodded and slipped her iPad back into her bag. When they walked into the sculpture garden again, Hanna was gone. For a while, there was only the sound of their footsteps. Halfway down the path, Noel stopped next to what everyone called the Slinky. "So I've been thinking about Olaf."

Aria felt her throat close. "Noel, I . . ."

He put his finger to her lips. "I was an asshole that trip, Aria. I felt jealous that I didn't know the Iceland side of you, and I was afraid that when you got there you were going to change and not be into me anymore. Instead of stepping up, I just acted like a whiny, ridiculous idiot. I should have just let you go with Hanna and Mike instead of coming along, too. I'm not happy that you hooked up with that guy, but I also sort of get it."

Aria blinked. It was the last thing she'd thought he was going to say. Just last week, she would have been flattered and touched—here was gorgeous Noel, worrying *she* was going to drop *him*. But now she felt hollowed out. Suspicious. Why was Noel forgiving her so easily?

Noel took her hands. "I still want to be with you. I

want to go on another vacation and do it right. We can even go back to Iceland if you want. This time, I'll ride one of those silly horses."

Aria knew she was supposed to laugh, but she couldn't muster the emotion. She looked away instead, a lump in her throat. Her hands felt like two dead weights. *Ali and Tabitha,* her mind screamed. *Maplewood. Hockey-player girl. Ask him.*

Noel cocked his head. "You seem miserable."

"I'm not," Aria said, her voice squeaking. "I just . . ." She trailed off. If only there was a way to bring Tabitha's name into the conversation without it seeming really random or suspicious. But *how*?

Noel pulled his hands away. "What the hell, Aria? Here I am, bending over backward for you, telling you everything, getting you the decor chairwoman spot, putting up with your weird moods, forgiving you for *cheating on me*, and you're still treating me like shit. It's getting kind of old, okay? The secrets, the strange behavior . . . it's like I'm not fully part of your life."

"Don't say that," Aria whispered. "I've just been distracted, that's all."

"With *what*?" Noel demanded.

Aria's throat bobbed. All she wanted was to exonerate him. But she couldn't just ask for the answers.

She stared at Noel. An indentation of something showed through the pocket of his jeans. It was his cell phone. A tantalizing idea wormed its way into her mind.

She took a few moments to center herself, then stepped

closer and cleared her throat. "I can't stop thinking about what I did to you. I still feel awful because of it. And with the explosion on the boat and almost dying out at sea, I've been a mess, Noel."

"Then *tell* me about it," Noel said. "Don't hide it. Don't hold it inside and make me guess."

"Okay," Aria mumbled, even mustering up some tears. "I will. I promise."

Then she pulled him into a hug. For a moment, she was afraid Noel wouldn't hug back, but he tentatively wrapped his arms around her. Aria's heart banged against his chest. She slid one hand down the length of his waist. Carefully, delicately, she pinched the top of the phone with two fingers and slipped it out one inch at a time, as deftly as a pickpocket. Noel shifted, but he didn't seem to notice it was gone.

Aria dropped the phone in the big pouch of her hoodie. When they broke away, Noel was staring at her lovingly again.

She swallowed hard and gestured to the barn door. "Well, they need me back inside."

Noel kissed her cheek. "Call me when you're done, okay?"

"Okay," Aria said shakily. In seconds, he was gone.

She couldn't get back into the barn fast enough; it would only be a few minutes before Noel discovered his phone was missing. She ran to her iPad and found a USB cord inside her bag. She plugged the phone in. A window appeared asking if she wanted to transfer data to the device. She stabbed

YES. Numbers flashed across the screen. In under a minute, a message popped up that the transfer was complete.

Aria yanked the phone from the USB, opened the barn door, and flung the phone into the grass. Hopefully, Noel would just think he'd dropped it.

She returned to the iPad. Noel's texts had loaded. She scanned them quickly, not expecting to find much—if Noel *was* A, he'd probably use a different phone with an unlisted number. Besides the texts Noel had sent to Aria about couple stuff, most of them were to his lacrosse buddies or family members. But as she skimmed farther down the list, there was something strange. Two Februarys ago, Noel had sent a text to an unlisted number. *Anything you need*, it said. The unlisted number had texted back. *Thanks for helping me. You know what to do.*

Aria did the math. February was when Noel and Aria bonded at the séance at that head shop in Yarmouth. It was bizarre he'd even saved this text—surely he'd had an earlier-model phone back then. He must have transferred it from that phone to this one. It must have been senti-mental. Could this text be from Ali? What did *You know what to do* mean?

Aria shut her eyes. This was all horrible conjecture. Was she really *doing* this? Had she lost her mind?

She clicked out of the texts, her limbs feeling heavy. Noel's e-mails had loaded, too, but Aria no longer wanted to look at them. Then a familiar name caught her eye. *Agent Jasmine Fuji.* It was from just two days ago. Aria felt dizzy. But Noel had talked to her last week, right?

There wasn't just one e-mail to Fuji, either—there were six in the thread. Words flashed before her eyes. *Thank you for your thoughts.* The next one: *I'm very sorry you lost your friend.* And the last: *We will speak more soon. I was very intrigued when you said not everyone is telling me the whole truth, and I hope you can elaborate.*

Someone laughed loudly behind her, and Aria dropped the iPad back to the desk. She stared around the room blearily, as if she were caught in a nightmare. Noel had lost his friend . . . as in *Tabitha*? Or Ali? And who did he think was lying? Aria? Was *that* why Fuji was frantically trying to speak with them?

She reached for her phone and punched in Spencer's number. This was getting out of hand. It was time to admit some of this stuff to her friends. The phone rang once, then twice.

"Hello?" Spencer answered. "Aria? What's up?"

A knock sounded on the window, and Aria jumped. Noel stood on the other side, his discarded cell phone now in his palm. He smiled at her so sweetly, so guilelessly, that Aria's heart cracked into a million pieces.

"Aria?" Spencer's voice came through the receiver.

Aria waved back to Noel, tears in her eyes. "Um, I–I butt-dialed you," she said to Spencer. And then she hung up, telling her nothing.

24

SOMEONE SLIPS

On Saturday afternoon, a few hours before prom, Spencer and Hanna sat in Hanna's bedroom at her father's house. A giant full-length mirror stood near the corner. The bed was strewn with makeup cases, hair dryers, and hair spray, and an assortment of bobby pins, clips, and curling irons lay on the floor like pickup sticks. Jewelry on loan from Spencer's and Hanna's moms sat on a velvet cloth on the bureau. Their gowns hung from hooks on the back of the closet doors, and their shoes sat at attention on the carpet underneath. The air smelled like perfume and that vague, chemical dry cleaning scent Spencer could never quite pin down. It made her feel a little sad that they *all* couldn't be here for pre-prom prep, but no one had heard from Aria, and Emily had, bizarrely, invited Iris as her date. They were getting ready at the Fieldses' house.

There was a knock on the door. Hanna's father popped his head in. "How's it going, girls? Anything I can do?"

"I don't know, Dad." Hanna smirked. "Want to help with makeup?"

Mr. Marin raised his palms and backed away. "That's not my territory." He smiled adoringly at Hanna. "You look beautiful, though."

"You *do* look awesome." Kate poked her head in next. Half her hair cascaded down her shoulders in tendrils, but the other half was still straight.

"Thanks," Hanna said, sounding surprised. "You do, too, Kate."

Then Kate and Mr. Marin disappeared into the hall. Hanna looked at Spencer. "Do you think I should have asked her to hang out with us?"

"Maybe." Spencer shrugged. Not that she was really into socializing. And Kate's simple, uncomplicated life would probably rub her the wrong way at the moment. That girl didn't have an A in her life. Or secrets she was hiding. Or a death threat on her head.

Hanna slumped back in the chair, making no move to go into the hall and call Kate back. "I wish Mike would call the house and let me know he's still my date." She eyed Spencer in the mirror. "Who's the guy *you're* going with, Spence?"

Spencer picked up an eyelash curler. "Oh, just someone I met."

"Where?"

"At the King James," Spencer said automatically, using the story she'd rehearsed in her head. "He works at that upscale men's boutique."

"Beauregard's?" Hanna's eyes lit up. "I thought about getting Mike cuff links from there. I'm totally going to hit him up for a recommendation . . . *if* Mike and I are still together."

"Um, I don't know if cuff links are his specialty," Spencer said, biting down hard on the inside of her cheek. She had a feeling this was going to be a long night. Hopefully Chase wouldn't want to chat with any of her friends.

Thinking of Chase, she pulled out her phone, leaned over Hanna, and showed her the picture he'd given her of Ali at The Preserve. "Look."

Hanna's lips were pursed. "Where did you get this?"

"I've been digging up stuff about her. You know where this is, right?"

"*Duh.* I'd know that dayroom anywhere." Hanna's brow furrowed. "Ali looks about our age, maybe a little younger." She pointed at the figure whose face they couldn't see. "Who's that?"

"I was hoping you'd know. He's with Ali, don't you think?"

Hanna squinted. "Too bad he's not wearing something distinctive. Everyone and their mother has a black hoodie, huh?"

"Noel has a black hoodie," Spencer said, coughing awkwardly.

Hanna gave Spencer a long, serious look. "It does seem like him, doesn't it?"

"I don't want it to be." Spencer sank to the bed and rubbed her eyes.

"But it seems like it, doesn't it?" Hanna asked softly. Hanna had told Spencer about how Mike didn't remember where Noel had been when the bomb went off on the cruise . . . and about how she'd seen Noel at the Bill Beach. She shook her head. "And I still can't believe you went into that apartment building in Philly by yourself. You could have been killed."

"I think A just wanted to scare me," Spencer mumbled, her stomach churning. It all seemed so obvious now: Ali and her helper had planted that address in the CVS system for Chase to find. They'd rigged the trapdoor to fall when Spencer snooped around. So did that mean A *knew* Spencer was snooping?

Spencer leaned into the mirror and blotted a bit of smeared eye shadow on her temple. "I wish I could go back to that building, but I'm way too scared."

"Why would you want to go *back*?"

"Because even if that's not where Ali's private nurse lives, Ali and her helper have been there, booby-trapping the place. And now that the trap has been sprung, there's a chance they'd go back and collect all the stuff they'd planted in that attic. Maybe that bowling ball is Noel's dad's. Maybe something up there can be traced to Ali."

"Huh." Hanna slowly ran a brush through her hair. "I never thought about that."

It was a theory Chase had raised. Spencer had begged

him to go in her place today to see if Ali or her mysterious boyfriend showed up, but he couldn't. He didn't explain why.

Her laptop beeped as if on cue. Spencer had a new e-mail in her top secret account. She glanced at the screen, shielding it from Hanna with her hand. *Looking forward to seeing you tonight, Britney,* Chase wrote, adding a winking smiley face. *And, by the way, I just found out something interesting about Alison.*

Her heart started to pound. *What?*

Another e-mail popped up. *Don't want to tell you online,* Chase wrote. *But I'll see you soon.*

Spencer gritted her teeth. She glanced at the clock on the bedside table. Only three more hours.

It was going to feel like an eternity.

Just as dusk was falling, Spencer and Chase, who met her back at her house, walked hand in hand to the limo at the curb. As Chase held the door for her, she gave him a bashful smile.

"You look amazing," Chase said, kissing her cheek.

Spencer tried not to swoon. "You look great, too." Chase's tux fit him perfectly. He'd been so polite when he'd handed Spencer her corsage and posed for the pictures. Even Amelia, who wrinkled her nose at everything, had gawked.

The limo turned out of the cul-de-sac and onto the country road toward Philadelphia. The front window was down just a little, blowing in the sweet-smelling spring air.

But even when Chase popped the cork of a bottle of champagne and handed Spencer a glass, she couldn't relax. She turned to Chase. "Now that we're alone, can you please tell me what you know about Alison?"

Chase sipped from his champagne flute. "I got some interesting footage from a friend. It's a surveillance video from a building not far from here. There's a girl in one of the shots who looks like Alison."

Spencer's skin prickled. "You're kidding." She glanced at Chase's phone, which was on his lap. "Do you have it on you? Can we watch?"

Chase stared at his phone, too. "I don't have it."

"Oh." Spencer slumped.

"Was that the only reason you came out with me tonight?" Chase's voice was froggy.

"Of course not!" Spencer cried. "I just . . . well, that sounds *huge*. I'd love to see it."

He took her hand. "This is huge too, though. Being with you, I mean. I just want a calm, normal night, one where we don't talk about Ali or stalkers or the shitty things that have happened to us. One where, like, you don't almost die from something falling on your head." He tried to laugh.

Spencer blinked. "But . . ."

"How about this." Chase squeezed her hand. "How about I access the video after our first dance. That's, what, an hour from now? I just want a little bit of time with this amazing girl I met named Spencer. Okay?"

Bubbles from the champagne fizzed in Spencer's nose. She gazed at the blurry highway lights above them. When *was* the last time she'd just enjoyed something? Even the cruise, which was supposed to be relaxing, had been a horrible, stressful mess. And it was kind of nice to be thought of as just Spencer, a regular girl, not Spencer the Pretty Little Liar.

"As long as you promise to show me everything as soon as that first dance ends," she said.

"I promise."

They shook on it. Chase rested his head on her shoulder. They looked out the window as the city of Philadelphia glittered on the horizon, and they started to talk. Spencer asked him about what his prom would have been like, and who he would have liked to have taken, and what he was thinking about studying in college next year. Then they talked about her upcoming semester at Princeton. Spencer even told him a little about the huge mishap at the potluck party the weekend she'd visited.

They talked the whole traffic-jammed ride into the city, and before Spencer knew it, they were taking the off-ramp near the zoo. Her pulse had slowed. Her cheeks hurt from laughing. Talking about everything but the case *was* a good suggestion.

Then, as they stopped at a light, the driver turned on the radio. *And now, turning to the murder investigation of Tabitha Clark. Investigators say they've made headway with their questioning and have several potential suspects.*

Spencer dug her nails into her knee. *Suspects?*

"That story is crazy, isn't it?" Chase crossed his legs. "I've been following it a little. A few people have sent requests for me to post about it on my site."

"Huh," Spencer said, shakily pushing a lock of hair off her shoulder.

Chase grabbed his champagne flute. "Actually, you were in Jamaica when Tabitha died, weren't you? Did you see anything?"

Spencer turned and stared at him, a cold feeling trickling down her back. "I never told you I was in Jamaica."

Chase blinked. "Yes, you did."

"No, I didn't." She started to shake all over. "I definitely didn't." It had been scary enough to admit who she really was. She wasn't stupid enough to tell him about Jamaica on top of that.

Chase drained his flute in one sip, his eyes not leaving hers for a second. His Adam's apple rose and fell as he swallowed. Slowly, he reached into his pocket for something. It was the same way someone threatened might reach for a knife, a gun. An entirely new reality formed in Spencer's mind. What if Chase knew Spencer was in Jamaica because he had been there, too?

Suddenly, Spencer's blood went cold and the whole horrible scheme clicked into place. How easy it had been to find his conspiracy theory blog. How willing Chase had been to feed her all those details about Ali, secrets no one could just happen upon. Those pictures he'd shown her were obviously from a private collection, too, not randomly mailed to him. And Chase was brilliant at hacking into computer systems, which meant he could have easily planted information on Naomi Zeigler's laptop on the cruise, Billy Ford's laptop, and the CVS system. If that address was even *in* the CVS system. Spencer had just taken his word for it.

He'd been the one who'd taken her to the booby-trapped apartment. And then he'd fallen against that door, knocking on it. He'd made it out to be an accident, but what if it hadn't been? Had he known that trapdoor was going to fall? Did he somehow trigger it to open with that knock? Or was it a signal to someone inside?

Could Chase be Ali's secret boyfriend? The other A? All this time, the girls had thought it was Noel . . . and she'd fallen right into Real Ali's trap.

Spencer's hand inched toward the door handle. Suddenly, Chase clamped down on her other wrist and pulled her toward him. His eyes blazed. His happy smile was gone. "There's something I need to tell you," he said sternly.

"I . . ." Spencer trembled. She pointed at something out the window. "What's that?"

Chase released her wrist and looked. Spencer twisted to the handle and wrenched the door open. By the time Chase realized the trick, she was on the pavement. A cold breeze zipped up her skirt. Her heel turned on the sidewalk, but she kept going.

"Spencer!" Chase called. "What are you doing?"

He tried to scramble out of the car, too. Spencer yelped and kicked the door with her heel, slamming it in his face. The light turned green. Cars behind the limo honked.

"Go!" Spencer screamed at the driver, who looked freaked out. Amazingly, the limo *did* go. Spencer turned and ran.

She zigzagged past a couple walking hand in hand and into an alleyway. This was in a part of the city she didn't know well at all. No cabs passed. People sat on their stoops, glaring. Kids disappeared around a corner, their charged laughter spiraling through the alleyway.

She grabbed for the burner phone, the only one she'd brought tonight. Maybe she could call a cab. The screen was already blinking. When she saw the jumbled letters and numbers in the sender line, her heart dropped to her feet.

You can run, but you can't hide, Spence! Kisses, A

Her phone beeped again. It was the same text. And then the same text again, and then again, jamming her phone until an alert warned that her phone had run out of memory. Spencer switched to the call function, but a new message appeared: OUT OF BATTERY. POWERING OFF.

The screen went dark. The sky seemed to darken around her, too, the shadows deepening. Spencer was cut off. A had won again.

25

WAKE-UP CALL

Hanna sat at the front window of her father's house, trying not to seem too eager and pathetic as she glanced at her phone one more time. Then she dropped it back into her little jeweled bag, crossed her ankles, and admired her brand-new Dior heels. They were five inches high; she'd had to practice walking in them all week. She'd also had to practice walking in her floor-length Marchesa gown so that she didn't trip over the hem. She'd fixed her prom crown so that the sides didn't pinch her head, and the scepter leaned against the couch, its faux jewels sparkling. Everything looked perfect. She was, literally, all dressed up with no place to go.

"Still nothing from Mike?" her father asked.

Hanna shook her head. Mike hadn't called her all day. They hadn't spoken since the weird pseudo-makeup I-don't-really-feel-better-about-anything conversation while she was at the burn clinic, right before Hanna saw Noel.

He hadn't written to say he'd picked up a tux. He hadn't texted to mention if he was bringing a limo. For all she knew, he wasn't going to show at all.

Her father turned a page of the *National Geographic* he was pretending to read. There was a clang in the kitchen; surely the pot roast Isabel had made for dinner was getting cold. They'd already seen Kate off with Sean, taking a zillion pictures. If *that* didn't prove to Mike that Hanna wasn't into Sean, what would? Why didn't he just believe her?

And what was with Noel telling on Hanna? That seemed like an A thing to do. . . .

Her old phone beeped, and she pounced on it. It was an e-mail from Agent Jasmine Fuji. *Can I stop by tonight?*

Hanna paled. The woman was relentless. *Sorry, it's prom night!* she replied, glad to have a legitimate excuse.

"Honey, are you okay?" Mr. Marin asked, noticing Hanna's stricken expression.

Hanna quickly exited the e-mail program. She tried to nod, but she felt tears filling her eyes. "Not really."

Mr. Marin walked over to her. "You know, I bet a lot of beautiful prom queens went stag. Think of all the starlets who go alone to the Oscars—it's really no different. It's alluring, actually. It means you can stand on your own." He picked up the cordless phone from the coffee table. "We'll call my driver. I'll have him stop at the florist's on the way there and order you the biggest corsage money can buy."

That just made Hanna cry harder. "Thank you." She snuggled into his large, solid body, inhaling the smell of his spicy deodorant and piney cologne. All of a sudden, it felt like the *old* Hanna and Dad, the relationship in which she could tell him anything. Before Isabel. Before Kate. Before *A*.

She took a deep breath and pulled away. "It's not really about prom, though. It's about . . . other stuff." She shut her eyes. "Things are kind of . . . a mess."

"What do you mean?"

Hanna licked her lips. If only she could tell him. If only he would accept everything she said as horrible mistakes that she totally regretted and that she'd never make again. If only he could track down A and just make this all stop.

But she couldn't say anything. If she told him anything, not only would his political career be ruined . . . his next job would be bending metal in a prison yard.

"Is this about prom queen?" Mr. Marin asked gently.

Hanna cocked her head. "Why would you ask that?"

Mr. Marin shifted his weight, looking guilty. "Don't be mad. But I heard you talking to Mike the other day about how you'd rather die than campaign against Chassey Bledsoe." His brow furrowed. "That's not really a nice thing to say, Hanna. Every rival is worthy of a good campaign."

Hanna's mouth fell open. A mix of emotions surged through her—betrayal, guilt, regret, embarrassment, frustration at A.

"It's not what you think," she admitted. "I didn't really mean it." But was that true, either? Part of her *had* laughed at Chassey as a competitor. Suddenly, Chassey's teary-eyed face when she'd lost flashed in her mind.

Mr. Marin put his hand over hers. "You know what I do think? That you're a good person. That you do the right thing—when you win *and* lose."

Then his gaze lighted on something out the window. Mike's car had pulled up to the curb. He stepped out of the driver's seat, dressed in a tux. He held a huge bouquet of roses in his hand.

Hanna shot to the mirror in the hallway and checked her makeup. She smoothed her dress and adjusted her crown. When the doorbell rang, she whipped it open. "Where have you been?"

Mike shrugged. "Sorry, I was running a little late. There was a crazy line at the florist's."

Hanna placed her hands on her hips. "Haven't you heard of calling? I've sent you a million texts today! I wasn't even sure you were coming!"

Mike looked her up and down and smirked. "You must have been *pretty* sure." He sighed. "I told you I was coming, Hanna. And you always jump all over me when I call while driving." Then he eyed Mr. Marin, who had drifted into the kitchen. "I shouldn't have been so mad about the burn clinic, either. I talked about it a little bit to Aria, and she made me feel like an idiot for even considering you might be with Sean. I should have just believed you."

Hanna eyed the roses. They were purplish-black, her favorite. Mike had a worried, pleading, please-love-me hangdog expression on his face, too. Maybe he *did* feel bad. Then she glanced at her father lurking in the kitchen. She *did* sort of want to take pictures.

"Fine," she said, primly kissing his cheek. "You're forgiven." And then she turned to grab her dad so he could take all those awkward pictures she'd always wanted.

After a traffic-heavy drive to the Four Seasons, Hanna walked into the large, ornate ballroom. The air smelled overpoweringly of grilled scallops. Girls in long silk gowns giggled in twos and threes. Boys in well-fitting tuxes looked almost like adults. A few couples were already slow-dancing, and there was a line for prom pictures in the corner. Every wall was awash with color, the Van Gogh masterpieces come alive. *Irises* took up the wall behind the dance floor. A huge *Starry Night* mural covered the space behind the tables, whose linens and plates were replicas of other works. The prom committee had bought huge stars and moons made out of papier-mâché and arranged them around the room in art installations.

"Whoa." Mike nodded appreciatively. "Trippy."

"Aria did a really good job in such a short amount of time," Hanna murmured, searching for her in the crowd. She didn't see her anywhere.

"Hey, Hanna, congratulations!" Jillian Woods said as she swirled past.

"Hey there, prom queen!" a group of boys called from a table. Hanna gave them a beauty-queen wave.

More and more people flocked to her. Heather Jonas, who'd had a thing for Hawaii since spending last summer there, placed a lei around Hanna's neck. Becky Yee and Olivia Kurtz, who were nerdy but sweet, asked to have their picture taken with her. Even Hanna's old friend Scott Chin, who was there with a tall guy who looked like a male model, gave her a huge bear hug. "You're a way hotter queen than that freak-show Chassey Bledsoe," he whispered.

Normally, Hanna would have laughed, but she pulled away, feeling prickly. After her conversation with her dad, she felt kind of guilty about how she'd treated Chassey.

Something off to the left caught her eye. There was an upright plywood replica of Van Gogh's self-portrait, a cutout where his face was. Phi Templeton's face poked through the hole. She crossed her eyes and shouted, "Ow! My ear's cut off!" Chassey Bledsoe, dressed in a shimmery gold raw-silk gown, snapped her photo and laughed.

Hanna ran her tongue over her teeth. Chassey looked awesome tonight. And she *had* worked harder than Hanna had for this.

Rolling back her shoulders, she broke away from Mike and walked over to Chassey and tapped her arm. The girl turned. Her smile dimmed a little as she saw the crown on Hanna's head.

Hanna undid the bobby pins in her hair, removed the

crown, and handed it to Chassey. "Here," she said. "This is for you."

Chassey stared at the crown in her hands, clearly not understanding. Hanna rolled her eyes. "Put it *on*, idiot," she said. She thrust the scepter at her, too.

Chassey blinked hard. "W-what?"

"Just do it before I change my mind," Hanna growled. And then she turned away, leaving the crown behind. But as she walked back toward Mike, a smile spread across her face like liquid. She caught a glimpse of her reflection in the mirror. She looked a million times better. That silver crown had really clashed with her skin.

"Ms. Marin?"

Hanna turned. A woman in a Four Seasons uniform stood behind her. "Are you Hanna Marin?" she asked. Hanna nodded, and the woman took her arm. "There's a call for you at the front desk. She says it's urgent."

Mike gave Hanna a curious look, then followed her out into the lobby. Hanna took the phone, her heart pounding with the possibilities. But when she said hello, a surprising voice spoke back to her. "Hanna?" a muffled girl's alto asked. "It's Kelly. From the William Atlantic."

"Kelly?" Hanna blinked hard. "What is it?"

"It's that guy you're friends with," Kelly said. "Graham. He's waking up. I called your house and your dad said you were at the prom, but you told me to call you whenever, wherever, so—"

"Thank you," Hanna cut her off, gripping the phone

hard. She gazed at the cabs just outside the lobby, her mind spinning in a million directions. "I'll be there in fifteen minutes."

Then she hung up, trying to figure out the best route for a cab driver to take. Mike cleared his throat behind her. "You're going to be *where* in fifteen minutes?"

Hanna froze. Mike looked crushed . . . and confused . . . and worried. Then she glanced into the crowd. Suddenly, Aria swam into view, Noel at her side. She pictured Graham rolling around in his bed. Muttering things. *Remembering* things. They could solve everything in a matter of minutes.

She turned back to Mike. "Graham woke up. I need to talk to him."

Mike stepped closer to her. "Fine, let's go."

"*Let's?*" Hanna shook her head. "No way."

"You're not winning this one." Mike placed his hands on his hips. "I'm not letting you talk to that psycho alone."

Hanna searched his face. There was no way he was taking no for an answer. What did it matter, really? Everything would be out in the open soon. Maybe she *did* need the protection.

"If you insist," she mumbled. "But let's go!" And then she grabbed his arm and ran into the night.

26

WHO DO YOU LOVE?

"Aria!" Ryan, dressed in a fringed flapper gown and with her hair piled atop her head, ran up to Aria and gave her a huge hug. "This room looks incredible!"

Aria paused from taking photos, a part of her decor chairwoman duty, and peered around the Four Seasons ballroom as though she'd never seen it before—even though she'd been here since three PM setting up. "Thanks," she told Ryan. "But really, it was the other girls who did this. I just gave direction."

Ryan waved her hand dismissively. "It was your vision." She gazed at Aria's outfit, from her ringlets to her simple-but-elegant vintage black dress to the high velvet shoes she'd bought in France years ago for this occasion. "You look awesome, too." She turned to someone next to her. "*Doesn't* she?"

Aria flinched. Noel had appeared by her side sound-lessly. He looked dapper in his tux, his prom king crown askew on his head. "Amazing as always," he said, like a good boyfriend.

Was he a good boyfriend? Noel had said she looked beautiful at least twenty times tonight already. And he had gotten her the decor position, something she'd wanted. He even stood by her when she acted like a freak, like she was doing right now.

Or was it all a sham? Aria's mind hadn't stopped spinning in the same maddening loop of thoughts. It was possible that Noel knew Tabitha. In his e-mail with Fuji, he'd called her a friend—or had he meant Ali? If he *had* meant Tabitha, was that how he'd gotten her necklace? Was that why he'd told Aria to stay away from Graham on the boat? Maybe Graham had known that Tabitha and Noel were friends, too. Maybe Noel worried he might say something. He hadn't, of course—but he *was* going to tell Aria who was watching her.

And if Noel *did* know Tabitha, it meant he would have known her stepmother, Gayle, as well. He could have had inside information on Emily's secret baby. He could have lurked around Gayle's old mailbox, waiting for Hanna to return that cash, without seeming too suspicious—maybe he'd told Gayle he'd come over to pick up something Tabitha had borrowed before she disappeared. He might have kept in touch with Gayle after she and her husband moved to Rosewood—he would have known where to find her. And when Gayle saw Noel on the driveway the night Aria, Emily, and the others had gone to her house in fear that Gayle had kidnapped Emily's baby, he'd killed her before she could yell out his name and expose him.

It *could* make sense. Even Jamaica fit. Aria hadn't been with Noel every second of that trip—he could have snuck off and coached Tabitha about what she needed to do to freak out Aria and the others. *Get them all riled up*, he might have said. *Get them on the roof, and push Hanna over.*

Only it hadn't gone that way—they'd pushed Tabitha instead. But did Noel have it in him to kill Tabitha? Was it the same reason why he'd killed Gayle—because he worried she might tell on him? And was he really doing this all for Ali? Did he really love her *that much*?

Aria shut her eyes. No. Noel didn't love Ali. Noel was a good person, innocent. The pieces fit because she *wanted* them to fit, because A was forcing them that way, because even her friends had twisted and knotted and spun things into something that wasn't true. She *had* to believe that. She *had* to give Noel one last chance to explain all of this.

Ryan checked her Chanel watch, then slung her arm around their shoulders. "Stay close, you two. It's almost time for the photo session of the king and queen in the cemetery."

Aria looked around. "Where's Hanna?" She'd hardly seen any of her friends all night.

Noel peered around. "I just saw Hanna and Mike leave a few minutes ago. But I'm sure they didn't go far."

"I'll find them," Ryan said, heading off into the crowd. When she flitted away, Noel turned to Aria. "What do you say we get a drink in the bar across the lobby while we wait? No one will tell on a prom king." He winked.

Aria licked her lips. *Your boyfriend wants to get a drink with you*, she told herself. *He wants time alone with you. Because he* loves *you.*

Suddenly, a figure appeared in her peripheral vision. A woman in a gray suit slunk into the room, speaking quietly into a cell phone. *Agent Fuji.* What was *she* doing here?

She looked at Noel, more determined than ever. "Let's go."

They crossed the lobby and entered a dark bar. A bartender wiping down the surface with a cloth looked up. "What can I get you?"

Noel asked for a whiskey, and Aria ordered a gimlet. Then he turned his sweet, caring green eyes on her. "Are you *really* okay?"

Aria swallowed hard. Thankfully, the bartender chose that exact moment to deliver their drinks. At least she had something to do with her hands.

"If you think I'm freaked about the Olaf thing, I've put it behind me. I even get it, Aria. I really do."

"I still feel terrible about it," Aria said into her chest. "I don't know what I was thinking."

"It's okay," Noel said emphatically, touching her wrist. "It doesn't change what I told you, though. About Ali, I mean."

Aria flinched at the sound of her name. "Really?"

"She kissed *me*." He gave her wrist an emphatic squeeze. "I wanted nothing to do with her. I hope you understand that—for *real*." He scooted the chair closer. "You mean so much to me, Aria. I can't even explain how in love with you I am. And if something happened to us—if we broke up again—I would be devastated." His chin started to wobble. "I might even die. No one else has ever made me feel that way. You *have* to believe me."

Tears pricked Aria's eyes. Noel's voice was thick with tears. He was telling the truth. She was sure of it.

Noel started digging through his pocket. "And actually, I have something I want to give to you." Something shiny caught the light, and before Aria knew it he was fastening a gold chain-link bracelet around her wrist. A tiny TIFFANY & CO. label was embossed on the link closest to the clasp. "I felt so bad about that other necklace I found for you on the cruise going missing, so I wanted to give you something special at prom." Noel touched one of the links. "You asked me why I was late to class the day they announced you were decor chairwoman—I was picking this up. I had my dad's art dealer find this for me in New York, and he was only in Philly for a few hours. It's vintage," he explained.

"Oh my God," Aria said, holding it up to the light. "You shouldn't have gotten this for me."

"Of course I should have." Noel snaked his arms around her and pulled her close. "You're everything to me, Aria."

Aria rested her head on his shoulder. It was all she wanted to hear. Noel hadn't snuck into her bedroom that day to plant the painting in her closet; he'd been with a jewelry dealer buying her an amazing gift. Suddenly, she knew that everything else she'd discovered could be explained, too—it was just a matter of sorting it out. Even what Noel had told Agent Fuji. Even that he'd known Tabitha. It was a misunderstanding that A had twisted into something terrible. Noel wasn't out to get her.

She shot forward and kissed Noel hard on the lips. He kissed like he always did, softly and sweetly and with abandon, as though Aria was the only girl he'd ever kissed in his life. She shut her eyes and let herself sink into the moment, never loving Noel so much as right then.

She pulled back and sniffed hard. "Hey . . ." Noel wiped a tear off her cheek. "Why are you crying?"

Aria fumbled for a napkin to wipe her eyes. "I'm really happy." She lifted her wrist. "And this is so beautiful." And just like that, a weight was lifted off her shoulders.

"You're welcome." Noel squeezed her waist and lowered his voice. "What do you say we get some *real* alone time now? No bars, no people, no crying—just you and me, *happy*?"

Aria smiled slowly. "That sounds wonderful," she said in almost a whisper.

But she knew it would be difficult, too. She would tell Noel everything tonight, she decided. About A. About Real Ali. About the painting. Even about Tabitha. No more sneaking around. She needed him as an ally, not someone she feared. All of this would be out in the open, and they'd fight A together.

The volume in the bar rose. More people filled the seats next to them. It was far too noisy in here—and too public in the ballroom. Aria drained her glass and stood, suddenly hitting on the very place where they could talk about everything without anyone hearing. "Come on," she said, offering her hand to pull Noel off the stool. "Let's go to the graveyard."

27

THE MOST IMPORTANT SYLLABLE

Mike pulled the Montgomerys' old Subaru into the parking lot at the Bill Beach. Hanna had told him to drive fast, and they'd gotten here from Philly in nine minutes and forty-three seconds, which was probably some kind of record. Hanna was pretty sure he'd done a hundred miles per hour up the expressway.

Mike circled the lot once, then again. Every space was full. "Something will open up," Hanna said, gripping the door handle. "Let me off at the front door and meet me inside."

Mike twisted his mouth like he didn't like that idea much, but Hanna was already out the door before he could protest.

As she crossed the parking lot, her phone beeped a few times, but she ignored it. She couldn't waste any time right now. She had to get to Graham.

The receptionists beamed at her gown, heels, and

makeup, but Hanna swished past them without a word. After scribbling her name at the front desk, she took a sharp left and took off down Graham's hallway. TVs flickered in the overstuffed rooms. Visitors sat placidly on couches. But at the end of the hall, where Graham was, nurses flooded his space.

Kyla was sitting up in bed just outside Graham's partitioned-off space. She waved when she saw Hanna. "What's going on?"

Hanna shrugged, then ducked inside Graham's area. She gasped. Graham's breathing tube was gone. He writhed back and forth, his eyelids fluttering. His dry lips mouthed a word. "Graham?" a nurse shouted into his face.

"Graham?" Hanna leaned over the bed, too. "Are you awake?"

A nurse glared at her. "Who are you?"

Hanna blinked.

"It's okay," Kelly said behind them, trundling into the curtained-off space with a tray of needles and medication. "Hanna's a volunteer." She looked at the other nurses. "I can handle this for a minute. You guys check on his parents. They said they were on their way."

The nurses disappeared. Kelly touched Graham's forehead, then looked at his monitors. "He woke up about a half hour ago," she told Hanna. "We lowered his dose of pain meds to see if he'd talk, but he still seems out of it."

"Kelly?" someone shouted behind the curtain. "Mrs.

Johnson in one-seventeen is having a seizure. We need you on it."

Kelly's eyes darted back and forth. "What a night," she muttered. She placed a hand on Hanna's shoulder. "Watch him for a sec, okay?"

Hanna blinked. "And do what?"

"Just don't touch him. I'll be right back." Then Kelly vanished down the hall. Hanna turned back to Graham, who was still writhing. His fingers curled and uncurled. He pawed at the IV tubes in his hands and made unidentifiable grunting sounds.

"Graham?" she said softly. "Can you hear me?"

Graham's eyelids fluttered. A scratchy whisper of a word came out. "Y-y-y . . . ," he struggled to say.

Hanna's heart thudded fast, then she picked up one of his hands. "Squeeze one for yes, two for no, okay? You were in an explosion on a cruise. Do you remember that?"

Graham squeezed once.

A bell pinged in the hallway. Hanna froze, watching white nurse shoes pass under the curtain. "It was in the boiler room of the ship," she goaded. "You were talking to Aria. Do you remember Aria?"

Again, Graham squeezed once.

"Good. You were trying to tell her something. Was it that someone was watching her?"

Graham's lips pressed together. He closed his eyes tight and winced in pain. "Y-y-y . . ."

Hanna's heart pounded. "Did you see her face?"

Graham struggled with a syllable, his lips gummy. "N . . ."

"No? You didn't?"

He shook his head, as if this wasn't right. Suddenly, Hanna hit on something. "Was it a *him*, not a her?"

Graham squeezed her hand once.

Hanna felt light-headed. She took a deep breath and continued. "Do you know his name?"

Graham opened one eye all the way. His iris was bloodshot. His teeth pressed together, his tongue wedged between them. He tried for a syllable, and then collapsed, exhausted, on the pillow.

"*Please*," Hanna pressed. "Please, tell me his name."

Graham tried again. "N-n . . ." He scrunched his eyes shut, looking frustrated. "N-n-n!"

Hanna leaned closer. "N . . . *what*? Noel?"

A woozy look crossed Graham's face. He made the *N* sound again. His jaw started to tremble. "N-n-n," he kept saying. "N-n-n!"

"Squeeze if it's Noel, Graham! Squeeze once if it's Noel!" Hannah urged.

But suddenly, his neck arched back unnaturally. His eyes rolled to the back of his head. His limbs started to tremble, his feet kicking wildly. The machines started to wail.

Hanna backed up, terrified. Had *she* done this? Had she pushed too hard?

The beeping continued. Graham's body shook with spasms. "Oh my God," Hanna whispered. She stepped out from behind the curtain and looked down the hall. It was empty, not a nurse to be seen. "*Shit*," she mumbled under her breath. Now Graham's machines were making horrible buzzing sounds.

"I just saw someone go that way," Kyla's voice called behind Hanna. She shakily pointed to the left. Hanna nodded at her, then dashed down the hall. But that nurse's station was empty, too. After checking three more corridors, she finally spotted a woman in pink scrubs tending to a patient near an exit door. "Help!" she shouted. "A patient's machines are freaking out!"

The nurse came running. Hanna led the way, her high heels clacking awkwardly on the slippery floor. She rounded the corner to Graham's room. The sounds of the machines carried all the way down the hall.

The nurse pushed past her and yanked open the partition. Her mouth hung open. "Oh my God," she whispered. "He's coding." She spun around and yelled for more help.

Hanna poked her head inside, expecting Graham's spasms to be even bigger and scarier than when she'd left. But his body lay limp on the bed. His head was twisted strangely to the right, his tongue lolling out of his mouth. The bandage over his eye had fallen, revealing blistered, pink skin. All of the IV tubes were out of his hands, and blood spurted everywhere. And on the machines was a single flat line. There were question marks where the blood pressure and pulse levels should have been.

More nurses appeared. Instantly, they began CPR and stopped the bleeding. A second team appeared with a crash cart, and a doctor ripped Graham's gown off to expose his bare, blistered chest. Voltage snapped through the paddles, and when they shocked him, his body arched off the bed. Hanna screamed. Graham slumped back onto the mattress, but the monitors remained unchanged.

The doctors and nurses shocked him three times. Someone gently pushed Hanna out of his curtained-off area. She stood uselessly in the hallway. There was a sound behind her, and Kyla was sitting up in bed, her eyes black under the gauze. She looked as shocked as Hanna felt.

The defibrillator stopped. Someone called out a time, and several nurses pushed back the curtain and walked down the hall. Hanna covered her mouth with her hand, fearful she might throw up. She looked at Kelly, who had just emerged from the curtain, too. Her scrubs were spattered with Graham's blood.

"Is he . . . ?" Hanna couldn't even say the word out loud.

Kelly lowered her eyes. It was clear she couldn't say the word out loud, either—but she didn't have to. Her drawn, pale, astonished expression, however, said it all. Graham, who had just been communicating with Hanna, who had seen A, who could have known *everything*, was dead.

SEEK, AND YE SHALL FIND

At the same time, Emily, dressed in a blue strapless dress she'd bought at the King James, swung her arms and twisted her waist in the middle of the Four Seasons dance floor. Swirl-painted silk banners surrounded her. Asterisk-shaped stars loomed above. Even the dance music seemed energized and psychedelic. It was like being in the belly of a Van Gogh painting.

Iris, who was wearing Emily's pale pink gown from last year's Foxy benefit, scampered over from the buffet. "*Look!*" She held up a silver crown. PROM QUEEN, it read across the front in sparkly letters.

Emily frowned. "Did you get this from Hanna?" She'd only seen Hanna for a second, and then she'd lost her. But she was probably having alone time with Mike.

"It was from that girl over there." Iris pointed to Chassey Bledsoe.

Emily blinked hard. "Maybe you should give that back to her. Or find Hanna."

Iris rolled her eyes. "Please. Everyone deserves a chance to be queen. Didn't we all dream of this when we were little?" Then she positioned the crown on her head and skipped onto the dance floor again. She even grabbed the royal scepter and waved it in front of her face like an oversized glow stick. A couple of kids stopped and grinned at her. Iris did a twirling dance around Dominique Helprin and Max McGarry, one of those couples who would probably never break up. Then, when the song ended, she removed the crown from her head and placed it on Emily's head.

"Now *you're* queen for a song!" she proclaimed.

The crown's teeth dug into Emily's scalp. Iris handed her the scepter. "Come on, girl! Work it!"

At first, Emily refused, but then the beat infected her body. She moved one foot, then the other. She wiggled her fingers. After a moment, she waved the specter around like it was a baton at a parade. Dancers followed behind her around the floor. Halfway through the song, Emily broke into a line dance the whole school had learned in seventh grade—and everyone *still* remembered.

"Go, Emily! Go, Emily!" Iris chanted.

Emily grinned. She'd never dreamed of being prom queen, but it was fun for a song.

When a new song came on, Emily removed the crown from her head and passed it to Kirsten Cullen. A cheer went up, and a couple of boys on the soccer team tossed Kirsten into the air, crown, scepter, and all.

Emily grinned at Iris. "That was a good idea to share the crown with everyone."

Iris shrugged. "Just trying to make prom fun."

"I'm glad you came," Emily said, really meaning it.

"Me, too, you crazy bitch." Iris threw her head back to laugh, but suddenly she pulled her bottom lip into her mouth and gazed out the window. "My last hurrah in Rosewood, right?"

Emily touched her arm. "Are you okay about going back?" Iris had scheduled for a cab to pick her up at the Four Seasons and transport her back to The Preserve. She wanted to show up looking fabulous in a prom dress, she said, to prove to the other patients that she'd had a blast on the outside. This time, she was going to work hard to actually get better . . . so they'd release her for real.

Iris made a brave face. "Who knows? But I guess I have to try." She peeked at Emily. "You'll really visit me?"

"Of course," Emily said, then nudged her. "I'll even take you shopping, as long as you promise not to steal anything."

"Deal." Then Iris glanced at the clock over the grand, scalloped doors that led to the lobby. "Hey, it's almost ten."

"Oh, is it?" Emily said nonchalantly, as if she hadn't been obsessively watching the clock all night.

Iris frowned. "How are you going to know what your surprise from Jordan will be? It could be anything . . . anywhere."

"I'll just know," Emily said as they walked off the dance floor. Only . . . *would* she? Jordan could have hidden a secret message in one of the four Van Gogh–decorated cakes around the room. She could have stitched it into a hand towel in the bathrooms. She could have subliminally recorded something on one of the DJ's tracks. It was like looking for a needle in one of Van Gogh's *Haystacks*.

She looked around the room for the fifty-millionth time. Jordan would know what a daunting task it was and try to make the surprise something Emily would gravitate toward anyway, right? Then again, everything in the room was interesting and worthy of another look. The bouquets of flowers on the tables. The animal ice sculptures. The teenager-height, papier-mâché stars. The henna tattoo artist in the corner, the fortune-teller by the stairs.

"It's conga line time, everyone!" the DJ called out, breaking Emily from her thoughts. A large easel was wheeled to the front of his booth. "Where are our prom king and queen?"

"I is prom queen!" called Klaudia Huusko, the exchange student, her words slurred. She staggered toward the stage, the prom queen crown askew atop her golden locks. When she was almost at the DJ booth, she tripped over the hem of her dress and the crown went flying. Everyone giggled. Klaudia's dress slipped down her body, showing off a push-up bra and—horrors—a *girdle*. Everyone guffawed.

Emily's gaze returned to the fortune teller. Their second day at sea, Emily had used the ship's slow Internet to log onto an astrology site to get her daily horoscope. When she told Jordan that she did it every day to see if things were going to be good or bad, Jordan had looked at her like she was crazy. "What if the horoscope tells you not to leave the house?"

"Then I don't," Emily joked. She gave Jordan a playful shove. "But they never say that. Even if you're going to have a bad day, they say it'll be *challenging*. Or *a learning experience*."

"And you really buy all that stuff?" Jordan asked.

"I do," Emily had said.

Jordan had touched the tip of her nose. "I love finding out things about you."

Now, Emily checked the clock on her cell phone: 9:53. As most of the kids on the dance floor were forming a long conga line, she drifted toward the fortune-teller's table. The woman had long, scraggly, gray-streaked brown hair, a mole on her nose, and oblong-shaped glasses with purple lenses. She eyed Emily calmly and steadily, like she was drinking Emily in slowly, all the way to the last sip.

Finally, she smiled, grabbed Emily's hand, and kneaded her palm. "You have smooth fingers, which means you're artistic," she started out. "Your thumb is strong, which means you're logical. And you're in good shape and able to overcome obstacles, aren't you?"

Duh, Emily thought. *That* was an understatement.

The woman went on to say that Emily would have a love affair but never marry and that she'd live a long, happy life. Emily kept waiting for some sort of reference to Jordan, but the woman didn't mention her. After about five minutes of kneading, she patted Emily's hand. "There you go. Go forth and be happy."

Emily cocked her head. "So . . . you don't have anything else to tell me?"

The woman frowned. "No, that's all." She pulled out a rubber stamp from under the table, pressed it on an ink pad, and stamped Emily's hand. "It marks that you've been here already. I don't do repeats."

Emily stood, unable to hide the disappointment on her face. This challenge suddenly felt like the I Spy books she used to look at in the school library. She would drive herself crazy trying to find the hidden snowman or tiny lamb charm or pink apostrophe in the cluttered photos, feeling unobservant and unintelligent when she failed. Or maybe Jordan just didn't know her that well. Maybe Emily didn't know *Jordan* that well.

She trudged over to Iris, who was marching in the conga line. Iris let Emily cut in, then looked at her strangely. "What's on your hand?"

Emily peered at the stamp the fortune-teller had given her. "No repeats," she mumbled. But when the strobe light flashed on it, she noticed the stamp was a large black circle with the initials JR in the center. She stopped short. Could that stand for *Jordan Richards*?

She broke out of the conga line, held her hand directly under a recessed light by the buffet, and squinted hard. The mark looked like a stamp on an envelope. Around the initials was the word *Bonaire*. Could that be some kind of clue as to where Jordan was? Was Bonaire a post office? A town?

Emily darted out of the ballroom and into the hall, where the light was much brighter, and fished out her old cell phone. The clock at the top said ten PM exactly. Luckily, the WiFi signal in the hotel was strong, so when she typed BONAIRE into the browser, quite a few results immediately popped up. Bonaire was a little island in the Caribbean. Emily clicked on a Chamber of Commerce page. According to the site, Bonaire was a popular spot for snorkeling. The site showed a slideshow of images: tropical fish, people playing in a turquoise ocean. Then, a photo of an old-timey movie theater flashed on the screen. On the marquee, instead of the coming attractions, were the words I MISS YOU, EMILY.

Emily's heart almost stopped. She stared, unblinking, at the website, worried she was seeing things. But then the image appeared on the slideshow again. I MISS YOU, EMILY. She gasped. "I miss you, too, Jordan," she whispered.

She watched it scroll through six more times. Then, at 10:01, it disappeared. Emily felt dizzy. It was the most romantic thing anyone had ever done for her. If only she could book a flight to the Caribbean tonight and find Jordan. But she was sure Jordan was much too smart for that. Even if she had been in Bonaire, she was most likely long gone by now.

"*There* you are, Miss Fields!"

A cold, slender hand landed on her bare shoulder. Emily jumped and looked up. Agent Fuji's smile was unfriendly. Her conservative gray suit looked out of place among all the tulle and silk. "Have you been avoiding me?"

Emily's mouth immediately felt dry. "Um . . ."

"I wanted to give you a chance to explain something," Fuji cut in. "Maybe we could talk right now."

Emily's mouth fell open. Explain . . . *what*?

Without waiting for Emily's consent, Fuji guided Emily to the end of the hall, where it was quieter. "I received an anonymous tip that you are harboring priceless art in your house," she said sternly. She leaned closer. "Do I need to get a search warrant, Miss Fields?"

Harboring priceless art? "There's no art at *my* house!" Emily blurted out.

Fuji raised an eyebrow. "Is it in someone *else's* house you know? I was told *one* of you girls had something we should know about. If it's not you, who is it?"

The music pounded in Emily's ears. She'd spoken before thinking. A had told . . . but A hadn't told everything. It was a brilliant scheme: She was relying on Emily to spill the rest.

She looked at Fuji again. "I-I don't know what you're talking about."

"Oh really?" Fuji placed her hands on her hips. "Are you sure about that?"

Emily shook her head faintly, trying her hardest to stand her ground. After a moment, Fuji pulled at the strap of her briefcase and spun on her heel. "You better not be lying," she warned.

She strode away, her phone glued to her ear before she'd even left the building. Emily felt hot, then cold. What had she just done? Where was Fuji going? As soon as the cops found that painting, they were done.

She ran back into the ballroom and looked around for her friends, but she didn't see any of them anywhere. Her burner phone was at the bottom of her clutch; she whipped it out and dialed Aria's number. "Not it!" she screamed after the voicemail beep. She tried Spencer next, then Hanna. Nothing. "Not it, not it!" she yelled at both of them.

"Are you okay?"

Iris was behind her, breathless from the conga line. Emily dropped her phone back into her clutch, feeling scattered. "Um . . ."

"Did you get your surprise? You ran out of here so quickly, and . . ." Iris trailed off abruptly, her eyes widening at something across the room.

"What is it?" Emily followed her gaze. Was Fuji back? Was there a SWAT team here? The only people on the dance floor were kids in gowns and tuxes. The DJ was now heading the conga line, bopping his head back and forth.

Iris started to tremble. "I can't believe it. That's the guy who visited Ali at The Preserve."

Emily frowned at the DJ. He had a scruffy goatee, beady eyes, and a fireplug of a body. "*Really?*"

Iris nodded, her gaze fixed. "I would recognize his picture anywhere."

Suddenly, Emily realized she was looking at a picture on the easel. ROSEWOOD DAY MAY DAY PROM KING AND QUEEN! read swirly lettering at the top. Beneath it was the picture of the king and queen in their crowns. *This* year's king and queen. A king Emily knew very, very well. Her gaze fell to the gold watch on his wrist. It was the same gold watch she'd seen in that photo from Tripp's house. The one that had been taken of Ali at The Preserve.

She stared at Iris, all feeling leaving her extremities. "Noel Kahn? Are you *sure*?"

Iris nodded gravely and with authority. "I'd bet my life on it."

29

BEFORE IT'S TOO LATE

It took Spencer forty-five minutes, several hiding spots to avoid the dicey-looking locals, and a fifteen-block walk in the direction of the city before she found a cab that would take her to the Four Seasons. She'd brought some emergency cash and her credit card—A hadn't found a way to shut *that* down. She'd tried to power on her phone again and again during the ride, but it was useless. A had jammed her in-box.

Something hit her, too: A *knew* of her in-box. Which meant A knew this phone number. Of course A did: A was Chase. He'd probably peeked at her phone when she was hanging out with him. She'd stepped right into his trap, and her friends were going to die because of it.

She glanced out the window as the Art Museum swept past. Couldn't the driver get to the hotel any *faster*? She needed to find Aria, Hanna, and Emily before Chase found them first.

Finally, the Four Seasons appeared on the right. "This is fine!" Spencer shouted on the corner, shoving some money at the driver and launching out of the backseat. She ran haltingly down the block in her narrow-fitting maxi gown. Several cabs and limos were parked at the hotel entrance. A familiar black car screamed past Spencer, lifting the ends of her dress. Was that . . . Fuji?

Spencer peered into the tinted windows but couldn't see the driver or any passengers. Were Hanna, Emily, and Aria already in there? Had Fuji already gotten them?

She barreled into the Four Seasons lobby and then into the ballroom. The first person she spied was Reeve Donahue, one of the girls on the decorations committee. "Have you seen Aria Montgomery?" she asked breathlessly.

Reeve looked Spencer up and down, curling her lip at Spencer's torn hem and mussed hair. "That girl has been AWOL all night. She *so* didn't deserve to be decor chairwoman."

Spencer eked out a thank you, then did another round of the dance-floor perimeter. Naomi Zeigler was dancing with Henry Bennett. Sean Ackard and Kate Randall were whispering at a private table in the corner. Iris had her head on James Freed's shoulder.

Spencer was about to run to Iris and ask her where Emily was when Emily herself appeared in front of her.

"Oh my God," Emily said, grabbing Spencer's forearms. "Where have you *been*? And what happened to you?"

"It's a long story," Spencer said. "But I have something to tell you."

"Ali's boyfriend was most definitely Noel," Emily blurted out at the same time.

Spencer backed up and looked at her. "Wait, what? Are you sure?"

Emily nodded. "Iris made the connection that Noel visited Ali nonstop at The Preserve."

The strobe light flickered across Spencer's arms as she canvassed the ballroom. If Noel was Ali's boyfriend . . . then Chase wasn't. She'd been wrong. She squirmed uncomfortably, not sure if she should feel horribly embarrassed . . . or relieved . . . or still annoyed that Chase knew about Jamaica another way.

"Where is Noel now?" she asked absently. "And Aria? And Hanna?"

"I'm here," Hanna said behind them, rushing into the room as breathlessly as Spencer had a moment before. Her face was drawn, and her hands were shaking. "We came back as fast as we could."

"Back from where?" Emily asked.

"The Bill Beach." Hanna's voice swooped up and down. "Graham woke up."

"And you took Mike?" Spencer was horrified. She peered around the room again. "Where is he now?"

"He's . . . somewhere." Hanna looked around, too, then shrugged. "I didn't tell Mike what was going on. And he stayed in the car—he didn't see anything. But guys,

Graham saw A. That's what he wanted to tell Aria."

"Was it Noel?" Spencer demanded.

Hanna nodded. "Well, all he said was *N*. . . . I'm sure he meant Noel. But then I had to get the nurse, and when I came back, he was gone."

Emily stepped back. "Gone, as in *died*?"

"Jesus," Spencer whispered.

Emily looked at Spencer. "What did you have to tell me?"

Spencer's stomach clenched, her mind on Chase again. "Uh, nothing."

"Guys, we have to go to the cops with all of this," Hanna said, peering around the room. "Noel might have a spy at the Bill Beach. He could know we're on to him. We've got to go to the police *now* and tell them everything we know."

"We need to go to the police for another reason," Emily said. "Fuji knows that one of us has the painting . . . but she doesn't know who. She thought *I* was hiding it—she asked if there was any reason they should search my house."

Spencer slumped against the wall. "Which means she might want to search my house next. Or Hanna's."

"Or *Aria's*," Emily whispered.

"Where *is* Aria?" Spencer asked worriedly.

Everyone scanned the room. Then Hanna strode toward a girl near the buffet. She wore a black tiered flapper gown and a 1920s hat, and she was holding Hanna's prom queen scepter in her hand. A pin that read

ROSEWOOD DAY ALUM was on her breast. She smiled when Hanna approached.

"Hey there, queen!" she trilled, offering the scepter back to Hanna. "I love how you made everyone else queen for a dance!"

Hanna grabbed the scepter, then frowned. "I did?"

"*So* innovative—I love it!" Ryan held up her hand for Hanna to high-five. "It's too bad the decor chairwoman didn't get pictures, though."

Spencer and Emily exchanged a look. *Aria* was the decor chairwoman. "Do you know where she is?" Spencer demanded.

Ryan cocked her head. "Actually, I thought she was with Hanna. Didn't you see her in the graveyard for your picture? She and the king left for there about fifteen minutes ago."

Hanna's eyes widened. "I wasn't *at* the graveyard."

"Oh." Ryan looked confused. "I saw you leave, so that's what I assumed."

Spencer stiffened. "So Aria is at a dark graveyard with Noel . . . *alone*?"

Hanna swallowed hard. "Oh, God."

Ryan's eyes searched them. "What?"

Spencer wheeled around and ran for the lobby. The others followed. All sorts of terrible things swirled in Spencer's mind. Aria was with Ali's coconspirator right now, the very person who'd helped burn and ruin and kill. Ian's lifeless body swam into her mind. That horrific fire in the woods. That twisted laugh they kept hearing high above the trees.

They spilled into the front drive of the hotel and stared out at the busy city street. Spencer turned to Hanna. "Do you know where this cemetery is?"

Hanna nodded shakily. "I-I think so. It's about a ten-minute walk."

"Then let's go," Spencer said, heading for the sidewalk. "I just hope we aren't too late."

30

DIGGING HIS OWN GRAVE

Even though the Rittenhouse cemetery was off a busy section of the Ben Franklin Parkway, there was something about the way the buildings hemmed it in that made it seem like Aria and Noel were in the middle of the countryside. Twisted vines surrounded the small space. Centuries-old gravestones jutted out of the ground like crooked teeth. Mist swirled around a large stone statue of an angel. An old, rusted fence surrounded the whole place. A loud squeak sounded from the hinges when Noel and Aria opened and shut the wrought-iron gate.

Aria gazed at the names on the gravestones, then ran her fingers along a large stone cross. Her bracelet glittered in the dim light. She ran her fingers along the links again, and they tinkled together.

Noel came up behind her and snaked his arms through the crooks in her elbows, lacing them around her front. "So what did you want to talk to me about?"

"Well . . ." Aria touched the top of an angel's wing. A bit of her confidence had flagged since sitting at the bar. Was this place *really* private? It certainly wasn't a panic room. What if A was listening?

But then she turned around and tried to focus. This would bring them together. And they could fight A as one. "You know I love you, right?" she began.

Noel's eyes softened. "I hope you do. You've been acting so strangely."

"Of course I do," Aria breathed. "I've been acting strangely because I've been keeping things from you, though." She spoke into her chest, too afraid to look Noel in the eye. "Big things. For your own good. I didn't want anything bad to happen to you."

Noel nudged Aria's chin back up so she would look at him. "Haven't we gone over this? You can tell me anything. No matter how bad it is. No matter if it puts me in danger." Then he stepped away. "Are *you* in danger?"

"I . . ." At that very moment, her new cell phone beeped. Aria peeked into her clutch at the message that had popped up on the screen. *Get away from Noel!* Spencer wrote in all caps. *He was Ali's secret boyfriend! We have definite proof!*

Another text popped up from Emily: *Noel visited Ali in the hospital. Iris knows it for a fact.*

And then from Hanna: *Graham just told me that Noel was the one who was watching you on the boat!*

Aria clapped her hand over her mouth. *No.* It couldn't be. There had to be an explanation.

"Aria?"

When she looked up, Noel was staring at her. His gaze drifted down to her open clutch, too. Aria snapped it shut, the breath leaving her lungs. Had he seen the texts?

She backed away, running into a grave marker. Noel stood where he was, his hands crossed over his chest, a weird smirk on his face. Or was it just the light? She closed her eyes tightly, trying to recenter herself. As much as she tried to purge the texts from her mind, to twist this into something innocent—a misunderstanding—a siren rang in her head again and again.

She swallowed hard and looked up at Noel, who still hadn't moved. "Do you remember that séance we did together?" she blurted out.

Noel smiled. "What do *you* think? That's where I got you to like me."

Aria winced. She didn't like *that* wording. "Do you remember when I got locked in that bathroom? Someone turned out the lights on me, maybe trying to freak me out?"

Noel nodded. "I guess."

"When the light came back on, I saw Ali's *Missing* flyer. For a while, I thought *she* had done it to me. But later, I figured it was someone else."

Noel searched her face. "Yeah, I don't know," he said finally. "Maybe that place was haunted." He leaned over and smelled a bouquet of flowers someone had left on a grave.

"Why did you come to that séance?" Aria demanded.

Noel righted himself and squinted at her. "I told you—because of my brother."

"But why *that* séance. Did you know I'd signed up? Were you following me?"

Noel shrugged. "So what if I was?"

Aria stared at him. *Because it matters*, she wanted to say. *That was how I fell for you. I need to know if it was for real or not.*

All she saw, in her mind, were those texts from Noel's phone. *Anything you need*. And, *Thanks for helping me*. What if Ali made Noel follow Aria? What if Ali had whispered, *Go in there, Noel, and hit on her. Get on her good side. You have to do what I say. Then I'll love you forever.* Maybe he'd balked when she told him to shut her in the bathroom and turn off the lights . . . but he'd done it anyway.

Noel leaned against a tall headstone. "What does this have to do with what you had to tell me? Is this what you've been keeping from me?"

Aria shut her eyes. "Kind of."

When Noel touched her arms, she tried not to flinch. "Whatever it is, just *tell* me. I love you, Aria. I can take it."

I love you, Aria. Something about the way Noel said it right then ignited a memory in her mind. Aria remembered lying in that little bed in the Icelandic guesthouse the night everything happened. Feeling the throb of guilt for kissing Olaf and stealing that painting. Sensing Noel shift beside her, trying to get comfortable. There had been an ocean of space between them, emotionally as well as physically. She had felt, in that moment, that they might never reconnect.

But then Noel had rolled over and taken her into his arms as though everything was right between them. "I love you, A . . ." he'd murmured into Aria's ear. Aria had thought he'd meant to say *Aria*, but he hadn't. He'd said someone else's name instead.

I love you, Ali.

Aria studied his face in the dim light. She suddenly felt like she was looking at a stranger. *I love you, Ali.* It was as clear in her mind as though it had only been a few moments ago. Maybe he *had* loved Ali. Her heart felt like it was tumbling down a long, dark grave. Noel had betrayed her, really betrayed her. She had trusted him, and, deep down, he hated her guts.

Slowly, she unclasped the bracelet and let it fall to the ground. Noel stared at her, his brow crinkling. "What did you do that for?"

"Do you love Alison DiLaurentis?" Aria whispered haltingly.

Noel froze. "*What?*"

"You visited her in the hospital after she killed Courtney, didn't you? The Preserve."

Noel turned away sharply, placing his palm on the flat part of a headstone. "Why does it matter?"

Tears began to cascade down Aria's cheeks. "What is *that* supposed to mean? Of course it matters! Did you realize she was the one who killed Courtney? How long did you visit her? How long have you *loved* her?"

Noel turned around to face her, his mouth an ugly triangle. "No one else was. I felt bad for her. She didn't seem crazy at the time. And of course I didn't know she'd killed her sister."

Aria was so angry and scared she was actually trembling. She'd never heard anything so insane in her life. And suddenly, it dawned on her: That was what the *Thanks for believing in me* note on the back of the ticket stub meant. Noel believed all along that Real Ali wasn't crazy. He was the only one who thought she'd been locked up unfairly. He'd been the only one on her side.

She raised a shaky finger at him. "You didn't visit her because you felt bad for her. You visited her because you loved her. Just admit it."

Noel blinked at her, his mouth hanging open. But he didn't deny it.

"And you *know*, don't you?" Aria whimpered. "You know she's still alive. And you knew Tabitha Clark long before we went to Jamaica. That's why you didn't want me to hang around with Graham—you were afraid he'd say something to me, connect you to her. Or that you and Ali were secretly together."

Noel made a strange noise at the back of his throat. "Yeah, I knew Tabitha Clark. But it was only in passing years ago. She seemed familiar to me in Jamaica and on the news, but I didn't really know, and—"

"And you're *working* with Ali," Aria cut him off. "All

this time you've been with me, it was only because she told you to be. She made you go to that séance. She had you scare me in the bathroom. She had you get close to me and then betray me so I'd go to the Poconos with her."

"Whoa." Noel stepped toward her, his arms outstretched.

She ducked away. "You're the one we've been after all this time. You're the one who tormented Spencer and Emily and Hanna and now even *me* with the stuff we did last summer. And now you're framing us for killing Tabitha—even though that was something *you* did. You told Agent Fuji on us, too. For Tabitha? The painting? Maybe everything—because you're A!"

"Aria!" Noel darted toward her again.

Aria lurched out of the way. Her gaze swung around the cemetery, but there was only one way out—the closed gate. She shot for it, but her heel twisted in the wet grass. Noel clamped a hand around her ankle and tumbled on top of her. He pressed all his weight on her. She struggled beneath him, kicking and clawing.

"Aria, just stay still!" Noel pleaded. "Just listen to me!"

Aria wrenched around to look him in the eye. A memory suddenly flooded her mind: a time at Noel's house when he'd flopped on top of her, yelling, "Steam roll!" and they'd both laughed until there were tears in their eyes. But he'd loved Ali the whole time.

When he accompanied Aria to all those cooking classes, dutifully making sauces and chopping vegetables, he'd loved Ali, too. When they first had sex, which had been so tender and sweet and important that Aria could barely imagine it now. The whole time, Ali, Ali, Ali.

He'd helped almost kill them.

Noel's body was heavy on top of her, and Aria gasped for a breath. "Where is that bitch?" she bellowed. "Tell me where she is so I can kill her!"

"I don't know what you're talking about," Noel said.

"You do, and you know it!" Aria shrieked, flailing her arms and legs. "Just admit you love her! Just admit you know where she is!"

Noel let up for just a moment, resting on his elbows. His head twisted away, shrouded in darkness. "I loved her."

Aria scrambled out from under him and stared into his eyes. "And is she alive?"

Noel looked pained. "Aria . . ."

"Is she alive?"

A brisk wind made the gate bang. Cars honked on the streets. Far up in the sky, a jet's headlight blinked. Noel turned away. "I don't know," he said quietly in a tone that indicated otherwise.

It was as good as an admission. Fury flooded Aria's veins. She leapt to her feet and headed for the gate, stumbling over the haphazard gravestones, the hem of her dress filthy from the mud. Strong hands wrapped around her waist, and she fell again, then felt the crush of Noel's body on top of her. Noel breathed hotly into her ear.

Aria screamed and tried to get out from under him, but Noel was too heavy. "Stop acting so crazy so I can explain everything," he begged.

"I hate you," Aria wheezed, Noel's weight crushing her lungs. "I will never, ever listen to you again."

"*Damn* it, Aria," Noel said, holding Aria steady beneath him. He sounded feral and dangerous. Aria swiped at him some more, but without oxygen, her limbs started to tingle. A desperate wail escaped from between her lips. She was going to die. The boy she thought loved her was going to be her murderer.

Whack.

Noel screamed in pain and rolled off Aria. Aria staggered to her feet and scurried behind a gravestone, unsure of what had just happened. As she gulped in breaths, several figures swam into view. Spencer stood next to Noel, the prom scepter raised over her head. Emily and Hanna loomed behind her, their eyes wide.

Emily spotted Aria and ran to her, hugging her tight. "Are you okay?"

Aria tried to nod, but her gaze was still on Noel. Spencer raised the scepter to hit him again, but he jumped to his feet and moved away. "Don't you dare run!" she warned.

"What the hell?" Noel's voice cracked. "You people are insane!"

He wove through the gravestones toward the entrance. Spencer tried to chase him, but her dress prevented her from moving too fast. She stopped a few paces past a row of gravestones and blinked in the darkness. Noel was gone.

Then Spencer ran to Aria. "Oh my God. Did he hurt you?"

She was staring in horror at Aria's cheek. It was wet—Aria hadn't even realized. When she pulled her hand away, she saw blood. Tears flooded down her face. "I'm sorry, guys," she blurted. "There were things I knew about Noel, things I didn't tell you. I should have. And now it's too late."

Hanna hugged Aria tight. "Don't say that. It's okay."

"I just didn't want it to be him!" Aria sobbed. "I wanted it to be anyone but him."

"We know." Spencer ran her hands through Aria's hair. "We wanted it to be anyone but him, too."

"But at least you're safe now," Emily whispered. "At least he didn't hurt you for real."

Aria sniffed and nodded, then looked into the dark distance where Noel had disappeared. She wasn't sure if what Emily said was quite true. Noel *had* hurt her for real.

He had broken her heart into a thousand pieces.

31

FORGIVENESS HAS A PRICE

Spencer walked in the woods behind her house. Dusk had fallen, and prickly branches and split logs littered the forest floor. A stream rushed in the distance, and birds called from the trees. All of a sudden, the night grew darker than it had been even a few seconds before. Something howled close by. Then she heard a low, growling sound, then the crunch of footsteps.

A figure emerged from the trees, pushing back the stray branches. It was a blond girl with a heart-shaped face and glittering blue eyes—*Ali*.

Spencer gasped. Ali's face was blistered with burns. She walked with a limp, and her right arm hung lifelessly by her side. She smiled at Spencer nastily. "I thought I might find you here."

"Stay away," Spencer warned, shielding her face and taking a big step backward.

Ali chuckled. "But haven't you been looking for me?

You were close, you know. Closer than I ever thought you'd get." She covered her mouth with her hand. "But you didn't find me!"

"H-how did you know I was looking for you?" Spencer demanded.

Ali rolled her eyes. "I know about everything. *He* tells me everything. He's my lifeline."

"Noel, you mean." Spencer backed up so that her spine was pressed against a tree trunk. "We know everything, too. We know Noel's been working with you."

A proud smile spread across Ali's lips. "Spencer, you're so cute. Such a little Sherlock Holmes."

"Are we right?" Spencer demanded.

"Sorry." Ali shook her head. "If I told you, I'd have to kill you. Actually, that's a good idea anyway."

She lunged for Spencer and covered her like a net. Spencer screamed and sank to the mucky ground. Ali's nails dug into Spencer's flesh. She touched her shoulder with her charred hand. "Open your eyes," she demanded in Spencer's ear. "Open your eyes so you can see what I'm doing to you."

Spencer opened her eyes with a gasp. Suddenly, she wasn't in the woods anymore, but in a sleeping bag on the floor of her den. Emily leaned over her, touching the exact spot on Spencer's shoulder where Ali's hand had been moments before.

"Wake up," Emily urged. "You're having a dream."

Spencer sat up and tried to catch her breath. Emily

rested on her haunches. "Were you dreaming about Ali?" she asked.

"Yeah," Spencer whispered.

"I could tell," Emily said.

Aria and Hanna wriggled out of their sleeping bags. The clock on the cable box read 7:46 AM. Their prom dresses lay in a pile in the corner, shed haphazardly when they'd arrived here late last night after rescuing Aria. Shoes and bags were in a jumble near the door.

Aria lunged for her phone and winced when she saw the screen. "No messages or texts from the Kahns," she croaked. Last night, she'd called Mrs. Kahn to ask her to call her if Noel showed up at home—she said he'd left prom without her, making it sound like a drunken evening instead of a scary almost-murder in the cemetery.

Hanna hugged her knees. "I guess that means he isn't back. I doubt his family is trying to cover for him or anything. They probably don't know a thing."

"We need to tell the cops, guys," Emily urged. "Noel tried to kill Aria last night in the graveyard before running off. They should know he's dangerous."

"And risk Noel retaliating by telling on us?" Spencer said. "Or worse—the truth? Aria's *still* got that painting at her house . . . and Fuji knows about it. And we're still connected to Tabitha. It's too risky."

Aria raked her fingers through her messy, hair-spray-sticky hair. "So you think it was Noel who told Fuji about the painting?"

Emily pulled a quilt around her shoulders. "I think so."

"Why wouldn't he just admit it was me, though? Why would he say it was *one* of us . . . and make Fuji threaten to search *all* our houses?"

"Because he's A," Spencer said. "It's just another way to torture us."

"This whole thing feels like a ticking time bomb," Hanna said in a hushed voice. "After he left the cemetery, I bet Noel went to strategize with Ali about what to do. Maybe the best thing to do is to go to Fuji and come clean about everything before he gets to her first. Or what if he and Ali plan to *hurt* us? That note said *we* were next."

"I say we nail Noel to the wall this minute," Spencer said. "We have enough proof, from what Aria told us and from all our evidence, that he had something to do with all of Ali's diabolical schemes—*and* now that he assaulted Aria, we have something to bring him in on."

Hanna nodded. "The cops can do the rest of the forensic work to link him to the murders. I agree—we need to end this."

There was a pained sound to her left. Aria covered her eyes with her hands. The girls exchanged a sympathetic look.

"Aria," Emily said softly, shuffling over to her.

Hanna slung her arm around Aria's shoulders. "It sucks, doesn't it? It happened to me, too, remember? With Mona?"

"I just don't want it to be true," Aria sobbed. "I keep

thinking he's going to turn up and explain all of this to us in a way that makes sense."

"I didn't want to believe it was Mona, either," Hanna said softly. "But Noel *admitted* he loved Ali. He knew about the switch for so long . . . and he never said a word. You shouldn't feel sorry for him. You should feel angry."

Aria nodded. "I know I should, but . . ." She gazed around at them, her eyes wet and red. "Can we give it a day? If I can't track down Noel by then, we'll tell Fuji everything."

Spencer shut her eyes. "What if Fuji decides to search your house? Then what?"

"I'm willing to take that chance," Aria said shakily.

Spencer leaned back on her palms. Hanna picked at a hangnail on her thumb. Emily gazed nervously out the window.

"How about six hours?" Spencer said. "So by"—she checked her watch—"two PM, if we don't hear from Noel, we're going to have to do something."

Aria's jaw trembled. "That's no time at all!"

"If he's innocent, he'll reach out, don't you think?" Spencer said.

"But . . ." Aria looked back and forth. Then she smoothed the tassels on the end of the afghan. "Okay," she said. "Six hours."

The girls stood and gathered up their belongings. After some coffee and toasted bagels, they headed out the door. Just as Hanna, Aria, and Emily pulled away, a black Jeep

stopped at the curb. Spencer peered out the window, surprised someone was visiting that early. It was a guy she
didn't recognize.

He stepped on the porch and rang the bell. Spencer
waited a beat, then pulled the door open. The guy in front
of her wore jeans and a striped button-down. He was about
Spencer's height and well-built, and he had sharp green
eyes and a sensual, pink full-lipped mouth. There were
ugly white scars across his cheeks. There were more slashes
on his hands. One of his ears was shriveled, barely there.

"Hey, Spencer," he said.

She backed away from him. "W-who are you?"

"I'm Chase," the guy said.

Spencer paused, waiting for the punch line. "No,
you're not," she spat. "I know Chase." She didn't know
what to think of Chase—even if he wasn't A, maybe he
was somehow working with Noel and Ali. How else could
he have known about Jamaica?

She went to shut the door, but the guy caught her arm.
"Actually, you know my brother. His name is Curtis. I
sent him to meet you in my place. I'm the one you've
really been talking to online. I'm the one who set up the
Alison DiLaurentis website."

Spots formed in front of Spencer's eyes. A horn
honked on the next street over, matching the dissonant
sounds in her brain. She grabbed the cordless phone that
sat on the table next to the door. "Leave right now, or I'll
call the police."

The boy raised his hands in surrender. "Look, I'm sorry I lied to you. But we had such an amazing connection online, and I was so jazzed about you, but when I went to the Mütter Museum and saw how pretty you were, I just couldn't go in there looking . . . you know . . . the way I look." He gestured to his face, his ear. "My brother was in the car with me. So I sent him in instead, told him to be me. I told him what to say about the case. But he fell for you. And then when we found out that you were Spencer Hastings . . ." He paused and shook his head. "Then I *really* couldn't show you who I was. I've had a crush on you since I read about you in *People*."

Spencer didn't know whether to laugh or cry. "You're not making any sense."

"I know." Chase looked tormented. "But it's the truth, I swear. Curtis texted me what you said during the meetings, and I told him what to say. We were both into you—Curtis and I actually got into a huge fight the night of prom because I thought we should come clean and he didn't want to."

Spencer's head was whirling so fast it actually hurt. "He mentioned something I never told him—*either* of you."

Chase blinked. "What did he bring up?"

Spencer swallowed hard. "Something about Jamaica," she admitted. It hardly mattered who she told now—Noel was the guilty one, not her.

Chase's brow furrowed, then a light came on in his eyes. "Oh—you were in Jamaica when Tabitha Clark died, is that it?"

Spencer's eyes flashed, but she said nothing.

"I've gotten some requests to put the Tabitha Clark murder on my blog, since it's local," Chase said. "I looked into it a little. I also peeked at your Facebook page—some of your photos are public, including a few from The Cliffs in Jamaica last spring. Curtis was in the room when I was searching, and I might have said that you were there at the same time Tabitha was—it was such a weird and sad coincidence." His big eyes filled with remorse. "But I'm sorry, Spencer. It's a huge invasion of privacy. I should have never Googled you, never stalked your Facebook page. I should have been honest with you from the very start."

The sun came out from behind a cloud, illuminating the scars on Chase's cheek. Spencer shut her eyes and tried to process what Chase was saying. In some ways, it wasn't really so different from what Their Ali did to them. She'd convinced them—*everyone*—that she was someone she wasn't. And people trusted her because of it. People bought into her lies.

"Why should I believe anything you're telling me?" she said stiffly. "You could be stalking me, too."

"I'm not." Chase shook his head. "I promise, Spencer, I'm not. I would never do that. This has happened to me, remember?"

"Exactly!" Spencer cried. "You know what being stalked was like. Or was that a lie, too?"

Chase set his jaw. "*Look* at me, Spencer. I'm not lying to you. And I'll never lie to you again. My roommate slashed me—and even *then*, people didn't believe he could do such a thing. You're right: I shouldn't have invaded your privacy like that, but I was just trying to help. As far as sending my brother in my place, tell me you wouldn't have slunk away, creeped out by the scars. I saw your face when you met Curtis. We all judge a book by its cover. It's just how life is."

A gust of wind blew her hair sideways. How *would* she have reacted? Was she really that superficial?

Chase sighed heavily. "Look, I don't expect to ever see you again, but I do want to assure you that everything on my site is for real. And I was serious yesterday when I had my brother say I found a picture of Alison on a surveillance video from a building not far from here. Look."

He rummaged in his messenger bag. Spencer shifted, having forgotten what Curtis had mentioned in the car. Chase extracted a silver laptop, opened it up, and clicked on a folder. "I'm friends with a bunch of cops in Rosewood, Yarmouth, and a couple of other towns outside Philly. I was actually researching that case about the Rosewood Stalker—remember that? Someone thought they'd seen the stalker near Hollis. A cop friend gave me some surveillance videos, and I hit on this."

The folder opened, and several pictures loaded. Spencer leaned down to look. A grainy, black-and-white shot of a Hollis street appeared. Garbage cans sat at the curb. A girl in a leather jacket was getting into her VW

Beetle. There was nothing interesting in it, as far as she could tell.

But then Chase pointed to two shadowy figures in the top right corner. "Doesn't that girl seem familiar?"

Spencer squinted. Even in black-and-white, she could make out the girl's long blond hair. She had a heart-shaped face, too, and there was something about the angle of her chin that made her heart seize.

She stared at Chase. "*Alison?*"

"It looks like her, doesn't it?" Chase clicked to the next photo. This one showed Ali's back and more of her helper. The person was taller that she was, and broader, too—definitely a guy. Spencer pressed her face so close to the laptop her nose was almost touching the screen. It was impossible to tell, but that could definitely be Noel.

Nausea washed over her. She ran her hand over her forehead. All this time, Ali was in *Hollis*? This was a huge lead. She needed to show this to the cops. Or maybe she needed to stake Ali out on her own. She had to do *something*.

Chase shut the laptop and dropped it back into his bag. "I thought you should see that stuff. But as of now, I'm discontinuing the Alison investigation. I think it's for the best."

Spencer blinked hard, not expecting him to say that. "Oh," was all she could murmur.

He looked up at Spencer, his eyes full of sorrow and longing. "I wish we could be friends, but I totally get why you never want to see me again. I just hope you find peace in all this. I hope you guys can nail her for real. That girl did terrible things to you. You're too awesome to deserve something like that."

Then he spun on his heel and stepped off the porch. His messenger bag banged against his hip as he headed for the car. His head was still down, and halfway across the yard, Chase's shoulders rose and fell in a sigh. It tugged at Spencer's heartstrings. Okay, so Chase was a little misguided, and he never should have Facebook-stalked her, but she could feel in her heart that he wasn't a bad person. And if it weren't for Chase and his connections, she wouldn't know where Ali was potentially hiding.

And, if she was being honest, she'd tried to Google-stalk him, too.

"Wait!" she called after him. Chase stopped and turned. "We figured out that Ali's boyfriend is definitely her helper," she said. "It's this guy who goes to our school, Noel Kahn."

Chase's eyes widened. "What are you going to do?"

The wind chimes knocked together. Leaves swirled on the street. "I don't know," Spencer admitted. "But maybe you shouldn't stop the investigation so soon. We might need you." *I might need you*, she was too afraid to add.

Chase walked back to her. "I'll do anything."

"Well, do you know the exact address of that house you just showed me?"

Chase nodded. "It's on Atherton Street."

"Maybe we could go there tomorrow. Just to see."

"Of course. No matter how small or big. I'm here."

Spencer pulled her bottom lip into her mouth. She needed someone like that right now, didn't she? Someone who truly cared. Standing on the path, the sun at his back, Chase simply looked like he was a handsome college kid who liked her—*really* liked her. Slowly, her icy interior started to melt.

"Have you really had a crush on me since you saw me in *People*?" she asked in a small voice. And when she peeked up at Chase's bashful, heartfelt, lovesick face, he didn't even have to say anything. She already knew the answer.

32

CRAZY LOVE

When Emily pulled into her driveway, her mom was bent over in the front flower bed, spreading mulch. She brushed off her hands and smiled at Emily as she got out of the car. "Did you have fun at prom?"

Emily pretended to rub at an invisible stain on her dress. *Fun* wouldn't quite describe it. She still couldn't wrap her mind around what had happened. All this time, A had been right in front of them. At their parties. In their bedrooms—well, Aria's, anyway. She couldn't get the image of Noel's body on top of Aria's in the graveyard out of her mind, either. He'd looked so . . . desperate. Angry. And then he'd run off . . . to where? Ali? The police? Was it crazy that they'd given Aria six hours to find him?

Mrs. Fields pushed the wheelbarrow to the garage, breaking Emily from her thoughts. "Where's Iris?"

"She went home," Emily mumbled.

Mrs. Fields pulled off her gardening gloves. "It was

nice having her here. I think she was good for you, too."

Emily nodded. "She was," she said distantly, realizing she meant it. In the end, Iris had been a good confidante. She was glad she'd shared Jordan's secret with her. *And* she'd made the Noel connection in the nick of time. Emily felt bad for not seeing her off to The Preserve last night, but by the time she'd returned from the graveyard, Iris had been gone. It wasn't like Iris had a cell phone, either—Emily couldn't text her and make sure she got there okay. She headed toward the front door, suddenly dying to know.

She grabbed the cordless phone in the kitchen and dialed The Preserve's front desk. "I want to check if a patient got in all right last night," she said after a receptionist answered. "Her name is Iris Taylor?"

The receptionist typed something, then made an *mm* noise. "Yes, Miss Taylor returned safe and sound."

"Okay, thanks." Emily pressed the receiver closer to her ear. "Maybe I could set up a visit next week, then."

After arranging to visit Iris next Wednesday, Emily hung up the phone and slumped into a kitchen chair. She felt good that Iris returned like she said she would. Maybe this time, she'd actually take her stay at The Preserve seriously.

Emily conjured an image of The Preserve with its Grecian columns and small terraces, then pictured Noel pulling his SUV up the drive to visit Ali, his secret girl-friend. Had he set appointments with "Courtney" like

Emily just had with Iris? She still couldn't quite wrap her brain around the fact that he and Ali had been working together for all these years. Watching Emily and her friends' every move, plotting to bring them down.

She shivered, thinking of all the intimate moments Noel had spied on. How carefully had he watched Emily and Jordan on the cruise? Had he seen them on that glass-bottomed boat in Puerto Rico? Had he seen them kiss on the top deck? She'd known that A had been watching, but that A was someone they knew so intimately hurt even more. It had been Noel who'd called the FBI on Jordan. And it was because of Noel that Jordan had to swan-dive off the top deck, risk those treacherous seas, escape the country forever. Sure, maybe Ali had told him to do it, but Noel had actually *done* it. He hated them that much.

And he loved Ali that much.

Lost in her thoughts, Emily climbed the stairs and padded into her bedroom. She sat down on the bed and stared into the middle of the room, a memory suddenly coming to her. She'd been in the Rosewood Day locker room. The girl she'd thought was Courtney had sidled up next to her and acted devastated that Emily had been with her sister on the night she was killed. Emily had taken pity on Courtney, saying that if she ever needed anything, Emily was there for her.

Courtney's face had lit up. *Maybe we could get together after school tomorrow?* she'd asked. *If it's not too weird, that is. With Ali, I mean.* And Emily had said yes, of course, that would be fine, and when she'd looked up at Courtney again, the girl had a gleam in her eye, a twist of a smile on her lips. *Is she flirting with me?* Emily had thought, stunned. Courtney had winked, like she knew exactly what she was doing. And something resembling lust had rumbled in Emily's chest. Those old feelings had started to stir. That old love.

But even if *she* was the one Ali wanted, she would have never done for Ali what Noel had. She would have never hurt innocent people, her friends.

She whirled around and kicked the bedpost so hard her toe ached. Maybe it was a bad idea that they hadn't told Agent Fuji about A—both of them—immediately. Because if Ali and Noel were out there, they needed to find them. *Now.*

33

WHO'S THAT GIRL?

"So you haven't heard from Noel at *all*?" Hanna said into her burner cell as she walked through the Bill Beach's back entrance—all the parking at the front was filled again. The entrance bordered one of the community rooms. The place smelled like stale coffee. A baseball game was on the TV in the lobby, and several visiting family members were gathered around in Phillies jerseys.

"Nope," Mike said on the other end. "Though Aria asked me about it, too. What happened between them last night?"

"It doesn't matter," Hanna said nervously. "Just a stupid fight."

"Really?" Mike cleared his throat. "Hanna, all those questions you asked me about Noel and that bomb—"

"I can't talk about it right now," Hanna interrupted. Mike would find out soon enough, after all. She didn't want him knowing anything before he had to. It was going to break Mike's heart that his best friend had tried to kill his sister *and* his girlfriend.

Hanna still couldn't believe what they'd come upon in the cemetery last night. She also couldn't believe Spencer had the guts to hit him with that scepter. And had Noel been hurt? He'd gotten away, but his run had been stumbling and strange.

The most worrying moment of all, though, was the sense Hanna got just after Noel ran off. Even though the cemetery seemed deserted, she couldn't shake the feeling that someone else was there with them. She hadn't mentioned it to her friends, though—and none of them had said anything to her. It was probably all in her mind.

She pulled open the door to the women's staff room— which, strangely, was empty. Usually there were a couple of nurses hanging out there, watching soaps. "My shift starts soon, so I'd better go."

"So how long are you going to work there?" Mike asked.

"Actually, I think today's going to be my last day." Hanna grabbed her scrubs from her locker and began unbuttoning her jeans. Her investigation into Graham was done. "I'll call you later."

She hit END. Her phone rang again a split second later. It was her dad's number. When she answered, her father sounded furious.

"Hanna, someone named Agent Fuji showed up at the house this morning with a team and a search warrant for *your* bedroom," he said. "I was able to have my lawyers send them away, but they'll be back. What the hell's going on? What are you mixed up in?"

Hanna froze. *A search warrant?* Spencer had been right: Fuji was systematically going to each of them, trying to find that painting. At least she hadn't picked Aria as her next victim.

"I-I have no idea," she lied. "What was the agent looking for?"

"She didn't say." Mr. Marin's voice was strained. "Is it drugs? There were rumors you had a suicide pact—was it a gun? I can't believe a news van hasn't shown up here yet. The last thing I need is an FBI vehicle at the house and a bunch of agents searching the place and me not knowing what to say."

Tears filled Hanna's eyes. She couldn't have her father getting caught up in this. "Whatever she's looking for, she won't find it in my room," Hanna bleated. "I'm sorry you had to go through that . . . but it was just a big mix-up. I'll be home soon, okay?"

She hung up the phone and took deep breaths. If her father had sent Agent Fuji away, she might try someone else's house. Like Aria's, maybe. And then what?

There was no way she could continue her shift now. She walked down the hall and turned toward the lobby, ready to tell Sean she'd do a makeup day another time. It was filled with people, tons of voices shouting at once. Mr. Ackard was speaking to two official-looking men by the front desk. A police officer spoke into a walkie-talkie. A man with a news camera walked in, followed by a reporter in a suit. In the corner, another reporter interviewed Sean, whose face was laced with concern.

Hanna's stomach soured. Was this for Graham?

Kelly stood at the edges of the group, her hand to her mouth. Hanna tugged her sleeve.

"What's going on?"

The nurse gawked at her with wide eyes. She opened her mouth to speak, but no sounds came out.

Hanna glanced down one of the patient hallways. "Can I go back there and talk to Kyla?" Maybe *she* could explain what was happening.

A nurse standing next to Kelly widened her eyes. "Honey, get in line."

Hanna blinked hard. "D-did something *happen* to Kyla?"

Kelly's mouth dropped open. "We thought you knew," she said in a hushed voice. "Honey, Kyla's dead."

"*What?*" Hanna backed away from them and bumped into someone. When she turned around, it was Sean. "What's going on?" she demanded shakily.

Sean's eyes darted back and forth. Then he stepped closer. "Someone found a body in a ditch behind the facility early this morning. It was a girl wearing a hospital bracelet from the clinic. Her name was Kyla Kennedy."

Hanna pressed her hand over her mouth. "*No.*" Her face felt hot with tears.

She collapsed into Sean's arms, and he patted her shoulder. "It looks like she was killed a few days ago and dumped there," Sean said mournfully.

Hanna shot back up. "Wait. That's not possible. I saw Kyla last night. She was in the bed in the hall, near Graham's room."

An uncomfortable look settled across Sean's face. "That's the thing, Hanna. I don't think that was Kyla. It was . . . someone else. This is such a horrible mistake—a huge legal and publicity nightmare."

"*What?*" It felt like her brain matter was leaking out of her ears. "What do you mean?"

"The police are certain that the *real* Kyla, our patient, died several days ago at least. But nurses—and you, obviously—remember *someone* in Kyla's bed after that."

"But . . . I *talked* to her!" Hanna gasped. "We bonded!"

Sean looked like he was going to be sick. "Last night, the nurses discovered Kyla gone. When the body turned up, we thought that was that, but the coroner's data is solid. The theory right now is that whoever that was in the bed murdered the real Kyla and put bandages on her face to get into the burn clinic for some reason. And then, for some *other* reason, she just . . . left."

"That makes no sense!" Hanna wailed. "Why would someone *do* that?"

"I don't know," Sean said quietly.

Flashbulbs popped around the room. A clump of nurses stood in the corner, crying. A man with a jacket that read FORENSICS began to cordon off some of the room. Hanna leaned against the table and tried to catch her breath. As she shifted, something sharp poked her side. It was something wedged inside the pocket of her shirt. Hanna frowned and pulled out a neatly folded piece of paper. She didn't remember leaving anything inside her scrubs the last time she wore them.

She unfolded the paper and saw tiny, loopy letters. Familiar loopy letters, in fact. Her stomach started to gurgle. This looked like *Ali's* handwriting.

Dear Hanna, it began. *I can explain everything, especially why I did what I did. But I think I know what you're after, and I want to help you. The answer you want is in the Rosewood Day storage shed. It will give you the proof you need and put everything to rest. Go there NOW . . . before it's too late. Love, Kyla.*

Her face must have been pale, because Sean touched her wrist. "What's that?"

Hanna pulled the note to her chest. "Nothing," she croaked. And then she turned around and ran out of the building.

34

SURPRISE INSIDE!

At 1:30, Aria paced back and forth inside her mom's house, the news blaring on the television. She checked her phone at 1:31 and 10 seconds, and then 24 seconds, and then 45. Nothing from Noel. She peered out the window for the zillionth time, but of course Noel wasn't walking up the front steps. She'd already cruised around Rosewood and Hollis, as if he'd just be strolling up and down Lancaster Avenue or walking on the Hollis Great Lawn without a care in the world.

He's with Ali now, she thought. But something in her brain still fought against it. Noel loved her. She could *feel* it. When he said he loved Ali last night, he'd been confused. He was holding on to something that wasn't there, just like Emily had. He hadn't *helped* her. He hadn't colluded with her. This was a mistake.

But he admitted it, she thought. *He's lied and cheated and killed for her. Facts are facts.*

She picked up an Icelandic horse–shaped paperweight from the end table and considered hurling it at the TV screen, but suddenly something caught her eye. *Multiple hoaxes in art theft case,* said a headline.

Horrifyingly, *The Starry Night* appeared on the screen. "There has been a frantic search to recover the study for *The Starry Night,* which was stolen from a chateau outside Reykjavik, Iceland, last year," said a reporter. "Baroness Brennan, who is handling the estate while Baron Brennan recovers from a long illness, recently had the painting insured for twenty million dollars, and thankfully, the insurance company won't have to pay out. The painting was recovered about an hour ago, and we're just getting news of it now."

The paperweight dropped into Aria's lap. Her mouth went dry.

A shot of a few men wearing police uniforms walking into a quintessential Reykjavik row house appeared on the screen. "Even though there were rumors that the painting had made it to the United States, authorities tracked down the study in a basement in Reykjavik. Baroness Brennan identified it immediately, and the painting is now safe and sound back in her home."

The image on the screen switched to a gray-haired woman in a fur coat standing in front of the very chateau Aria had broken into. Aria leaned forward as if sitting closer to the TV would reveal a different picture. If the study painting had been recovered in Iceland, then what was the painting in her closet?

She ran upstairs, pulled open her closet door, and unfurled the canvas. The Van Gogh stars twinkled. The drip-castle spires made dark shapes against the bright sky. It looked just like the study painting she'd seen on TV. Then she grabbed the Van Gogh art book she'd brought home from the library to use for the prom decorations and opened to the *Starry Night* spread. As she compared the two side-by-side, the colors in Aria's painting suddenly looked a little . . . different. The whirls weren't as whirly. The brushstrokes were choppier, less calculated. From afar, glanced at quickly, it looked utterly believable, but up close, it was kind of a mess.

The painting was a fake. Aria wasn't going to get in trouble for it. Fuji couldn't arrest her. It was possible Fuji wasn't even after her now that the real painting had been found. A had done all this to scare her.

What other lies had A been telling?

Aria headed back downstairs in a daze, eager to call the others and tell them the news. Something else on TV caught her eye. She looked up, her heart in her throat once more. Was that *Olaf*?

The anchor's face was large on the screen. "The painting was among an older woman's things, though she has no memory of how it might have gotten there. Ms. Greta Eggertsdottir, age sixty-six, is a landlord, and says she has many tenants going in and out of the row house on a monthly basis, so it's probable one of them brought the painting and left it in the basement. When shown a picture of Olaf Gundersson, the alleged thief who stole it from Baroness Brennan's estate, Ms. Eggertsdottir was quite sure she recognized him. Mr. Gundersson was reported missing after an alleged attack in January, though authorities now believe that might have been a hoax. The hunt is on for Mr. Gundersson, but there are no leads so far as to where he might be."

Aria sank down to the couch. This story was getting more and more bizarre. So Olaf had faked his attack? It made sense, sort of—maybe he'd realized the cops were on to him and needed a way to escape. And maybe A saw the article and pounced on the opportunity, never trekking to Iceland and stealing the painting at all. It had been a lucky break for A . . . though not for Aria.

Her phone bleated. She squealed and stared at the screen. *Hanna.* "Did you just see the news?" Aria cried.

"No . . ." There was a swishing sound on the other end; it sounded like Hanna was driving. "But you've got to meet me. Something weird is going on."

"Something weird is *definitely* going on." Aria gripped the phone hard. "That painting from Iceland is a fake—which means the police have nothing on us. And even weirder? Olaf isn't dead. He faked the whole attack. I just saw it all on CNN."

The line crackled. "Huh," Hanna said. "So you think A just caught wind of the story, used it to her advantage, and forged the painting?"

"Yeah." Aria stared blankly out the window at the

birdhouse her mom had carved last year. "It means we can go to the police right this second and not worry about being in trouble. Even if A brings up Jamaica, we still wouldn't be punished in the same way we would have been if the painting was a real Van Gogh." She cleared her throat, feeling a pull in her chest. "Not that *I* want to go to the police." She couldn't bear the thought of the police going after Noel. Or maybe she could. She didn't know.

"Well, actually, I think A has forced our hand. I got this note at the burn clinic about some critical evidence that will put all of this to rest. I think it was from Ali."

"What?" Aria's skin prickled. "*How?*"

"I'll explain everything when I see you. You have to meet me at the storage shed behind Rosewood Day. Maybe she's there."

Aria gripped the doorjamb. "Oh my God. What if it's a trap?"

"That's why I called the cops to come with us. And before you freak out, Aria, I *had* to. This has gone too far. If Ali's there, if we can catch her, we have to have the police involved. Meet me there in ten minutes."

"Okay," Aria whispered, hitting END. She stood in her silent house for a few moments, staring at the dust motes in the air. Too much had happened in the last few minutes for her to handle. She knew she had to meet Hanna . . . but what if Ali *was* there and Noel was with her? What if the police arrested Noel, too? Then again, maybe that was what Aria wanted. He'd lied to her for over a year. He'd never loved her. Right?

She grabbed her keys from the hook in the hall, a heavy weight crushing her chest. She just *couldn't* hate him, even after all this. She could only hope that whatever happened, it would be like pulling off a Band-Aid—fast, and painless.

Aria left the radio off on the drive over and kept the window cracked. Her gaze darted back and forth from one side of the road to the other, hoping—fearing—she might see Noel there. Finally, she turned into the Rosewood Day parking lot. There were only a few cars in the spaces; the boys' soccer team had Sunday practice. Aria spotted Hanna's Prius in the back and headed for it. Emily's Volvo and Spencer's Mercedes were there, too. Spencer and Emily were wearing sweats and sneakers, and Hanna had on pink scrubs and clogs from the burn clinic. As far as Aria could tell, the cops hadn't arrived yet.

"Here's the note." Hanna shoved it at Aria when she reached their circle.

Aria looked down and recognized the tiny, even letters immediately. It was the same handwriting from the hateful letter Ali had slid under the bedroom door in the Poconos, just before she'd lit that match. *The answer you want is in the Rosewood Day storage shed. . . . Go there NOW . . . before it's too late.*

"Jesus," Aria whispered. "She has to know that we'd

recognize her handwriting. And now we're just going to go and do exactly what she wants?"

"We still have to check it out, don't you think?" Hanna asked. "The police will be here any minute."

Spencer peeked at the note again. "How did you get this, anyway?"

"From this patient I met at the burn clinic." Hanna paused for a moment, peering over the hill. Sirens began to wail. A police car appeared over the crest. Aria's stomach twisted.

Hanna turned back to the girls and explained about the body the cops had found behind the hospital. "Her hospital bracelet said Kyla Kennedy," she whispered hurriedly. "I think Ali killed her, then *became* her. The girl I met was completely covered in bandages."

Spencer collapsed against the hood of Hanna's car. "It *totally* sounds like Ali. Who else would murder a burn victim and swap places with her?"

Hanna nodded, looking tormented. "Kyla's bed was outside Graham's room. And when Graham was spasming, Kyla sent me in the wrong direction to get a nurse. When I came back, he was dead."

"So she was keeping an eye on Graham, making sure he didn't say anything?" Aria whispered.

"I can't believe I didn't suspect it sooner. I thought I would have been able to spot Ali from a mile away," Hanna said, choking back tears. "Kyla was just so . . . *cool*. Now I feel like an idiot . . . *again*."

"If she had bandages all over her," Spencer said, "it would have been easy to fool anyone."

Suddenly, Aria realized something. "You guys, if it *was* Ali at the burn clinic . . ."

" . . . then that explains why Noel was there, too," Emily finished for her.

By this time, the cop car had pulled into the parking lot, and two officers Aria vaguely recognized from Ali's trial walked over to them. Their name badges read COATES and HARRISON.

"Hanna Marin," Harrison, the taller one, who had a broad face, a flat nose, and long eyelashes framing his green eyes, said gruffly. "You said you got a threatening letter?"

"Yes." With shaking hands, Hanna passed it to them.

Coates and Harrison scanned it, then frowned. "*Proof you need*?" Coates, who was shorter and wirier and had a jutting Adam's apple, repeated. "What is this all about?"

"We'll explain everything, we promise," Hanna said, walking toward the sports fields. "We just need you to check this out. We're too scared to do it on our own."

The cops shrugged, then walked ahead of them to the shed, their walkie-talkies squawking every few seconds. Aria glanced at Hanna worriedly. Was it a good idea to get the cops involved? What if Ali was watching at a distance? What if she had a bomb in the shed—and when she saw the officers, she detonated it?

Suddenly, Aria's phone beeped. Hope flared inside

her, followed by a pinch of terror. What if it was Noel? What if it *wasn't* Noel?

Then she looked at the screen. The text was from a jumble of letters and numbers.

Her knees went weak. "Oh my God," she whispered, glancing back up. The cops were several yards ahead of them. She signaled to her friends.

Spencer, Emily, and Hanna shot over to her and stared at the message.

> You bitches think you're so clever, getting new phones, try-
> ing to hide from me.

Then everyone's phones beeped. This time, a picture message loaded. When Aria opened it, she screamed. It was a picture of the suspects list they'd created in the panic room. All of the names were crossed off . . . except for Noel's.

Spencer's face had turned white. "How did A get this?" she shrieked, looking at the same picture on her phone.

The cops swiveled around and stared at her. "Is everything all right?" Coates asked.

But none of the girls could answer. Another text came through. And then another, and then another. The note was so long it was several texts.

> The most darling part was when you went to that panic room
> and went all James Bond to figure out who I was. But guess

what, bitches? I've been a step ahead of you this whole
time. I've known where you were. I've known where you
were going. I call the shots, not you—in ways you can't even
begin to imagine. But don't worry—you'll see soon enough.
Just open the shed. —A

Hanna's head shot up when she finished. *"Just open the
shed?"*

"Guys, it's definitely a trap." Spencer's hands trembled.

"Maybe it's dangerous that we're even here," Emily
whispered.

"Girls?" Harrison loomed over them, hands on his
hips. "What's going on?"

Aria was about to answer, but then her gaze focused
on the shed. To her horror, one of the soccer players was
jogging toward it. His hand reached out for the doorknob.

"Wait!" Aria sprinted for him. "Don't open that!" Her
mind whirled with all the possibilities of what could be
inside. Explosives. Wild animals. Ali *herself.*

"Don't open it!" Aria screamed again. Spencer, Emily,
Hanna, and the two officers followed, yelling at the boy
as well.

But it was too late—he was already pulling on the
handle. The shed door creaked open, the bottom getting
caught on the tall grass.

Coates pushed the boy aside and tried to shut it
again, but then he paused, his face going pale. *"Shit,"* he
whispered.

Aria peered inside. For the first half second, all she saw was darkness. Then, shapes began to form: balls, sticks, mats, hurdles, goal nets. When she saw the object sitting on a chair in the back of the room, she thought that it was just another piece of sports equipment—a speed bag, maybe, or a blocking sled for Rosewood Day's less-than-stellar football team.

Then an arm appeared. Two feet. A head hung limply on a neck. Aria took a step closer, knowing a split second before seeing his face who it was going to be. She sank to her knees and let out a howl. Hanna gasped. Spencer screamed. Emily took a few big steps back, her mouth frozen in terror. The soccer boy spun around and threw up in the grass. Coates and Harrison shooed the other players away.

"Is that . . . ?" Spencer wailed.

Mercifully, she didn't say his name. Aria stared at the top of Noel's head. He was still in his tuxedo jacket, and his arms were pinned behind his back, his ankles tied to the chair. There was a big strip of duct tape over his mouth. His skin was eerily pale, and there were huge gashes on his cheeks, like he'd been badly beaten.

It felt like cymbals were crashing in her head. *This isn't happening. This can't be happening.*

"I need an ambulance!" Hanna screamed into her phone. "*Do* something!" Spencer bellowed to Coates, who was shouting something into his walkie-talkie. But Aria hardly heard them. She lay on the splintered ground of the shed, unable to move any closer to Noel, petrified to see whether he was dead or alive. All she saw, in that moment, were the shiny shoes on his feet. She'd been with him when he bought those shoes. He'd tried on a bunch of pairs in the store, just like a girl. *A stylish girl deserves a stylish guy*, he'd told her with a wink.

Her phone beeped in her ear. Somehow, she had the sense to sit up and look at the screen. Behind her, her friends were scrambling around, trying to make sense of what they were seeing. But as their phones beeped, each of them paused to look at the heartbreaking message on their screens.

Twinkle, twinkle, little liars,

Your situation has become quite dire.

Sleuths you're not; you haven't solved shit.

Noel as A? Not it!

—A

WHAT HAPPENS NEXT . . .

So the liars finally figured out there are two of us. Took 'em long enough. But they still didn't get the story right. They were too hung up on investigating Noel to see what's right under their pert little noses: *us.* But the noose is tightening and soon *they'll* be the ones hanging on by a thread. . . .

Hanna may have been voted queen of the prom court, but the next court she's in will be of the criminal variety. Last time we checked, hitting-and-running is still a felony. . . . Once Daddy's constituents find out, Hanna won't be the only loser in the Marin family.

Spencer went *chase*-ing conspiracy theories, and entre nous, she got a little too close for comfort. But Spence still has a lot to learn about stalking. Like, it's not actually sneaking up on us if we see you coming.

So Emily's pretty little girlfriend is in Bonaire. We can think of a few people who might be interested in that tidbit, starting with Special Agent Jasmine Fuji. Emily better get started on a bucket list of her own—it's only a matter of time before she and Jordan end up behind bars. Or worse.

And then there's Aria. Noel may not be A, but he's as two faced as they come. What did she expect from a Typical Rosewood? So what will Atypical Aria do? Our money's on an artistic retreat to Europe. But doesn't she know all tortured artists die young?

Tick tock, ladies. Live each moment like it's your last. Because soon enough, it will be.

Until next time . . .

—A & A

ACKNOWLEDGMENTS

Thank you so much to my wonderful editor, Lanie Davis, for her thoughts and encouragement. And to the other awesome people at Alloy Entertainment, including Josh Bank, Les Morgenstein, Sara Shandler, Kristen Marang, Katie McGee, and everyone in art and media. You guys make my life so much easier.

Thanks also to Kari Sutherland at HarperCollins and Andy McNicol and Jennifer Rudolph Walsh at William Morris. Kisses also to the fans in the Twitterverse who love PLL so much—and who always take part in the book chats and answer my random questions when I need to know the perfect name for a character or what sorts of foods people eat during Hannukah. A big shout-out to all the fans at South Hills Village who attended my reading this December—it was so awesome to see every single one of you! Much love to K, Shep and Mindy, Ali, Caron, Beth, Greg, Eloise, and Rex, the Lorence family, and the

Gremba family—including Calli, Ryan, Talon, Brayden, Jordan, Brock, Ashton, and of course Michael, the biggest and most lovable kid of all. Also a shout-out to my buddy Chris Ferguson and his family in Texas. Chris, I hear you have some betting winnings coming your way. (Just a hunch.)

Finally, a lot of hugs to Marlene King—it was scary to put PLL into someone else's hands, but you've been so loving, careful, and thoughtful with the show. Hats off to you and your inimitable talent, and I hope we can have another long, wine-filled dinner soon.

Don't miss a single scandal!

EVERYONE IN ULTRA-EXCLUSIVE ROSEWOOD, PENNSYLVANIA, HAS SOMETHING TO HIDE . . .

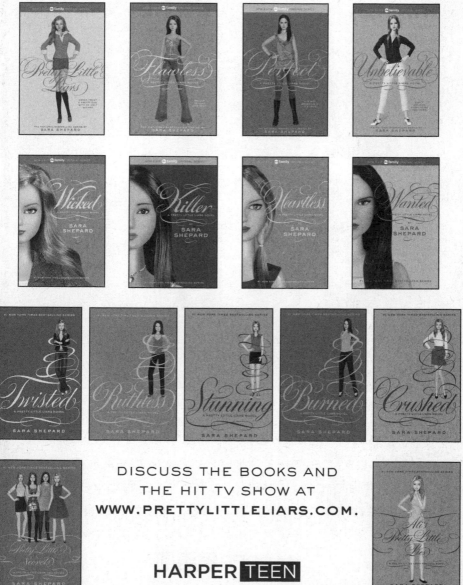

DISCUSS THE BOOKS AND
THE HIT TV SHOW AT
WWW.PRETTYLITTLELIARS.COM.

PRETTY GIRLS DON'T PLAY BY THE RULES...
THEY MAKE THEM.

DON'T MISS SARA SHEPARD'S
KILLER SERIES THE LYING GAME—AND CHECK
OUT THE ORIGINAL DIGITAL NOVELLAS
THE FIRST LIE AND *TRUE LIES* ONLINE.